Praise for *USA TODAY* bestselling author Katherine Garbera

"Katherine Garbera's latest keeper
is an absolute must-read: dynamite characters
leap off the page with witty dialogue
and comical yet sensual scenes."
—*RT Book Reviews* on *Overnight Cinderella*

"Katherine Garbera knows how to aim for the heart
with her tales of love and happiness.
Not only was this an emotional read
but it was hot and sexy as well."
—*The Best Reviews* on *Tycoon for Auction*

Praise for *USA TODAY* bestselling author Day Leclaire

"Day Leclaire does it again with her trademark
larger-than-life characters, quirky scenes, brilliant
story line and just absolutely wonderful romance."
—*RT Book Reviews* on *The Marriage Project*

"The story is fun and hot all at the same time."
—*TheRomanceReader.com* on *Dante's Blackmailed Bride*

KATHERINE GARBERA
is a strong believer in happily-ever-after. She's written more than thirty-five books and has been nominated for career achievement awards from *RT Book Reviews* for series fantasy and series adventure. Her books have appeared on the Waldenbooks/Borders bestseller list for series romance and on the *USA TODAY* extended bestseller list. Visit Katherine on the Web at www.katherinegarbera.com.

USA TODAY bestselling author **DAY LECLAIRE** is described by Harlequin as "one of our most popular writers ever!" Day's tremendous worldwide popularity has made her a member of Harlequin's "Five Star Club," with sales of well over five million books. She is a three-time winner of both a Colorado Award of Excellence and a Golden Quill Award. She's won *RT Book Reviews* Career Achievement and Love and Laughter Awards, a Holt Medallion and a Booksellers' Best Award. She has also received an impressive ten nominations for the prestigious Romance Writers of America RITA® Award. Day's romances touch the heart and make you care about her characters as much as she does. In Day's own words, "I adore writing romances, and can't think of a better way to spend each day." For more information, visit Day on her Web site, www.dayleclaire.com.

USA TODAY Bestselling Author

KATHERINE GARBERA

Sin City Wedding

USA TODAY Bestselling Author

DAY LECLAIRE

The Forbidden Princess

HARLEQUIN®

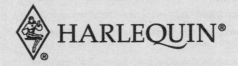

TORONTO • NEW YORK • LONDON
AMSTERDAM • PARIS • SYDNEY • HAMBURG
STOCKHOLM • ATHENS • TOKYO • MILAN • MADRID
PRAGUE • WARSAW • BUDAPEST • AUCKLAND

ISBN-13: 978-0-373-68806-7

SIN CITY WEDDING & THE FORBIDDEN PRINCESS

This edition published by arrangement with Harlequin Books S.A.

For questions and comments about the quality of this book please contact us at Customer_eCare@Harlequin.ca.

www.eHarlequin.com

Printed in U.S.A.

CONTENTS

SIN CITY WEDDING 9
Katherine Garbera

THE FORBIDDEN PRINCESS 181
Day Leclaire

SIN CITY WEDDING

Katherine Garbera

One

Larissa Nielsen had imagined how she'd look when she saw Jacob Danforth again. None of her ideas involved wearing her oldest pair of leggings and a tie-dyed Florida T-shirt. But the early-morning call from Jasmine Carmody, a reporter with the *Savannah Morning News*, had left Larissa no choice. She needed to talk to Jake before Jasmine told the world who Peter's father was.

Now Larissa was sitting in her car in front of Jake's Savannah town house like some crazy ex-girlfriend stalker. She wished she were just waking up back at her house in Riverside. She wished their morning routine wasn't disrupted and she and her three-year-old son could welcome the day on their dock overlooking the Savannah River. Instead, she was about to do something, her conscience reminded her, she should have done a long time ago.

She shone the light of her tiny flashlight on the pages in front of her. A collection of Robert Frost poetry had always been her saving grace. She'd used it to escape from life more than once and this morning, while she waited for time to creep by, it provided the escape she desperately needed from her chaotic thoughts.

A rap on the car window startled her. She glanced up to see the faint outline of a man. The man leaned down and she looked into dark brown eyes she'd never forgotten. His tough-guy look faded, replaced by a welcoming smile when he recognized her. She unlocked her door and Jake opened it.

Larissa wasn't a person anyone would call timid. But suddenly she felt like the Cowardly Lion. And it wasn't anything like the green floating head of the Great and Powerful Oz that scared her. She knew the man behind the curtain and she knew he would be royally pissed when she told him he had a three-year-old son.

Peter slept quietly in his car seat and she double-checked that his favorite blanket was tucked next to his chin before getting out of the car. The March morning air was chilly. She shivered a little and rubbed her hands on her arms, praying the tinted windows wouldn't reveal her son until she had a chance to tell Jacob herself.

"What are you doing parked in front of my house at seven in the morning?"

Jake was dressed in running shorts and a sleeveless T-shirt that was stained with sweat. He must have left before she'd arrived. She smoothed her hair down, wishing she'd had the time to make herself look more presentable.

He looked as good as she remembered. Would he feel as good? Somehow she knew he would, despite the fact that it had been almost four years since she'd had sex. She forced her gaze from his muscled chest to his face.

"It's a long story."

"About four years long?"

"You have no idea."

"Well, then let's get comfortable. Come inside and I'll make you some coffee. You know I'm famous for it."

She couldn't help but smile. Even when they'd been nothing more than friends, Jake had always been able to make her laugh. But she couldn't leave Peter sleeping in the car.

"Actually, I have something to tell you."

"And you can't do it inside?"

"Well…no."

She leaned back against the driver's door and tried to find the right words. She swallowed once then licked her lips. "Um…this is harder than I thought it would be."

"I wish I could help you out, Larissa, but I have no idea what you're trying to say."

She shook herself. She'd be matter-of-fact. She was known for her practicality. "Remember that night at the reunion?"

"How could I forget?" he asked, running the tip of one

finger down the side of her face. Shivers of awareness coursed through her. Jake had always elicited a response from her even when he wasn't trying to.

"I haven't forgotten it either," she said.

"Is that why you are here?" he asked. He leaned closer toward her, surrounding her with the heat of his body and his earthy scent. His dark eyes focused on her lips and she felt them tingle. Without thinking, she licked her bottom lip and he tracked the motions with his gaze. Dammit, this was getting out of hand. His touch on her face moved to her mouth, stroking her bottom lip with his thumb.

"Larissa Nielsen on my doorstep. I can't quite figure out why. Why now? Why are you here, Larissa?"

"A reporter contacted me about your uncle's senate bid." Larissa knew the only way to the truth was through the story of what had happened. Because the reason she'd been keeping Peter a secret hadn't changed and if Jasmine Carmody hadn't called her, Larissa would still be at home in Riverside watching the sun rise and drinking D&D Coffee's special morning blend.

"Those damned reporters. They won't leave any of us alone." Jake ran his fingers through his thick curly hair in a gesture she'd seen her son make when he was on the verge of a meltdown.

"I'm sorry," she said, knowing Jake treasured his privacy above just about anything else.

"Hey, babe, it's not your fault. So why are you here?"

"She knows about our one-night stand," Larissa blurted out.

"I wish you wouldn't call it that. I wanted to see you again."

He'd called her several times, but she'd dodged his calls. Eventually she'd moved to Atlanta with her college roommate to make sure Jake never found out their one night had consequences.

Jake hadn't been ready for fatherhood then. D&D's, the coffeehouse Jake had co-founded with his cousin Adam, had been about to go national and Jake hadn't really changed all that much since college. He was still the fun-loving, Saturday-morning-soccer-playing guy he'd always been. And she knew from bitter experience that a woman who tied a man down became a burden. She'd vowed long ago to never become a burden.

"I had my reasons for not meeting you in Cancun." She nibbled her lower lip. Just tell him.

"Our one night together isn't really that newsworthy, honey. Don't worry about that."

"Actually, it is," Larissa said.

"Why, did the reporter have pictures?" Jake asked with a bad-boy grin that brought that night back in vivid detail. It had been a steamy summer night, and in his arms she'd felt like the most beautiful woman in the world, not the plain Jane she'd always been.

"Yes, but not of us."

"Then who?" he asked, becoming exasperated.

Oh, God. "Our son."

Jake staggered back from her. "Did you say son?"

"Yes, his name is Peter, Peter Jacob, and he's three years old."

Jacob reached for the back door but it was still locked. "Unlock it."

She did and he opened the door and looked down on their sleeping son. Peter's curly hair was the same dark shade as Jake's. He reached out for Peter's head with a touch so gentle that she knew she'd made a mistake in not telling him sooner.

But the past had taught her a bitter lesson, and she'd always dreamed that her life would be sit-com perfect. Instead reality was very different. All the excuses she'd made to herself for the past three years sounded lame now and when Jake glanced up at her, she knew he'd think so, too.

"My son," he said, looking down on Peter with a wealth of emotions that she hadn't suspected Jake could feel.

His son. He still couldn't really take it in. Parenthood was an alien concept to Jake. He reached for the buckle on the car seat but couldn't figure out how to operate it. Nothing in his life had prepared him for this. He'd have to give his brother Toby a call later; he was the only expert on fatherhood he knew.

"Get him out," he said to Larissa. His hands were shaking. He was a father.

She brushed past him. Her slender body had remained unchanged over the years since they first met. Her clear blue eyes had always struck him as the most honest he'd ever looked into—until today.

Larissa put her hand on his back and leaned into the car. One of her breasts brushed against his side and arousal moved through him like lightning. He felt the heat from her hand on the small of his back burn through his shirt.

She pushed against him as she leaned into the car, balancing herself with the touch on his back. Reaching out, she ruffled Peter's hair. "Morning, sleepyhead."

"Morning, Mama," he said.

They had a bond. A bond that Jake had never wanted but now suddenly envied. Maybe this was what he'd been searching for lately. Maybe this would fill the restlessness that his work and partying couldn't.

Jake reached for his son and the boy recoiled, pulling a ragged-looking bear and a tattered blanket closer. Tucking the edge of the blanket between his lips, Peter looked at Larissa.

"It's okay, baby. Jake's a friend." Larissa turned toward him, her breath brushing across his cheek. Her mouth was fuller than he'd remembered.

"He's kind of shy around new people," Larissa said.

"The word Dad is foreign to him?" Jake asked, to remind himself that Larissa wasn't the sweet girl from his memories. She was the woman who'd had his child and kept it a secret.

"He's only three. Some things take time to remember."

"Did you have a problem remembering too?" he asked sarcastically.

Jake had always loved women. He'd never had any trouble with them. Women were meant to be protected, he knew, even though his track record on this front wasn't great. But how did you protect someone who had betrayed you?

She sighed. "If you're going to treat me the way I deserve to be treated, I'm going to take Peter home and come back by myself. To him you're a stranger who's mad at his mom."

He realized she was right. For better or worse, Peter's entire world revolved around Larissa. And making Larissa cry or angry probably wouldn't help Peter to like him. He straightened from the car and took the two steps back to the sidewalk.

She lifted their son out, brushing a soft kiss against the top of his head and rubbing his back before setting the boy on the sidewalk. It was obvious how deeply Larissa cared for her son. He shouldn't be surprised. She'd always had a nurturing quality about her. Originally it was what had drawn him to her.

Peter clung to the back of Larissa's leg, watching Jake with the same intensity that his mother did. Why hadn't she trusted him enough to tell him he had a son?

"Did that reporter follow you?" he asked.

"I don't think so."

"Let's go inside just to be safe."

She nodded and bent to pry her son's hands from her thigh. She took the small hand in her own and as

Jake watched them, he realized the two of them were watching him. Waiting to see what he'd do. Frankly, he was out of his element.

He bent down on one knee and held out his hand to his son. Peter hesitated, then handed Jake the bear. "Oh, he's giving you Mr. Bear. That means he likes you."

"I'm glad one of you does," Jake said.

Larissa watched him with those soulful eyes of hers. And he felt like a big mean bully. He tried to get past his anger so he could remember all the reasons he liked her but he couldn't.

"Oh, Jake, this isn't about liking you," she said, softly.

He glanced up at her. "Then what is it about?"

"Me not being the right woman for you."

"Well, I do tend to like a different sort of woman."

"I know. Tall, blond and built."

"Nice opinion you've got of me, Rissa. But I'm not that shallow. I meant honest. I like my women to be honest."

She flushed. He knew that anything else he said now would be mean and sarcastic, but sending her away with the son he'd just discovered wasn't an option.

He pivoted on his heel without saying another word. Unlocking the door to his town house, he turned left and entered his living quarters. The living room was sleek and sophisticated. All chrome, glass and Italian leather. The entertainment center was top of the line and he'd just had a new large-screen plasma TV installed on Friday.

Larissa and Peter stood in the doorway as if afraid to enter. How old was his son? He knew she'd told him, but he'd been trying to grapple with the fact that he was a father and hadn't paid attention. It had been almost four years since he'd seen Larissa so Peter would have to be about three. What did kids that age do?

"Does he watch TV?"

"Yes. But only PBS."

Figures, Larissa would be all about educational television. He looked at the serious little boy.

His son. He felt a stirring so deep inside that it made his anger pale. This was his son. His future was tied to this little boy, and he knew he had to make the situation right.

He knelt in front of Peter again. The boy had his eyes. He studied Peter until the boy reached out and touched the stubble on his chin. "You're prickly."

"I didn't have time to shave yet."

Peter glanced up at Larissa. "How come you don't feel like that?"

"Girls don't," she said.

"Girls are different," Peter said, turning back to Jake.

"They sure are."

"You got any food?" Peter asked.

"Peter."

"It's okay. Come on, I'll fix us some breakfast." He stood and led Peter down the hall to the kitchen. "Then your mom and I need to talk."

Jake seated Peter at the large butcher-block table and

checked the pantry for something a little boy might want to eat. He had two jars of martini olives and a box of water crackers. The fridge held several bottles of wine, a six-pack of Coors and an opened bottle of champagne. Maybe Wes had eggs in his fridge. His best friend lived upstairs.

"I probably should have found a sitter for Peter," Larissa said.

He turned to look at her. Peter was occupied at the table with an electronic book that Larissa must have had in that big purse of hers.

"I'm glad you didn't," he said.

She was so close he could smell the fragrance of her shampoo. She wore no makeup. But then she rarely did. Her skin was smooth and fine, creamy looking. Lust surged inside him, which further enraged him. He didn't want to want her.

She swallowed and he knew that she still wasn't sure letting him know his son was a good idea. He wondered how much of it stemmed from his reputation and how much of it came from her knowledge of him.

He'd never really taken responsibility seriously. Everyone in the family knew it. And thanks to the media coverage of his uncle's senate bid, most of the public knew it too. He was the fun-loving, thirty-year-old millionaire with the Midas touch. But Larissa should know better, especially when she'd found out she was having his son.

"What do you want to eat, sport?"

"Pancakes."

"Uh…let's see what I've got." Jake had no idea how to make pancakes. He could scramble eggs but there weren't any in the fridge. "I can run upstairs to see if Wes has some eggs."

"Your college roommate Wes?"

"Yeah, you remember him."

"Don't bother. Surely you have some cereal."

"Frosted Sugar Os and Captain Crunch."

"He'll have toast with butter."

"Educational TV and healthy food. Larissa, does our boy get to have any fun?"

"Of course, he does. Just not bad influences."

"Is that why you never called me?" he asked.

"What?"

"Am I a bad influence for our son?"

"No. Never."

She closed the distance between them, reaching up to touch him, and then dropped her hands. "The reasons are complicated. Let's get Peter settled, then we can talk."

He nodded. He'd wanted her to touch him. Needed her to in a way that made him feel vulnerable, reminding him that he was just a man and had more weaknesses than he wanted to acknowledge.

The toast was buttered and eaten in short order. Jake grabbed a soccer ball from the closet, and now that the morning sun was shining brightly, they took it outside. Peter kicked the ball, chasing it from one end of the yard to the other.

He gestured for Larissa to sit down on the chaise and

dragged over one of the Adirondack chairs he'd made last summer.

He watched his son running after the ball on pudgy legs. Larissa had taken something from him that he could never get back. Though deep inside he allowed he probably wouldn't have been ready for fatherhood three years ago, he still felt betrayed.

Jake suddenly thought of his father. God, the old man was going to be extremely disappointed when Jake told him he had a three-year-old son. Just one more screwup from a son who never measured up.

Larissa sat there looking much the same as she had in their college days. A sweet innocent who didn't really fit in at Georgia Tech. He'd befriended her because she'd reminded him of his younger sisters and he would've wanted Victoria and Imogene to have found a guy who'd do the same.

But all of that faded when he glanced at their little boy. "I'm so angry I want to shake you."

Two

Larissa had been hoping that Jake would just jump on the problem with the reporter, but she should've known better. He was a detail man who liked to get all his facts in order before making a decision. Many times during their college days, he'd used her as a sounding board for his theories and ideas before drawing a conclusion. She leaned back in the lounge chair and took a sip of her coffee.

"Stalling is not going to make me less angry," he said.

"I know." She watched her small son chasing the ball across the yard and tried to find the words to tell Jake that she'd kept Peter a secret for herself and for him. She hadn't wanted Peter to grow up in a household similar to the one she had.

Her parents had married because her mother had been pregnant. From her earliest memories Larissa was aware that if she hadn't been born, her parents wouldn't have been married. Theirs was an unhappy house. So she sought refuge in a world of books, creating her dreams from the stories she cherished. Tales of epic love and vanquishing heroes.

But the real world wasn't full of those epic love stories she'd dreamed of for her life. And instead of being a fair lady waiting in her tower to be rescued, Larissa's fate had become her mother's.

"I'm waiting," Jake said, his voice quiet and deep with suppressed emotion. Her heart ached because she knew how hard it had always been for Jake to express his emotions. To the outside world he presented his devil-may-care bachelor image but Larissa knew that Jake's emotions ran deep. He was anything but carefree.

She studied Jake's face. He was so familiar to her, not just because of his resemblance to their son. But because she saw his face every night in her dreams. Even before Peter was born, Jake had been the one man she'd never been able to forget.

Perhaps it was because of their friendship. She'd survived her college years at Georgia Tech because of him. Unlike the other guys who'd looked right through her, Jake had seen her.

He'd been her first male friend. The first man she'd trusted. The only man she'd ever really been comfortable with.

She couldn't tell him that she'd kept their son a secret

because she'd been afraid that one day he'd leave her for a more glamorous woman and perhaps take their son with him.

"Everything about Peter is complicated."

Jake sat on the edge of her lounge chair and touched her face carefully. She knew in that instant that however Jake saw her, it wasn't the way other men did. "It doesn't have to be. Just level with me."

When he touched her she couldn't think. Shivers of awareness spread throughout her body and she'd never been more aware of Jake's maleness.

The fact that he was filled with rage at the secret she'd kept for too long didn't make it any easier to stop her skin from tingling, her nipples from tightening, or the warmth from pooling between her legs. She closed her eyes. But that only intensified his touch. It brought the entire focus of her world down to the two of them and the warmth of his fingers on her face.

"I'm waiting, Rissa."

Rissa. Jake was the only person who'd ever cared enough to call her by a nickname. To the world she was the serious librarian who could find any fact in record time, but to Jake she'd always been…she wasn't sure what she'd been to him. Or what she would be now.

She opened her eyes and his face was barely an inch from hers. His breath brushed her cheek and she knew if she leaned the tiniest bit toward him, he'd take control of this unexpected embrace. His lips would touch hers and she'd give up reason and sanity to experience again the magic they'd shared on that long-ago night.

She cleared her throat and leaned away from him. He rubbed his fingers, which had just been touching her face, and looked at her with regret.

"I'm not sure where to begin. The reasons are long and complicated. And you're too angry to really listen."

"Any man would be."

"I'm not saying you shouldn't be. I just don't want to become a victim in your quest for vengeance."

He watched her for a moment then stood in a rush, cursing under his breath. She realized she was right.

She should have known better. She'd never been more than a rather average-looking woman and Jake…well, Jake was used to prime cuts of womanhood. Tall, leggy blondes with D cups and flawless complexions. The closest she'd come to a D cup was after Peter had been born and her milk had come in.

"Then let's get this talk about our son over with."

She took a deep breath. She felt even more vulnerable than she had when she'd arrived at his house this morning. "I don't know what to say."

"For God's sake, woman, you graduated from Georgia Tech with honors. How hard can it be for you to find the words?"

"I wish it were easier, but it's all tied to my feelings."

"About me? I didn't force you that night."

"Jake, I was there, remember? It was an incredible night. I don't have any lingering resentment from that."

"I knew it."

"Good thing we're outside."

He quirked one eyebrow at her in question.

"So that your swelled head has room."

"Start from the beginning. I thought I used a condom."

"I think it broke."

"What?"

"I was a little sticky the next morning. So I took a test as soon as possible."

"You knew when I called to ask you to go to Cancun?"

"Yes."

Jake turned away from Larissa, intent on leaving before he said something he'd regret. Larissa was watching him with tears in her eyes and his head told him there was no way she'd intended to hurt him with her decision. But right now his heart told him he didn't care.

He felt betrayed because he'd always trusted Larissa. If any of the other women he'd slept with had shown up on his doorstep with a child in tow, he'd know they were there for money. He was always careful about protection because he knew that his name and his money left him vulnerable to ambitious women.

But Larissa was the sweet girl he'd felt comfortable talking to in the late hours at the library. The woman who'd come back to their five-year reunion looking like the embodiment of every female fantasy he'd ever had.

The woman who'd come to him today for help whether she admitted it or not.

And he was in no mood to help. He had to shake the fury pumping through him with every beat of his heart.

"I'll be back," he said, and walked into his house.

He headed down the hall to his tae kwon do workout room. In the corner was a bag he used for kickboxing practice and for sparring when Wes wasn't available to work out. He closed off his thoughts. Centered himself and focused all of his energy on the punching bag. Twenty minutes later he was dripping with sweat and still not sure he was ready to talk to Larissa. But they didn't have the luxury of time. There was a reporter who was determined to flash his face across the front page of every paper with the word father in the headline. He had to step up to the plate. He had to drop the safety of his carefree existence and really make his life count.

He bit back a savage curse. He wasn't ready for this. Didn't know that he ever would be. But Peter—that little boy—and his family deserved better. His uncle had enough to worry about with his campaign and some vaguely threatening e-mails. Jake wasn't going to add Larissa and Peter to the mix.

Grabbing a monogrammed towel from the rack near the door, he walked through his house. His town house had been featured in Modern Architecture as the ultimate bachelor pad. He grabbed a bottle of water from the fridge before stepping out on his patio. He wasn't sure what he expected to find when he returned.

He knew it wasn't Larissa sitting on the grass with their son in her lap. Both of them had their eyes closed and faces turned to the sun. He thought they were sleeping but then realized that Larissa was speaking softly. The words were familiar to him. Robert Frost's poem Stopping by Woods on a Snowy Evening.

He'd never felt more inadequate for the task before him than he did at this moment. Sure, *Fortune* magazine had called him and Adam the golden boys of the coffee bean world, "taking a tried and true idea and making it new and fresh."

But fatherhood was different. It involved emotions and all kinds of variables that didn't work in a solid business plan. And emotion was the one thing he'd always felt most uncomfortable with.

He guessed that was partly why he had a son with Larissa. The night of the reunion he'd realized she'd become more than just a smart girl who'd listen to him ramble on about what he wanted to do with his life. And he'd been uncomfortable with all she'd made him feel. Except for the passion she'd evoked in him. Passion was one area he was extremely comfortable with. So he'd seduced her under the stars.

Watching mother and child now kindled a desire for something that he hadn't realized was missing from his life. He wanted to be a part of that golden circle of light. Of that deep bond between mother and son. He wanted to insure that Rissa and Peter could always find a patch of sunlight to sit in. He set his towel and water bottle down on the table and crossed to them.

Not questioning his actions, he sank to the ground behind Larissa and settled himself around her. He left a couple of inches of space because he knew that in spite of his feelings of betrayal, he wasn't above using sex to manipulate her. He wanted her like hell on fire. And if he touched her again, he wasn't going to be able to control himself.

He put his hands over Larissa's and felt her stiffen. Peter's small hand moved to rest on his wrist and Jake felt something close to peace for the first time since he'd been old enough to know that he was a Danforth.

He liked the sound his deep voice made added to Larissa's soft tone and Peter's childish one.

"The woods are lovely, dark and deep
But I have promises to keep
And miles to go before I sleep
And miles to go before I sleep."

They finished the poem together and Peter leaned around his mother to watch him with wide questioning eyes.

"How did you know the words?" Peter asked.

"Your mom taught them to me," he said, softly. The boy continued to watch him with a focus that was unnerving.

Peter broke into a wide grin and said, "Cool." The boy hopped to his feet and ran across the yard toward the ball.

Jake turned his head a quarter and met Larissa's

clear blue gaze. For a moment they were back in the uncomplicated days of college. Life was just about doing what felt right and making each moment count. Victoria had still been safely at home, and he hadn't yet fathered a child. But times had changed and Victoria was gone—disappeared at a concert so long ago. And though everyone warned them she was dead and would never return, Jake's family kept hope alive.

Larissa smiled at him and his groin tingled. She was so close that her scent filled his nostrils with each breath.

"I did, didn't I?" She licked her lips nervously and he leaned closer to her. Her mouth had always fascinated him. Her lower lip was fuller than the top and he knew from that one brief night how sumptuous her mouth would feel under his own.

He leaned farther toward her. "Yes, you did," he said to Larissa.

"That seems like so long ago."

"It was a different life," he said.

Peter kicked the ball over to them with more energy than skill. Jake had always been very good at soccer and his son showed…none of Jake's aptitude.

"Where'd you go before?" Peter asked, coming over to them.

"To my workout room. I needed to clear my head."

"Is it clear now?"

"Almost," Jake said, ruffling his son's hair.

He stood and helped Larissa to her feet. He still wanted to know why she hadn't told him she was having his child, but he'd save that conversation for later when they were alone. Right now they needed to figure out what to do next.

But Peter was watching him and he didn't want to have an uncomfortable conversation in front of the boy. "Let me show you how to kick the ball like the pros do."

"What's a pro?" Peter asked.

"A professional player. You know someone who gets paid to play the game."

"You can get paid to play?" Peter asked.

"Only if you're really good."

Jake showed his son a few basic kicks and then got out his practice goal net and left his son playing.

Larissa had returned to her lounge chair and watched him warily as he walked toward her. He didn't like the look on her face. He didn't like it at all.

Larissa tried not to stare as Jake walked over to her, but she couldn't help it. Sweat glistened on his neck and she knew that if she got close to him, he would smell earthy. She wanted to indulge herself in him once more. But he needed answers and she'd come here this morning intent on giving them to him.

She closed her eyes. While Jake had been gone, she'd found the words she needed to tell him. She'd have to sacrifice her pride, but Peter was more important than pride.

Jake returned and sat on a chair facing her. He braced

his elbows on his knees and leaned toward her. She took a deep breath.

"Jake, I—"

"Larissa, I—"

She laughed. In the old days when they'd been friends, often they'd both started talking at the same time.

"You first," Jake said.

Knowing that Jake had never been anything but good to her, she sorted out the pieces of her troubled past and took a deep breath. "The reason why I didn't tell you about Peter is that I wanted to manage parenthood on my own."

"You always were pretty stubborn about that. Why don't you save the rest of the tale for a time when we are alone? Let's talk about what we do now."

She appreciated the reprieve, but she was curious. "What made you change your mind?"

He shrugged massive shoulders. "Something about you looking at me like I was an ogre."

"I didn't."

"Sweetheart, you have the biggest, most innocent eyes I've ever looked into, and it only takes one instant for you to make me feel like a bully."

His words made her feel special. "I didn't mean to."

"I know. Let's fix this reporter problem and then we'll talk. We'll find a sitter for Peter and we can learn each other's secrets."

"I don't have any secrets."

"Peter's it?"

"Yes, just Peter. I felt so...panicked when Jasmine Carmody called and said she knew you were Peter's father. There's nothing I can do to protect him from anything she writes for her newspaper. At least he can't read."

"How did she find out about Peter? Am I listed on the birth certificate?"

"No. She said she'd talked to Marti Freehold. Do you remember her?"

"She's the biggest gossip I've ever met."

"Yes, she is. Marti mentioned she'd seen us leaving the reunion together. And that we'd looked, well, like we needed to find a private room and quick."

"Sounds like Marti," Jake said.

"Jasmine Carmody has Peter's birth certificate and she knows you're not listed on there, but she also has a picture of you when you were the same age as Peter. They're practically identical."

Jake leaned back in the chair and Larissa tried not to stare at him. She knew that he was trying to solve a very sticky problem. And she shouldn't be lusting over him at a time like this.

Finally he cleared his throat. "I think I may have come up with a solution that will take the sting out of any article Jasmine Carmody writes."

"What?"

"We'll live together as a family."

"Will that work?"

"Sure it will. What she's doing is just a step above blackmail. If we acknowledge it and move on, then she can't hurt us with whatever she writes. I think it's the perfect solution."

"But living together? I don't think that's necessary."

"I do. I want to get to know my son. We'll be a family unit and once she knows I've acknowledged Peter is mine, she won't be able to hurt us."

"Jake, we hardly know each other."

He raised his eyebrow at her. "I'd say we know each other pretty well."

"That was just one night."

"Rissa, I was talking about all those late-night conversations in the library."

She flushed, knowing good and well what he'd been referring to. She wasn't sure what had changed while Jake had been gone, but his workout had brought back the man she knew. The man she was comfortable with. The man who wasn't so angry at being left in the dark where his son was concerned.

"Still, we've never lived together. I mean, where would we live?"

"I don't have every detail planned. I'd like to live here because I'm close to D&D's and I go into the office every day when I'm not traveling."

"Well, your place isn't much farther than mine from the library. But I don't know that I'd feel comfortable in your house."

"We'll hire a decorator to do the place over."

"I don't know. That seems like a big expense for..."

"For what?"

"For camouflage."

"Camouflage?" he asked.

"We aren't in a relationship. Are you sure about this?"

"One-hundred-percent certain."

"Would we be like roommates?"

"What did you have in mind?" he asked, waggling his eyebrows at her.

She didn't know if she could live with Jake and not give in to the lust surging through her. This was probably the dumbest idea ever but deep in her heart it felt right.

"Not what you're thinking. I mean we're both adults. We can keep our hands to ourselves. We're living together for Peter's sake, not for ours."

"It's precisely because we are adults that I think we're going to have a hard time living together and not sleeping together."

"Jake, are you trying to say I can break your willpower?"

"Sweetheart, do you really want to start a battle over this?"

"Why, don't you think I could win?"

"Not if I put my mind to it."

"It's not your mind that tempts me, Jake."

He threw his head back and laughed. Her heart clenched and her entire body ached. She wanted to be in his arms again. But she knew better than anyone did what a relationship based on a child was like. She also knew that when it came to lasting relationships, the odds of her and Jake making it work were very slim.

Her only chance at sanity was to make sure he stayed out of her bed and her heart.

Three

Jake knew there was no way he'd be able to live under the same roof as Larissa and keep his hands to himself. But if she wanted to pretend a platonic relationship was all she wanted, he'd let her. Passion and proximity were two things that couldn't be ignored.

He'd been celibate for a while now. Though he still casually dated, sleeping with women he hardly knew had lost some of the excitement it had held. And his business took most of his time. Becoming a millionaire in his own right before he turned thirty had taken all of his concentration.

The spark that had been kindled at their college reunion almost four years ago hadn't died after one night together. This morning had proved that the fire between them still burned strongly. But he was willing to bide his time until they had everything settled between them before he made any moves toward Larissa.

He knew that in time she'd be in his bed. Everything else about the future seemed uncertain, but there was a sense of rightness in his soul when he thought of the two of them together. Just to be certain that he never lost his son again, he made a mental note to call Marcus, his cousin and family lawyer.

"You can move in today. Do you need my help to get your stuff?"

Larissa got to her feet and paced around the patio. Peter was still playing by the soccer net Jake had set up. Larissa watched her son for a few minutes, then turned back to him. "Not today. Let me think about this."

Jake moved near to her. She crossed her arms over her chest and stepped back from him. What was she afraid of? "What's to think about? No sex and we'll live here."

She bit her lip. "For how long?"

Jake shrugged. His experience with relationships said that most didn't last longer than it took to get your stuff settled, but Peter guaranteed they'd be together longer. "I don't know. Why?"

"What if one of us falls in love with someone else?" Larissa asked. The wind caught a strand of her hair, which brushed across her face. Larissa reached up and tucked it behind her ear.

Love was the one thing he'd never really found with any woman. It seemed elusive to him somehow. He wondered sometimes if love and happiness were going to be forever out of his reach. He was jaded enough to know that he wasn't going to find love through the intense desire that he felt for Larissa. "I doubt that would happen."

"Why not?" she asked, holding herself tighter while she waited for his answer.

He didn't like the barrier she'd built between them. Didn't like that she was comforting herself and that she was still hiding something from him. So he said the one thing sure to needle her. He remembered her soft heart and belief in happily-ever-after.

"Because love is part of the game that people play when they are searching for themselves. We're both secure in our place in the world."

She fisted her hands and put them on her hips. "That is the stupidest thing I've ever heard."

This was the Larissa he remembered. Eyes shooting sparks when he pushed her buttons. She'd been so sure she was a plain Jane who no jock would ever look at twice. But she'd caught his eye and held it longer than any of her peers back then. "Surely, you don't believe in love?"

"Of course I do. And I'm raising our son to believe in it, too," she said, gesturing to Peter.

"You're just preparing him for heartache."

"Is that what love means to you?" she asked. Despite her argument, he didn't think she believed in love, either. Because any woman who had a romantic outlook on life would have contacted her baby's father.

He didn't like the direction this conversation was

taking. "I don't know what love means to me. I can honestly say I've never really experienced it. Have you?"

"No."

"I don't think we'll have a problem with either of us falling in love. You're down-to-earth and so am I."

"I don't want to be a burden to you, Jake. I don't want to wake up one morning and find out you don't want us anymore."

"Why would that happen? I don't have time for anything else right now. D&D's keeps me busy and I'm not dating anyone."

"Right now, but you change women as often as you change your pants."

"That's not true. I haven't been with a woman in the last year and a half."

"Sure, you haven't."

"Believe what you want but I've never lied to you."

"Low blow."

"The truth hurts."

"I don't think this will work. Maybe I should take Jake and leave Savannah."

"You can leave if you want to, but you're not taking my son." Jake wasn't going to waste a single day of his time with Peter now that he knew he had a son. His dad, who'd always been busy with the shipping company, had made time for family. He wanted the opportunity to do the same.

She rubbed her eyes with the heels of her hands and then looked at him. He knew this was hard on her and he sympathized with her to a certain extent but they wouldn't be in this predicament now if she'd come to him when she'd first found out she was pregnant. "I don't know what to do. But I don't want to make things worse than they are now."

"I'll take care of everything for you."

"I'm not looking for a hero."

"Good, because I'm not much of one," he said. He'd always known his own faults.

He wanted to reach out and touch her. To take her in his arms and promise he'd shoulder her burdens, but he knew she wouldn't accept that. "Trust me on this, Rissa. I'll take care of everything."

"You aren't doing this for revenge, are you?"

"I don't follow."

"You know, make me move in here and then…do something to keep Peter and kick me out?"

"That's a nice opinion you have of me."

"Well, I wouldn't blame you if you tried it."

"You're important to Peter," he said. Larissa was the center of Peter's world and his son was the most important person to consider.

"People are going to say I trapped you."

"Let them talk. Anyone who knows you won't believe it."

"It's easy for you to say."

"Nothing about this is easy for me."

"I know. So we'd live with you until your uncle's campaign is over? Then the media scrutiny around your family will die down and we can go back to our normal lives."

"I'm not going to disappear after this reporter moves on to her next juicy topic." He realized the words were true as he said them. Larissa and Peter were his responsibility now and forever. And whether she lived with him or not, he'd always be involved in their lives. And that felt right to him deep in his soul.

"Promise?" The word was hardly out before Larissa bit her lip wishing she could take it back.

Jake closed the gap between them and cupped her face in his big hands. His brown eyes more serious than she'd ever seen them before, he leaned close to her. There were hidden depths to this man she'd scarcely explored.

She wondered what he'd do if she turned the tables on him—if she held his face in her hands and looked down on him with something like tenderness.

"I promise."

She shivered. This was the secret dream she'd harbored since she was a young girl. That she'd find a man, a big, strong, attractive man who'd make her feel that she was the center of his world. But her dream had always been a bittersweet one, because time and experience had taught her that being the center of any man's world was a fleeting thing.

"Oh, Jake, don't say things you don't mean."

"Woman, I don't know why you have such a low opinion of me."

"I don't. It's myself I don't trust."

"What's not to trust?"

"You. Saying things that I'll take to mean something you aren't feeling."

"This isn't the love thing again, is it?"

"Don't be flip."

"I can't help it. You make me want to be a better man than I know I can be."

She was flattered that he thought she had any power over him. And saddened to realize that Jake thought he wasn't a great man to begin with. "Really?"

"Really."

"There you go again, making me believe you could be my knight in shining armor," she said, feeling her control shatter.

"I thought we both agreed I was no hero."

"When you touch me I can't think of anything but you."

"Rissa," he said. Lowering his mouth to hers, he brushed his lips back and forth over her own. It was a simple, gentle kiss, but it shook the moorings of everything she believed about herself.

She brought her hands to his shoulders, holding on to him for balance in a world that was suddenly spinning further and further out of her control. He traced the shape of her mouth with his tongue, running it over the closed seam of her lips. She knew what he wanted—what they both wanted. She opened her mouth on a sigh. And he teased her with his tongue. Teased her by giving her a hint of what was yet to come.

She leaned into him, resting against his strong body.

She felt safe and in danger at the same time. Her breasts were heavy and she threw back her shoulders, rubbing their tips against him. He moaned deep in his throat, the sound feral and arousing.

Sliding his hands down her neck and then around to her back, his hold on her changed. He traced the line of her spine with his fingertips and she shuddered. She felt him tremble, too.

Jake pulled her more firmly against his body. His groin nestled into the notch at her thighs, her legs turned to jelly. She sank against him, totally caught up in his embrace. Jake supported her completely with one hand on her backside and the other behind her neck.

She moaned deep in her throat, tunneling her fingers through his hair to try to control their embrace. Or to at least be an active participant in it. He rubbed his tongue over hers and then pulled back.

Watching him intently, she couldn't help but wonder why she'd stayed away so long. But she knew the answer—because sanity was hard to come by and Jake threatened hers. She pulled away, tripping over her own feet in her hurry to put some distance between them.

Jake steadied her with one hand. His touch was warm but not soothing against her arm. She wanted to say the heck with her reservations and just indulge herself in a red-hot affair with this man. But there were too many barriers between them. Not the least of which was a little boy who deserved a happier childhood than Larissa had experienced.

She'd promised herself to protect Peter. No matter

what the cost to her. Peter hadn't asked to be born and it was up to her make sure he had the best life had to offer. And Jake, for all his playboy ways, seemed genuinely interested in being a father to his son.

She knew she couldn't keep Jake and Peter apart. She'd have to make sure that Peter never knew the circumstances that had brought Jake and her together. If things didn't work out between her and Jake, she didn't want Peter to feel it was his fault.

"Are you sure about the platonic part of this relationship?" Jake asked.

"You're the one who suggested it," she said. Less than ever, she thought. Her blood was racing through her body. Her nipples were beaded and aching for his touch. And her center was wet with desire for him. She wanted to take his hand and lead him into the house where they could be alone. Only the knowledge that her son was a few feet away kept her from taking such an ill-advised action.

"Rissa?" he asked, running his finger down the side of her face.

"Yes," she said. She had to get out of this place. Figure out what was going on in her life and make a plan to protect herself from the vulnerability that Jake brought out in her.

He smirked. "Whatever you say."

She knew he could make her eat her words, just prayed that he wouldn't.

"Mama, can I have some juice?" Peter asked, racing over to them.

"It's may I, sweetie," Larissa said.

"May I have some juice?"

"Sure," she said, going into the kitchen to her oversize bag and pulling out a juice box. She paused in the doorway before returning to the patio. Jake and Peter were in front of the goal net again and this time Jake was setting himself up as goalie. She watched the two of them together and realized she wasn't the only one who'd been missing a man in her life. No matter the cost to herself, she had to make this new arrangement with Jake work out. For Peter's sake.

"Here's your juice, Peter," Larissa said from the patio.

Jake ruffled Peter's hair, lifting up the boy to carry him back to the patio. It was the first time he'd held his son's small body. A surge of protectiveness roared through him.

This was his son. Peter rested his head on his shoulder and Jake met Larissa's gaze. Something passed between them and he knew she knew what he felt.

"We should get going. Peter needs a nap."

"I'll carry him out to your car. When will you be back?"

"I have to work this afternoon. I won't have time to get our stuff together until after I pick Peter up at the sitter's."

"Can he stay with me?" Jake asked.

"I...I don't know if he would. He doesn't really know you."

"I'm the boy's father. Isn't it time he got to know me?"

"Yes, it is. But watching him takes a lot of patience and attention."

"What do you say, sport?" Jake asked Peter. "Want to stay with me while your mom's at work."

Peter looked at his mom and Larissa took a deep breath and nodded. "It's okay with me, sweetie."

"Can we play soccer some more?"

"After you take a nap," Larissa said.

"Okay, I'll stay with you."

Larissa gathered her things and Jake carried Peter out to her car. She buckled him in the car seat and put Mr. Bear and his blanket around his face.

Jake stood waiting by the car when she turned around. "I'm not due at work until three. I'll bring Peter by around two-thirty."

"Why don't I come to your place for lunch? I can help you pack up your stuff. Peter can help me bring your stuff back here."

"Okay. Are you sure about this living together thing?"

"Yes. I have to do it because I'd feel like less than a man if I didn't."

"Why don't you think about it? I couldn't bear it if you had regrets."

"I wouldn't have asked if I wasn't positive this was the best course of action. Now that I know I have a son, nothing less than living under the same roof will satisfy me."

"Somehow I knew you'd feel that way."

"Knew it this morning or when you first discovered you were pregnant?" he asked.

He still wanted to know why she hadn't come to him to begin with. He would have done the honorable thing then. Even though she'd said she'd wanted to manage motherhood on her own, Larissa wasn't one of those staunch feminists. Sure she'd believed women deserved equal pay and equal opportunity, but she'd always had a sort of dreamy vision of what family life should be.

A vision that included a mother and father and two kids. A cute little cottage on the river. A big yard with room for soccer practice and a dock to fish from. Somehow his vision and hers had blended together in the early-morning hours when they'd talked about the future.

She'd always made him want to talk about the future and maybe he realized that was why her answer now was so important. He wanted to believe that she'd known he would have done the honorable thing three years ago, not because of what society would say, but because of the woman she was.

"I've always known it," she said, quietly.

Without thinking, he reached out and pulled her close in a bear hug. He held her tightly to him and knew deep in his soul he wasn't letting this woman or their son walk out of his life. "I hope this isn't a mistake."

Jake let her go. "It's what's best for Peter. So are you going to stop arguing and move in with me?"

She stared at him. Her eyes were wide and questioning, still holding secrets that he wondered if he'd ever uncover. "I will."

Satisfaction flowed through him. She belonged to him and so did their son. The sooner he had them under his roof the more settled he'd feel. "Good."

She crossed her arms over her chest again and he realized she was trying to put a barrier between them. She didn't realize that running only made him want to chase her. And catch her. His mind filled with images of what he'd do when he caught her. When he coaxed her willingly to his bed.

"I'm going to call Nicola, Uncle Abe's PR person and advise her of this current situation. My folks are going to want to meet their grandson. So after you get off work tonight, we'll head over there, if that's okay with you."

"I'm not sure I want to meet your parents."

"Why not?"

"They're bound to be mad at me."

"They're nicer than I am."

She hadn't even considered the family that Peter would now call his own. Her own dad hadn't spoken to her since she was six and her mom had died during her first year of college, so he'd never had any grandparents. "I doubt that."

"Don't worry about it. I'll take care of everything. Trust me," Jake said.

"You keep saying that."

"I'm going to continue to until you finally believe in me."

"I wish I could, but it's not that easy."

"What's not?"

"Trusting a man."

"I'm not just any man. I'm the father of your child."

"I know," she said. He couldn't know that made it even harder for her to trust him.

Four

After Larissa and Peter left, Jake called his lawyer and had a lengthy conversation to put in motion a bid for custody of Peter. The first thing Marcus had suggested was a paternity test to give them a legal leg to stand on. Jake didn't doubt that Peter was his son. He knew Larissa. And he'd looked into his son's eyes. Peter was his. But he liked the idea of having the documentation to prove it.

Nicola had been out of the office so Jake had left a message for her to call him. Then he drove to Larissa's house. Riverside was a nice suburb of Savannah and as he neared Larissa's house he realized she wasn't just eking out a living. She'd made a life for herself and their son that was comfortable.

He felt a little bad about the plan he had put into

motion with Marcus. But he wasn't going to give up his son now that he'd found out about him. Being a father felt right deep in his soul and if he had a few doubts that he wouldn't be up to the job, he'd get over them. There had never been anything he couldn't achieve when he put his mind to it. Except for gaining his father's respect.

Mindful that Larissa said she was going to give Peter a nap, Jake avoided the front door and walked around to the backyard. As he approached the side of the house he heard soft Asian music playing. He rounded the corner to the back of the house and found Larissa lying on a yoga mat in a shady area.

He watched her change poses. He admired her grace and style. But from his position he could also see her cleavage and any altruistic thoughts he had were banished by the rush of desire.

He waited until she finished her routine by sitting in a meditative pose. She looked peaceful and serene—untouchable. And she evoked in him a savageness he'd always tried to tamp down and hide.

Clearing his throat, he climbed the steps of the deck. Her eyes snapped open and she stared at him. There were beads of perspiration on her neck and chest. His first impulse was to lick them from her skin. His eyes narrowed. His breathing changed and he felt arousal spread throughout his body. Damn. This reaction to her didn't fit into his well-ordered plans for Larissa.

She scrambled to her feet when she realized he was watching her. The formfitting leggings and snug sleeveless shirt left little of her body to the imagination.

It was the first time he'd seen her in anything that wasn't loose and concealing. Even that night they'd made love, she'd insisted they leave the lights low.

Her legs were long and curvy. Her hips a real woman's and not a model's. Her breasts were pert and, he knew from experience, just the right size to nestle in his palms.

The spandex shirt clung to the full globes and Jake had to swallow when her nipples budded against the cloth under his gaze. She stopped moving and he glanced up at her face. A pink blush covered her neck and cheeks, but she didn't cross her arms over her chest.

"Are you sure about this platonic thing?" he asked, his voice husky with need.

"No, I'm not sure."

He took two large steps toward her, closing the gap between them. She didn't smell sweaty the way he did after exercise. It reminded him of how different the two of them were. How different men and women were and how exciting those differences could be.

Unable to resist, he traced with his finger a bead of perspiration that rolled down between her breasts, disappearing under her shirt. She shivered when he reached the border where skin and fabric met. He watched goose bumps spread over her skin and, hesitating only a second, he dipped his finger under her shirt.

She was just as soft to the touch as he remembered. Her breasts appeared a bit bigger than before and he let his finger slide under one of them. She bit her lip and tilted her head to the side, watching him with hooded eyes.

She swayed and he brought his other arm up around her waist, holding her the way he'd dreamed of since he'd opened her car door this morning. He pulled his finger free of her shirt and lifted it to his lips.

Her pupils dilated as she watched him and her breath rushed in and out as if she'd just completed a five-mile run instead of a yoga routine.

The salty taste of her on Jake's tongue only whetted his appetite for more of her. He leaned toward her. She gripped his biceps and rose on her tiptoes. Her breath fanned against his cheek.

He bent and captured her mouth. She opened for him with a sigh that told him she'd needed this embrace as much as he had. Her fingernails bit into his arms as she returned his kiss.

He cupped her bottom and brought her more fully against him. Her hardened nipples pushed into his chest. He swallowed her moan as he deepened their embrace. He reached again for her breast, sliding his hand up under her shirt this time. She shuddered when he palmed a nipple.

He slid his mouth from hers, down the slope of her neck until he could trace the V-neck of her shirt with his tongue. She trembled again in his arms, her hands clutching at his head.

The phone rang inside the house and Larissa pushed him away, stumbling, her eyes wide and wounded. She hurried into the house to take the call and he cursed under his breath. Pivoting on his heel, he walked to the edge of the deck.

He braced his hands on the railing, bowing his head and breathing deeply, searching for his control. Hell, what was he thinking? He hadn't come here to make love to Larissa. In fact, considering their situation it was the last thing he should be doing. Further evidence, as if he needed it, that he wasn't cut out for responsibility. Maybe he should rethink the custody suit. He knew it was male pride motivating him.

He heard her return, sensed her standing in the doorway watching him. She cleared her throat and he glanced over his shoulder at her.

She'd put on a large sweatshirt while she'd been in the house and crossed her arms over her chest. He didn't know what to say to her and he had the feeling if he opened his mouth he'd say something stupid instead of acting like the rather suave guy he liked to think he was.

Finally she said, "Peter's still sleeping. Why don't you come inside and I'll make us some lunch."

"I'm not hungry," he said.

"Oh. Okay."

This wasn't working out the way he'd planned it. "Larissa, sit down."

"Why?"

"We have to talk."

"I guess we do. Are you sure you don't want any food? How about some iced tea?"

"No. Nothing."

She sat down on one of the wrought-iron chairs around a small café-style table. He took one of the chairs, spun it around and sat facing her.

"What'd you want to talk to me about?"

"A couple of things. First off, I'd like to take Peter to get a paternity test."

Larissa laced her fingers together and stared at Jake. He was so familiar to her, yet at the same time a stranger with steely determination. This was the man who'd made D&D's coffeehouse the success it was today. And though Larissa had spent some late nights with Jake in college, he'd been more of a dreamer then than the man he was today.

The calm she'd tried to find through yoga had disappeared as soon as she'd seen Jake. She'd gone into his arms remembering the man she'd left earlier today. The man who'd told her she could trust him. This didn't feel like trust. This felt…this felt like betrayal.

"You don't think he's your son?" she asked at last.

He watched her with that intense dark brown stare that penetrated through the layers she used to protect herself. She flinched under his scrutiny, tucking a stray strand of hair back into her ponytail.

"I didn't say that," he said, running his hands through his thick black curly hair. She could still feel the texture of his hair in her hands. She clenched her hands and tried to concentrate on his words.

"Yes, you did. If you believed me then you wouldn't need a test." She'd known he'd be angry at her for keeping the truth from him but had never expected him to doubt he was the father.

"Don't make this about you and me, Rissa. This is a matter of practicality. I can't provide for Peter until I'm legally recognized as his father. Only a paternity test can prove that."

Practicality. She'd spent a lifetime being practical, realistic and sensible. She understood those things, but just once she wanted the fantasies she still harbored to come true. A million thoughts ran through her head. Jumbled and confused—a chaotic disarray of her view of reality. She pulled her legs up in the chair and wrapped her arms around them. Of all the things that Jake could say to her this was the one thing she'd never expected.

She wished now she'd run away this morning when Ms. Carmody had called. That she'd taken Peter and disappeared. Anything so she didn't have to go through this. She'd created a mess of complications she'd never considered when she'd kept Peter a secret.

Complications that had made her regret her actions a few times—things like medical history; Peter had asthma. Things like who would take care of her son if she died; Larissa had no family. Things like being a part of a wealthy family; Larissa made enough to provide for her son, but was she denying him the opportunity for more?

"Everything is so..." She trailed off, afraid of revealing too much to Jake. It would be different if they were just friends, if there wasn't that spark of sexual attraction buzzing between them.

He raised one eyebrow at her in question.

"Complex," she said at last.

His lips quirked and he reached across the small table to pull her hands off her legs. He twined their fingers together. "We'll take it one day at a time—together."

Together. The word scared her. She'd grown used to being independent, to being solely responsible for Peter. It was strange to think that Jake would have some say in Peter's life. Not necessarily in a bad way, she realized, which also scared her.

"I'm still not sure that us moving in with you is a good idea."

"Now that I've seen your place, I'd be willing to move here."

She didn't want Jake here in her house. This was her sanctuary from the world. The one place where it didn't matter that she'd never really had a father. "No, we better stay at your house."

"This is a nice place," Jake said after a while, gesturing to the house.

"Thanks. It suits us. We spend a lot of time out here or on the river."

"I never pictured you as an outdoorsy person," he said. He shifted her hands in his, his thumbs making lazy circles on her palms.

"Probably because I'm so bookish."

"Bookish?"

"What would you call me?" she asked.

"Intelligent but in a sexy way."

"I had no idea brains were a turn-on for men."

"I don't know about other men."

She smiled at him, unsure where this was going. She tugged her hands away from his and looked out at the Savannah River. She loved this house even though she'd inherited it from a man she'd scarcely known.

"Did you move here after Peter was born?" he asked.

"Yes, my grandfather left the place to me."

"I'm sorry for your loss."

"That's okay," she said. Her grandfather hadn't ever spoken to her when he'd been alive. The old man had disowned her mother when she'd first found out she was pregnant. "We weren't close."

"I remember your mom died when we were in college. Do you have any other family?"

"I have Peter."

"This must have been some fun place to explore as a kid."

She shrugged. She'd never visited here until the day they'd moved in. She'd sold her condo in Atlanta and moved here. Her grandfather hadn't kept any pictures of her mom or herself in the house. She'd found a drawer in the mahogany desk in the den filled with unopened letters from her mom. Only one letter had been opened—the one she'd sent to her grandfather telling him he had a great-grandson.

He'd never contacted her, but Larissa often wondered if that was why he'd left her this place. Not for her and for the sins of her mother, but for Peter. The great-grandson he'd never let himself know.

"I know you're an only child, but did you have cousins to play with?" he asked.

"Not every family is like yours, Jake. Some of us are only children of only children."

He put his hands up. "I didn't mean anything by it. This is a great place to raise a son. When you said he only watched PBS, I was scared you were turning him into a little brainiac."

"I'm trying, but he has your genes," she said, trying for a lightness that she didn't really feel.

He grabbed his chest. "Ouch."

She chuckled.

"I'll take that lunch you offered now," he said. Something had changed in his eyes that made a ray of hope blossom in her chest. She realized that there was no one else she'd rather share parenthood with than this man.

Larissa's kitchen reminded him of Tuscany. It was painted rich warm colors. He could tell she'd remodeled since she'd moved in. The houses in this neighborhood had been originally built in the fifties. But her kitchen was very modern. The large butcher-block island where she assembled lunch had a new look to it.

"Is salad okay?"

Not really. He'd still be hungry when he was done. But they'd reached a kind of truce on the deck and he didn't want to rock the boat. "Sure. What can I do to help?"

"Can you cook?"

He laughed. "No. But cutting up veggies isn't that hard."

"No, it's not. I'm making a Greek salad, so you can cut up olives and peppers for it."

She put on a Jimmy Buffett CD while they worked in the kitchen. The first time he'd noticed Larissa in college had been at a Buffett concert. She'd been the only one in their group without a grass skirt or Hawaiian shirt. And she'd turned eight shades of red when Buffett sang "Let's Get Drunk and Screw."

"I love this CD. I remember the first time you heard some of these songs."

"Me, too. I wanted to die, I was so mortified that ya'll were singing it at the top of your lungs."

"Wasn't long before we'd corrupted you and you were singing along. Remember the next concert less than a year later?"

She gave him a saucy grin, one he'd forgotten. For all her shy ways in a large group, one on one, Larissa was a sassy woman. "You always were a bad influence on me."

His track record with women wasn't the best. He'd gotten Larissa pregnant and not known it. In his defense, he'd been going through a lot then. His sister Victoria had disappeared and D&D's was starting to go big time. Jake didn't cut himself any slack for those things. Some men were inherently flawed when it came to women and he was beginning to believe he was one of them.

"Yeah, I guess I was," he said.

He felt her hand on his arm and realized he'd stopped cutting. "I was joking."

He put the knife on the counter, leaning his hip against it and staring down at her. Damn, he'd forgotten how small she was. He felt big—too big for her and for her kitchen. He also felt too hard for the woman who'd blushed at provocative song lyrics. "But there is an element of truth to your words."

She cupped his jaw. Her long fingers were cold against his skin. "Not really. You've never made me do anything I regretted."

There was something in her eyes that convinced him of her sincerity. He leaned down to kiss her. A quick embrace that held shared memories and the hope of finding some sort of peace for the future. She pulled away too soon for him.

"We better get back to work or we'll never eat," she said lightly, stepping away from him and moving around the island.

Did she really think one butcher-block countertop was going to stop him? He'd let her back away earlier when her phone rang but he knew they were going to have to come to terms with this sexual attraction between them before she moved into his place. "Maybe I'm not hungry for rabbit food."

"What are you hungry for?" She tilted her head to the side and watched him with eyes that knew their effect on him.

"Do I really have to tell you?" he asked, coming around the side of the counter and closing the gap between them. He backed her up against the countertop, not stopping until their bodies brushed against each other.

She tipped her head back, exposing her long elegant neck. He lifted one large blunt finger and stroked the length of it. She trembled under his touch and her pulse started to beat more heavily. Her eyes narrowed to slits.

"The only thing on the menu is Greek salad, Jake."

She wasn't ready for anything other than teasing, he thought. Right now, maybe that's all he was ready for too. Marcus had made some interesting points on the phone. A paternity test was only one of the things he wanted from Larissa. He also needed to know why she'd kept her pregnancy a secret.

He stepped away and went back to chopping olives. "Too bad. I had my sights set on something mouthwatering."

She said nothing but assembled the salad and led the way out to the deck overlooking the Savannah River. She was still nervous around him, afraid to trust him, and she was right to be. He had his own plans and she was only a means to an end. As cruel as that sounded, he couldn't curb his gut instinct, which told him an eye for an eye.

"Thanks for lunch," he said while she cleared the plates.

"It was only a salad," she said.

"It was delicious."

"Thanks. I'm not really much of a cook."

"Me either. Luckily I know how to dial for take-out."

"I can't eat take-out every night. And it's really not good for Peter. Or you."

"I run five miles every morning and play soccer on Saturdays."

"I...I've seen you."

"When?"

"Last fall. Peter and I were having a picnic at the park. We were packing up to leave when you guys arrived for your game."

"Why didn't you say something?"

"I was scared."

"Of what?"

"My reasons are personal, Jake."

"Honey, surely not too personal to share with the father of your child."

"Sarcasm doesn't become you."

"Neither do lies you."

"I'm not lying to you."

"Not today, right? It's funny how truth seems to be your ally when you need one."

"Ally? Are we enemies?"

"Only in your eyes."

"When did I make us enemies?"

"When you kept my son a secret," he said savagely.

"I can't believe we're going through this again."

"I'm waiting to hear these reasons of yours, Rissa.

Because I have to tell you I can't believe the sweet girl I knew in college would keep this from me. What other secrets are you hiding?"

Five

Larissa stood and walked into her house, unsure what to say but needing to escape. She paused inside the living room. Portraits of Peter lined the wall. She had spent a small fortune in film developing since he'd been born. She'd filled this empty old house with pictures of her son.

With pictures of the small family that she'd finally found. She scanned the pictures, stopping on one taken only two weeks ago, Peter on the dock with his fishing pole in hand. He'd been aggravated that he hadn't caught anything and he stared down into the water with the same determination she'd just seen in Jake's eyes.

She hurried past the photos and entered her kitchen, where she started cleaning. Cleaning had always been a chore that soothed her. It was simple and straightforward, and when she finished she could look back and see what she'd accomplished.

Unlike life, which seemed never to run smoothly. Every time she thought she and Jake had a chance at getting past her deception, his anger reared its ugly head. And she knew he deserved some answers, but the last thing she wanted to do was bare her soul to him.

Jake had always been the one guy she'd wanted. The one guy who'd made her feel like it was okay to be herself. The one guy who…she'd never been able to forget.

She sensed him behind her. She put the rest of the dishes in the dishwasher and turned to face him. He had that bulldog angry look on his face and his arms crossed over his massive chest that told her he wasn't budging until he got some answers.

She swallowed, twisting the dish towel with her hands. "You're right. I do have some secrets that I don't want to share with you."

"I'm trying to understand. But your lack of trust makes it damned hard."

"I know. Remember earlier when you asked me about my grandfather?" she asked, sorting through her past and finding one of the things that seemed safest to tell him. Jake came from a wealthy family with history and pride. And she'd never had a real family until Peter. She'd never felt she'd missed out until she'd had her son and realized what life could've been like.

He leaned against the doorjamb, no less intimidating in the more relaxed pose. "Yes."

His black T-shirt stretched across his chest and she wished she'd never left his arms earlier. He was too handsome for his own good. He could be dirt poor and he'd still have a legion of women after him.

If she'd stayed in his arms earlier, nature would have taken its course and she could have avoided this conversation. But she was vulnerable where Jake was concerned. She didn't want to create any further bonds between them and risk the chance that she'd be hurt when he left. And she knew he'd leave. No man had ever stayed. Starting with her grandfather, before she was even born.

"Well, I never knew him. He and my mom had a falling-out before I was born. He disowned her over her choice of husband."

"Your father?"

She nodded. No way was she ever going to call Reilly Payton her father. The man had made it clear that society may have demanded he do his duty by her mother, but father was one role he'd never wanted to play. She'd legally changed her name to Nielsen when she'd turned 18.

"What's that got to do with you keeping Peter's birth from me?"

She took a deep breath, mentally crossed her fingers and bowed her head. She'd learned early on that if she was going to tell a half-truth it was easier if she wasn't looking the person in the eye. "I didn't want your family to disown you because of me."

"Sweetheart, look at me," he said.

She glanced up at him, hoping he'd let the subject drop. "Yes?"

"That's the biggest whopper I've ever heard. You know Wes and I are brothers and he liked you. My family could care less about your past or where you came from."

She'd forgotten about Jake's college roommate and friend, Wes. Wes was still like a second son to Jake's parents. But she knew that his parents would have minded having a daughter-in-law who'd done the same thing to their son that her mother had done to the Payton boy twenty-five years earlier. And Savannah society would have remembered it too. The Paytons were old money and her parents had been the talk of the town. If there was one thing those Southern ladies liked, it was scandal and gossip. Larissa had decided long ago she'd had her fill of being fodder for them.

"I'm sorry. The truth is my mom got pregnant to trap my..." She didn't know what to call the man who'd married her mom and then refused to have anything to do with the child they'd created. Certainly not father. Never father.

"...her boyfriend into marriage. I couldn't do that to you."

Jake cursed savagely under his breath. He pushed his hands through his hair and watched her. He entered the kitchen, walking toward her with a slowly measured gait. He stopped when there was about six inches of space between them. But she still felt dwarfed by his physical presence. She tried to step back, but the counter stopped her.

"Did you get pregnant on purpose?" he asked her.

She couldn't gauge his mood. Suddenly she felt very small and awkward. Wrapping her arms around her waist, she stared at his chest and whispered, "No, I'd never do that."

Jake took her chin in his large, warm hand, tipping her head back until their eyes met. "Then why would I think you had trapped me?"

She couldn't think when his breath brushed over her cheek like that. When his eyes looked down on her with a tenderness she'd thought never to see in them again. When he pulled her into his embrace and wrapped his arms around her. Oh, God, this was what she'd been afraid of. Leaning on Jake felt right in the seat of her soul and she knew that he wouldn't stay, but she couldn't help herself.

Didn't want to step away. They didn't move from each other's arms until Peter came into the kitchen, rubbing the sleep from his eyes.

Her heart was heavy with fears and hope swirled together. She wanted to believe the promise Jake offered her, but she feared as soon as she did, she'd end up getting hurt.

Jake sat on the couch with Peter reading Jake's favorite book *Lord of the Rings: Fellowship of the Rings* to him. Peter was fascinated by the world of Middle-earth and was rapt in his attention.

Jake glanced at the mantel clock. What was taking Larissa so long? "I'm going to check on your mom. Do you want to watch some TV?"

"Yes, please, Daddy," Peter said with a smile.

They'd had a lot of fun this afternoon together. He and Larissa had told Peter that Jake was his father. Peter had been overjoyed at the news and had started calling him "Daddy" almost immediately. He said the word so often, Jake realized how much his son had missed having a father.

Jake turned the television on and left his son watching Arthur. Larissa had provided a long list of acceptable television programs on a laminated four-by-six-inch card for Jake when they'd moved in. He also had cards on acceptable words to use—apparently *shut up, stupid* and *idiot* were forbidden, as well as every curse word. There was an approved food list, which Jake had noticed was lacking his favorite cereal. He'd added it to the list with a Sharpie pen and put it on the kitchen counter where she'd see it when she fixed breakfast tomorrow morning.

He went down the hall to the guest bedroom he'd given Larissa. He didn't question it, but there was a sense of rightness to having her under his roof. And for him being responsible for her and their son.

It felt right in his gut. He sensed this was what his father must feel when the entire family was assembled at their home. It was the first time he'd ever felt anything in common with his dad and it felt…weird.

He rapped on her door. "You ready?"

"I don't know," she opened the door, and nervously stepped back.

"How do I look?" she asked.

She looked too damned good to be someone's mom. Her dress was a feminine bit of silk that teased him with its demureness. Teased him with the hint of sexuality beneath that flounced skirt ending just above the knees and the scoop neckline that hinted at her cleavage.

"You look fine."

"Just fine?" she asked, hurrying back over to the mirror and patting her hair once more.

"What's wrong with fine?" he asked, lounging against the door frame. He was fascinated to see the normally unflappable Larissa so unsure of herself. He'd never known her to worry about what she was going to wear.

"I'm meeting your family for the first time. Plus I'm bringing scandal down on them. I think I should look better than fine."

She did, but he wasn't going to reveal anything more to her. Her features were drawn and she looked more nervous now than she had in the doctor's office earlier when they'd had the paternity test done.

He left the doorway and entered the room. The bed was piled with discarded clothing. He wondered if this went back to what she'd said the other day about her grandfather. How did knowing your family had rejected you before you were born affect someone? For all his problems with his father, he knew the old man loved him and would always be there for him.

"What's this all about, Rissa?"

She sighed and sank down on the clothes strewn on the double bed. "I don't want to go."

He sat down next to her. Her perfume was faintly floral and sexy to him. But then everything about Larissa was. He reached for her hands, which she had clenched tightly into fists on her lap. He pried her hands open and held them loosely in his own.

She tipped her head to the side and looked up at him. It was a beseeching look that made him want to give her whatever she asked for. But at the same time, they were in this predicament because of her actions. He lifted one eyebrow in silent question.

She licked her lips and then turned her head toward her lap again. "It was hard enough telling you about Peter. I don't think I can face your family."

"There's no other choice. You have to go with me so we both know how to handle the media. Nicola was clear on that point."

"I wish Jasmine Carmody had never called me," she said, looking up at him again.

"I'm glad she did despite the trouble she's caused. Jasmine Carmody has given me my son."

Larissa said nothing, but her eyes revealed the truth. And the truth wasn't a pretty and nice thing. It was that this woman would have rather run away than face him with the news of his own son.

He cursed under his breath and stood, walking away from her. Every time he thought he'd forgiven her, he was reminded he hadn't. Spending two hours in the toy store with his son had gone a long way toward showing him what he'd missed out on all these years. And now she was telling him again that she regretted telling him the truth.

He clenched his fists and walked toward the front door. "Get your purse, Larissa. We're leaving."

"Jake…"

He didn't pause or turn to look at her. She'd made her decisions. Now he'd made his. He'd see Marcus tonight at Crofthaven and set the custody suit in motion. It was obvious to him, no matter what Larissa said, she couldn't be trusted where Peter was concerned.

He was willing to cut her a little slack because of her upbringing, and he understood that she'd had a rough shake early in life. But Jake wasn't responsible for another man's mistakes and he wasn't going to keep paying for them.

Her hand on his arm stopped him and he pivoted to face her.

"I'm sorry," she said suddenly.

He realized she was trying to tell him something else. But he'd never been good at reading minds and didn't think he was suddenly going to get better at it.

"For?"

"Everything."

"Don't be sorry for everything. That's too big a burden for your shoulders. We're both responsible for this mess and I'm not going to let you continue to carry it alone."

* * *

Larissa felt small and very out of place in the grand foyer of Crofthaven. Peter leaned closer to her and she stooped to pick up her son as Jake gave their coats to Joyce Jones, the housekeeper. Jake exchanged pleasantries with the woman and then cupped his hand under Larissa's elbow, leading her down the hall.

"Where are we going?" Larissa asked.

"To the library. Relax."

"I can't. This place is intimidating."

"It's just a house," he said.

"It's not just a house. It's a historical landmark. It's your family's mark on Savannah and I feel like an interloper."

"Relax," he said again. "I didn't grow up here."

He rubbed Peter's head and their son glanced up at him. "Ready to meet your family?"

Peter didn't answer, just stuck his thumb in his mouth and held tighter to her neck. "Maybe I should have gotten a sitter."

"We don't need a sitter," he said. "What a couple of cowards you two are."

"Am not," Peter said, squirming in her arms to be put down. "I'm just as brave as Frodo."

Jake ruffled his son's hair. "I knew you were."

Peter glanced up at Larissa. "Mommy's not so brave."

"Then we'll be brave for her," Jake said, stooping down to Peter's eye level.

Peter nodded and slipped his hand into hers. He

gripped hers tightly and smiled up at her. And she felt an infusion of love for her son and for his father. Jake was taking this task of being a father very seriously and she regretted that she'd waited so long to let him know he was a dad.

"Ready?" Jake asked.

She nodded and followed Jake into the library. The librarian in her was in awe. Private collections like this one were the stuff dreams were made of. She almost forgot her nerves. Despite his courageous words in the hall, Peter seemed to have picked up on her apprehension and now clung to her leg. She rubbed his back, focusing on Peter and not the others in the room.

There were five people in the room. Jake's uncle, Abraham Danforth, and Wesley Brooks were at the computer desk on the far side of the room. She knew Wes from college, "Honest" Abe from the articles she'd read in the newspaper about him and his family. Abe was the patriarch of the Danforths, a retired Navy Seal who was currently running for the senate.

There was a couple on the couch who stood when they entered. They had to be Jake's parents. There was too much emotion in their gazes for them not to be. They both eyed her and Peter with curiosity. The other woman with gorgeous red hair and bright green eyes was taller than she was and Larissa was no shorty at five-seven. She had to be Abe's PR manager.

"Is this our grandson?" Miranda Danforth asked, crossing the room. Jake's mom had blond hair worn in a sleek bob. Her eyes were a warm blue that made Larissa feel safe and comfortable.

"Mom, this is Larissa Nielsen and my son," Jake said.

Peter clung tighter to Larissa and wouldn't turn around and meet his grandmother at first. "I'm sorry," she said. "He's not used to meeting new people."

"That's okay," Miranda said, running her hand down Peter's back. "Why don't you come sit down with me?"

Larissa followed her across the room, conscious of all the others there. Wes Brooks, Jake's college roommate, looked up from the desk where he was working on the computer. He gave her a friendly smile and a wink. Larissa smiled back. She knew Jake's not officially adopted brother from their college days. And it was nice to see a familiar face in this sea of Danforths.

Miranda seated herself on a leather sofa and Larissa sank down next to her, pulling Peter onto her lap. Harry Danforth stood on the other side of the room. Jake had followed them and he sat on the other side of Larissa. He dropped his arm over her shoulders and she felt comforted by his presence.

As he'd said earlier, she wasn't alone in carrying this burden. But Peter had never felt like a burden to her. He'd always been her joy. And these people, Jake's clan, were lucky to have her precious son in their family.

"Jake called me earlier about your situation—" Nicola said.

"Pardon me for interrupting, Nicola," Miranda

Danforth said. "Peter, would you like to come to the kitchen with me for some cookies and milk?"

Peter lifted his head from Larissa's shoulder. "What kind?"

"Peter."

"That's okay, Larissa. Double chocolate chunk, I believe."

"Mama?"

"You can go, sweetie. Mrs. Danforth is your grandmother."

"Wow. A daddy and a grandmother."

Miranda smiled down at him. "You've got a grandfather as well as a bunch of other family."

"Really?" Peter asked.

"Really," she said. "I'll tell you all about them while we have our cookies and milk."

"Okay!" Peter said, taking Miranda's offered hand and following her from the room.

Larissa felt naked without her little boy on her lap. She laced her fingers together and tried not to pretend that she was the cause of an uncomfortable situation for this very important family.

"I've been thinking about this all afternoon and I've come up with a solution that I think will take the heat out of anything Ms. Carmody writes."

"Great, I'll help in any way I can," Larissa said.

Jake rubbed her shoulder, and she leaned back to smile at him. He didn't smile at her, but a warmth entered his eyes that made her acutely aware of every place where their bodies touched.

"Perfect. I think you two need to get married as soon as possible."

Jake surged to his feet. "No way."

For Larissa, the next few moments seemed to happen in slow motion and there was a ringing in her ears. She wasn't sure what she'd expected, but being forced to marry the man whose child she'd had wasn't it. She had the first inkling of what her mother may have felt all those years ago when she'd faced Reilly Payton and his family—trapped and doomed.

"Excuse me," she said, standing. She walked from the room, down the long hall and out into the night.

Any chance of forever happiness with Jake was gone in an instant, because no man could ever love a woman who'd forced him into a marriage he didn't want.

Six

Jake knew he'd screwed up even before he'd felt Larissa leave the room. But one look at the condemnation shining from his father's eyes was all it took to make him feel about fourteen again. Dammit.

He turned away from his father and focussed instead on Nicola.

"Is a marriage going to be a problem?" she asked.

Jake had no idea. He suspected that he was the last man Larissa would marry right now, after hearing his reaction to the suggestion. But the suggestion had taken him completely off guard.

"No, it won't be a problem, will it, Jacob?" His father, Harry Danforth, said. There were maybe two moments in his life when Jake had felt as if he'd pleased the old man. Once when he was six and won the all-city soccer kickoff, and once when he had made his first million with D&D's Coffeehouses. But for the remainder of Jake's life, he'd seen his father with the same look he had on his face now: one of disappointment.

Even Uncle Abe and Wes were looking at him like he'd screwed up. But he knew what his father meant. He'd made this mess, now it was time to clean it up.

"I don't know that Larissa wants to marry me," Jake said. Not much of an excuse but the only one he had.

"Then convince her," Harry said.

"I'll try." Jake stood and exited the room. He paused in the hallway and leaned back against the wall. His hands were shaking and he had that gut feeling that life was changing in a way he hadn't anticipated.

The hallways were lit with wall sconces and Jake figured Larissa hadn't gone out the front door, but out the back into the gardens. He pushed away from the wall and moved slowly through the house. Crofthaven was a showplace, unlike his parents' more modest house.

He stepped out into the spring evening and paused. What if he couldn't convince Larissa to marry him? He'd learned a long time ago that running away from problems wasn't a solution. But marriage? It wasn't as if he had anything against the institution, but he wasn't sure it was the right move for them.

He heard the rustling of leaves and a soft fall of footsteps. He followed the sound until he found Larissa. She was walking around one of the smaller formal gardens in the backyard. Hedges surrounded it and there was a very European feel to this garden. A marble bench was tucked off to one side and Larissa paused next to it, then sank down on the bench. He stayed in the shadows to watch her.

The full moon and landscape lanterns provided soft lighting to the area, revealing the woman who was bound to him in ways he didn't understand. It was more than that they shared a child. It was more than sharing college memories. It was a soul-deep feeling that made him flinch and that he found difficult to ignore.

He didn't know what to say to her. He wasn't really sure what he wanted from her. But he knew what duty demanded and he'd give it his best shot.

He was about to step from the shadows, when Larissa turned her head to the right and brought the blossom of a hibiscus close to her face, inhaling deeply. What was she thinking?

"Can I join you?" he asked.

She turned toward him. He stepped from the shadows and waited for her permission to join her.

She shrugged and crossed her arms over her chest.

He sat next to her, leaving space between them. Though it was only a few inches, he knew the gap here was miles wide. His next words would have to build a bridge over it. But he wasn't ready. He was still angry that she'd never told him about Peter before now. He knew he needed to get past the anger and thought he'd been making some progress in that direction.

But sitting in his uncle's library and knowing those closest to him knew the mother of his child didn't think he was good enough to be a father—well, hell, it hurt.

And he'd reacted the only way he'd ever learned—by lashing out and hurting back.

Hurting the one woman he wanted to protect. She looked fragile sitting here in the garden. But he knew she wasn't fragile. Larissa was a survivor. She rolled with the punches and kept plodding along with life.

She cleared her throat. "I'm sorry I ran out like that. I..."

Suddenly everything was clear and he knew, despite the anger and need for vengeance still pulsing through him, that marriage to Larissa wasn't just a right choice; it was a necessity.

"I'm sorry."

"It's okay. I know you don't want to marry me."

"The thing is, I'm not sure I don't."

"What are you saying?"

"I wasn't prepared to have everyone know you thought so little of my fathering skills."

"Oh, Jake, I didn't."

"Of course, you did."

"Didn't you hear anything I said to you earlier?"

"About what?"

"My family. I never thought about you as a father, Jake. I thought about you as a man trapped by circumstance. And I was right, wasn't I?"

He cursed under his breath and stood, then paced away from her. He was a man trapped, but not so much by circumstance as by his past. By all the lousy decisions he'd made to get to this point. All the time when he'd put feeling good and having fun in front of responsibility.

It was time to get his act together in his personal life and he knew it.

He turned back to Larissa, who watched him with wide, wet eyes. He knew he'd hurt her. Somehow he hadn't expected her pain to cut him. But it did.

He strode back to her and took her hands in his. He sank down in front of her on one knee and looked up into those pretty blue eyes. Those eyes that usually showed her wit and intelligence, but tonight were guarded and vulnerable.

"Larissa Nielsen, will you marry me?"

Larissa wasn't sure what to say. Marrying Jake, well honestly, it was what she'd been secretly dreaming of since she'd first met him in college. But she'd also dreamed they'd have a huge wedding in Savannah so the old gossips wouldn't be able to talk. She'd wear an elaborate white gown similar to Princess Di's and she'd be the most beautiful woman on that day.

It was a fantasy she'd devoted too much time thinking about. Despite Jake being down on bended knee, Larissa knew that responsibility was motivating Jake and not love or eternal devotion. And she knew that he was a good man. He'd already proved he could be a good father. And sometimes in life you had to take what was offered and kiss goodbye the secret dreams you'd harbored.

"Are you going to keep me hanging forever?" he asked, his voice low and husky. When she looked into those devastating dark brown eyes of his, she wondered if she'd ever be able to deny him anything.

She shook her head. He was doing his duty—darn it. She had to remember Jake was still angry with her for keeping Peter a secret for three years. Jake wasn't in love with her, and no matter what else happened, she had to protect her emotions from him. Because she knew from watching her mother's bitter experience that falling in love with an illusion was never a good thing.

"You don't have to do this," she said at last, forcing herself to look away from him. She looked instead out at the well-tended gardens. She and her mom had had a window box at the small duplex they'd lived in most of her life. One small box that they'd filled with annuals every year. And though Crofthaven wasn't Jake's childhood home, she knew this kind of garden—the kind that took a small army to maintain—was what he was used to.

Their lives were worlds apart and she wondered in her heart if they could ever make anything work between them. Even his original idea of them living together now seemed doomed. But marriage—marriage was sacred to her because she knew that when it wasn't right, too many people got hurt. Innocent little people that had no right being hurt by choices that adults made.

"Do what?" he asked, shifting closer to her on the ground. His arms circled her hips and tugged her closer to him. He didn't leave any space between them. She remembered what it was like to be in his arms and wanted to be there again. She'd never thought of herself as sex crazed until she met Jake. He made all her senses go on hyperalert.

He was so close and she remembered their earlier embraces. She still ached for him in this most basic way. She needed something from him that she wasn't sure she should take, because it would make her even more vulnerable.

"The down-on-one-knee proposal thing."

"It's for me as much as for you."

"Yeah, right. I heard you in the library, Jake. You don't want to marry me."

"Dammit, Rissa, you piss me off," he said, pinching her butt.

She swatted his hand away. "I know I do. So why are you asking me to marry you?"

He wriggled his eyebrows at her. "You also turn me on."

"Is this a joke to you?" she asked.

He cursed under his breath and then hugged her tightly. "I can't explain it, but there's something about you I've never been able to forget."

Her heart melted a little at his words. He let go of her arms and cupped her face, bringing her face toward his. He brushed his lips over hers, softly, gently…seductively. Making her yearn for deeper contact between them. But she knew what he was doing, what he was trying to say with this kiss. And she returned it. Took control of the embrace, kissing him deeply.

Jake stayed at her feet and it was a heady feeling to dominate him. He was totally at her mercy. His head tipped up to hers; his body was under hers. Her emotions swirled out of control. She wanted more from him than this. She wanted—no, needed—something that he wasn't offering.

Something more than duty. She broke the kiss, taking deep breaths to try to remember that despite the garden and the moonlight, this wasn't a love story. She wasn't the heroine in some happily-ever-after tale. Reality was that Jake hadn't wanted to marry her. It was only the pressure of the media and his family that had sent him out after her.

And despite his sweet words, she knew it was too soon for Jake to feel anything but anger toward her.

"What's going through that head of yours, Rissa?"

"Nothing you'd want to hear."

"I know I've screwed up one thing after another, but marry me and let me make this right."

"If we got married it'd be more business than romance, wouldn't it?"

"It would be what we made it. There's no one else in our relationship but us and Peter."

"I'm scared, Jake."

"Of what?"

"Of making the wrong decision and ruining Peter's life."

"I told you earlier that those shoulders of yours are too small to carry everything. Share that burden with me, Rissa, I'm not going to let you down again."

Promise? She wanted to ask but didn't. Normally she wasn't this needy. Normally she wasn't this timid. Normally she made her decisions and lived with the consequences. But it was time to stop clinging to girlhood fantasies and start living in the real world. A world that included more than her and Peter.

"Okay, Jake. I'll marry you."

Jake figured it probably wasn't the best acceptance in history, but he knew it was good enough for him. He stood, pulled Larissa to her feet and took her in his arms.

But her fingers over his lips stopped him. "No, Jake."

"Why not?"

"I want this marriage to work for Peter's sake."

"I've never heard that sex screwed up a marriage."

"I think it would screw up ours. I can't think straight when you kiss me."

"Good," he said, lowering his head again. But she turned away from him and his lips barely brushed her hair.

"Dammit, woman."

"You're not listening to me."

"You're not saying anything I want to hear."

"I'm sorry, but I think keeping things platonic between us is for the best."

"Woman, who are you kidding?"

"Maybe myself. But it's important to me."

"Hell," he said, letting her go. She took a step away from him, but it didn't change the way his blood was racing. He was still aroused and could tell from her shallow breathing and flushed skin she was too. If he pushed her, he could convince her she was wrong. He knew it. And he suspected she knew it.

Why then was she saying no?

"I'm not letting this go. Honestly, I don't think we can live together without sleeping together."

"You may be right. But I'd like us to try it."

"I don't understand."

"It's because we have to get married," she said softly.

He waited, sensing there was more she had to say. Here was the Larissa he'd known in college. The quiet and contemplative woman who'd spent hours discussing world politics but had never said a word about her upbringing. Would he ever understand this woman?

Finally she bit her bottom lip and looked up at him. "I don't want to start thinking there's more between us than obligation."

He knew she was being serious. He wanted to respond to that, to take this discussion even deeper, but instead, all he could think about was her lips. The bottom one she kept nibbling on as she thought about what she was going to say next. He wanted to suckle on it, to tease away her solemn mood with a lighter one. A safer one. Because he didn't like where this conversation was going.

"More? Like what?" he asked at last.

She crossed her arms over her chest and tipped her head to the side, watching him with those wide expressive eyes of hers. "Like love."

Oh, no, not love. If the topic didn't change soon, he'd

have to say to hell with it and force matters back into the physical realm, where he was more confident. "Just love?"

"The in-sickness-and-in-health, until-death-do-us-part stuff. I don't want to buy into this fantasy that I've had in my head for so long a time."

"What fantasy?" Did he have a starring role in this image in her head or was he a walk-on replacement? He suspected the latter.

"Oh, Jake. Don't make me tell you this."

He held his hands up. Far be it for him to force anything from her. "I'm not making you tell me anything."

"I know. Let's go inside and tell Peter we're getting married." She started walking out of the garden. Jake wasn't really ready to rejoin his family. Even though he'd convinced Larissa to marry him, he knew his dad still wouldn't be pleased.

"I'm not sure how much he understands," Jake said, letting her change the subject.

"He's pretty smart for his age. But you're right, I don't think he realizes we aren't married."

She kept walking and he had no choice but to follow her. Dammit, when had he become a coward? He took her elbow and led her up the path to the house. "He took to me being his dad really well."

"I'm sure the two shopping carts of toys you bought him didn't hurt."

"Hey, the kid had never been to Toys "R" Us, Rissa. I think that constitutes neglect," he said. Jake had never been to one, either. He and Peter had enjoyed their afternoon in the store immensely.

She pulled away from him and stopped. “Peter’s not neglected.”

“Hey, I was kidding. You’ve done a great job with our son. I’m proud to call him my boy.”

“Sorry about that. Must be the single mom in me.”

“Well, you’re not a single parent anymore.”

“No, I’m not. That’s going to take some adjusting for all of us. And for all his easygoing nature, you wouldn’t believe how stubborn he can be about things.”

“Sure I would. He’s your son.”

“I’m not stubborn.”

“What would you call it?”

“Determined,” she said with a faint smile.

They’d reached the house, but she didn’t enter. She stood there with her hands twisted together and waited.

He pulled her close for a quick hug and then opened the door to the house. Even though he’d never had any trouble sweet-talking women, suddenly he couldn’t find the right words to use with Larissa. He was out of his element here and he didn’t like it.

He led her back into the library. His folks were sitting on the floor with Peter, helping him put together a puzzle. Standing with Larissa at his side and watching his parents and son together, Jake felt like everything in his world had finally come together.

Seven

Larissa was glad to leave Crofthaven behind. She'd put Peter in the new car seat in Jake's big Suburban while he went to have a few last words with his father and Wes. It was odd to see Jake and Wes at Crofthaven, but they fit in there in a way she'd never imagined.

Nicola had recommended a Vegas wedding and would contact a few of the bridal magazines to come and photograph her for their spreads. Jake had taken over when they'd reentered the living room and she'd been happy to take a back seat to him. This whole marriage thing still felt very surreal.

She knew she was never going to sleep tonight. Too much had happened and she needed time to herself to figure it out. She'd never imagined that having a child with a man could make things so complicated. There were some papers she had to sign before they were married. The family lawyer, Jake's cousin Marcus, had recommended she get her lawyer to read them. Unlike the Danforths, she didn't have a lawyer. But she had a friend from college who'd become one.

According to Marcus, the papers were straightforward—your run-of-the-mill prenuptial agreement without too many complications. She understood why Jake had wanted a paternity test after reading it. Jake had more money and assets that she'd ever imagined.

She rubbed the bridge of her nose. She felt she was getting a migraine. She took Mr. Bear from her purse and tucked him into the car seat with Peter.

Though the hour was late, Peter was still awake. Meeting his family hadn't intimidated him at all. He was practically buzzing with excitement. She sat next to him in the back seat of the car.

"Did you know my daddy has two brothers and two sisters?" he asked her.

She pushed his hair back from his eyes. "Yes, I did."

"But one of my aunts is missing."

Victoria. Jake had told her a little bit about it earlier. They'd found a body in the attic at Crofthaven and the family refused to believe the remains might be Vicky's. But so far no proof had been offered. "I'd heard that as well."

"My grandmother—she said I could call her Granny—told me all about them."

"I'm glad. Do you like having all this family?"

"I guess. I'm tired, Mama."

"I know, sweetie. Why don't you close your eyes?" she suggested. He leaned against the side of his car seat. She had the idea it was going to take him a long time to settle down.

"Are they always going to be our family?" he asked.

She wondered at that. But she knew Jake well enough to know that he wasn't going to let Peter out of his life now that he'd found him. "They'll always be your family, kiddo."

"What about you?" he asked. He reached for her hand and she gave it to him. He tucked it between his face and the car seat, leaning on her hand.

Though the angle was awkward, she didn't pull her hand back. She loved these moments when he just needed to be touching her. "What about me?"

"Aren't they your family?" he asked.

Family. It was the one thing that had always eluded her. She'd created her own little safe unit with Peter, but anything larger scared her. "I guess so. When your daddy and I get married, they will be my family, too."

"What's married?" Peter asked as Jake opened the door and climbed behind the wheel.

"I'll explain more in the morning."

"Okay, Mama."

"You want to climb up front with me?" Jake asked.

"Sure," she said. She leaned over and kissed Peter, whose eyes were finally beginning to droop. She got out of the car and moved to the front seat.

As she closed the passenger door, she heard Peter's sleepy voice. "Thanks, Daddy."

"What for?"

"For my family."

Larissa felt a pain deep in her heart. Of all the gifts that Jake had given Peter, he wasn't impressed with the money he'd spent at the toy store. He'd been impressed by the one thing she'd never been able to give him. And it hurt to realize that she'd been depriving him of it all along because of her own fears.

"You're welcome, buddy," Jake said, his voice low and husky. He reached into the back seat and ruffled Peter's hair.

They started the car and drove back toward Savannah in silence. Larissa's thoughts troubled her. She'd never thought of herself as selfish, never realized that she'd put her needs in front of her son's. She never acknowledged that the fear she'd always secretly harbored had driven her to isolate herself from others.

"I know this is kind of rushed, but I promise we'll have a nice wedding."

She knew Jake was trying to ease her mind. But she was having a hard time acknowledging her past behavior and dealing with the guilt it now caused her. "I'm sure whatever you decided on will be fine."

He turned to look at her, his features stark in the dashboard lights. "I want it to be better than fine, Larissa."

She hugged herself, feeling more vulnerable than

ever, even more so than when she'd given birth to Peter alone in the hospital. "I'm not sure I deserve that."

"Why not?" he asked. He'd turned his attention back to the road and she was glad. She didn't want him to look at her.

"I just suddenly feel very selfish."

He didn't say anything, and she waited until they'd driven at least a mile before she spoke again. "I've been so afraid of getting hurt that I didn't think of Peter."

"You said it earlier—he's not neglected."

"Who's to say what constitutes neglect? I'd never realized how my own fears were shaping him. He really took to your mom."

"Yes, he did. She took to him, too. She offered to watch him when we go to Vegas," Jake said.

"I'm sure he'd love that."

"Good. That's settled." He reached across the seat and took her hand, holding it in his for a minute before placing it on his thigh. She felt reassured in ways she shouldn't because she'd promised herself that she wouldn't let herself care for Jake.

It was more important than ever that she make this marriage work. If she didn't, then they'd all end up hurt. And she wasn't going to be responsible for causing the men she loved any more pain.

It was midnight a week later and Jake was wide-awake. So he got out of his bed and wandered down the hall to the kitchen. He tried to pretend it was family concerns that disturbed him. Wes had been out at

Crofthaven all week trying to stop a computer virus that Uncle Abe had downloaded with his e-mail. His father hadn't called once but Jake knew the old man was disappointed. His mom had dropped by twice and Larissa had disappeared each time.

Too much had happened lately. It wasn't every day that he found out he had a son. And that was partly the reason for his restlessness. But he knew the true reason was the sweet blonde sleeping in the room next to his.

Larissa was more of a woman than he remembered. It wasn't as if he'd forgotten her in the almost four years since he'd last seen her. She'd always elicited a blend of bittersweet memories. He'd thought he'd scared her away that long-ago night with his lovemaking. Larissa had always been so innocent—having a one-night stand would have been enough to scare her.

He opened the fridge and stared at the contents. Larissa had bought groceries on her way home. He reached past the soy milk and grabbed the six-pack of Coors that had been pushed to the back of the fridge. He took the six-pack outside. He stretched out on one of the loungers, feeling the moisture that had developed from the night air saturate his T-shirt. He pulled it off and tossed it on the ground next to the beer.

Tipping his head back, he watched the stars. He remembered one time when Larissa had talked him into going to the observatory. They'd spent the night listening to Dark Side of the Moon and watching constellations.

Damn, that was a long time ago. Sometimes he felt years older than he was.

He heard the scrape of footsteps on the ground and turned to see Larissa silhouetted in the doorway. She wore a nightshirt that buttoned down the front. It wasn't meant to be sexy even though it did leave her long legs bare, but he found it so. To distract himself he took a long draw on his beer bottle. As a distraction, it was a piss poor one.

Jimmy Buffett had the right idea when he'd written "Why Don't We Get Drunk and Screw." Just mindless sex with Larissa was what he needed tonight. But he knew in the morning it would have consequences.

He ached for her. And having her here in his house made that ache deepen. He'd never had a woman here overnight. With all the traveling he'd done in recent years, there really hadn't been time for a relationship. Hell, that was an excuse. He could have had a woman the night before and he'd still want Larissa with this gut-twisting need.

He knew he wasn't going to sleep or have anything resembling comfort until they'd spent a few hours in bed together. But he'd agreed to a platonic marriage. He intended to try to honor it.

"Can I join you?" she asked. Her hair hung in waves around her shoulder, tousled and disheveled from sleep. He knew she was a natural blonde, but there were so many different shades in her hair that he used to suspect she dyed it. But dying her hair wasn't something that Larissa would do. She was always very genuine.

"Sure. You want a beer?" he asked, gesturing to the six-pack at his feet.

She shook her head and hesitated near his chair. "Are you getting drunk?"

What would she do if he was? "Nah. Just passing time."

"Are you okay?" she asked. She glanced around for somewhere to sit. The other chairs were damp with moisture. She picked his shirt up from the ground and used it to wipe down the seat of one of the lounge chairs. She dragged it closer to his lounger and put her feet on the bottom of his.

Such small, feminine feet. His looked big and rough next to hers. He wanted to explore all the ways they were different. To strip them both naked and take his time with the exploration.

"Why wouldn't I be okay?" he asked, to distract himself from her sweetly curved body and the images of her body dancing in his head. One night years ago wasn't enough.

"Well, it's after midnight and you're sitting in the dark drinking. Something about that doesn't seem like the confident man I've come to know." She ran her toe up his calf, teasing him. Her toenails were painted a deep luscious red that confirmed what he already knew. There was more to the prim librarian than she wanted the world to see.

He glanced up and realized she'd been watching him stare at her legs. "I can't sleep."

She ran her toes back down his leg and then tucked

her feet under her and tilted her head to the side. "Why not?"

"You don't want to know," he said, draining his bottle of beer. He leaned over to replace it in the carton and get a fresh one. He twisted the cap off and offered it to her.

She reached forward and took the bottle. Her shirt gaped open and he had a glimpse of the inner curve of her breast. His body hardened a little more, and he shifted his legs to find a more comfortable position.

She took a long sip of the beer and then handed the bottle back to him with a smile. "I wouldn't have asked if I didn't want to know what was keeping you awake."

"I'm hard with wanting you," he said baldly.

"Oh."

"I had a feeling you'd say that. Go back to bed, Larissa, before I forget my good intentions and seduce you."

She stood up and he felt a twinge of disappointment. "Who seduced whom the last time?"

She walked away before he could respond to her. And he watched the smooth swaying of her hips.

Larissa double-checked her seat belt and waved goodbye to Peter in Miranda Danforth's arms as they drove away. Ten days had passed since she'd let Jake know he was Peter's dad. Tears burned the backs of her eyes and she stared out the window until she had her emotions under control. Jake drove away from his parents' home through Savannah and headed to the airport.

Jake's family home was just as luxurious as Crofthaven, but a little smaller in scale. It was also homier. The walls in the family room had been covered with pictures of Jake and his siblings at various ages. And there was a display that was practically a shrine to the trophies Jake had won playing soccer.

"What happened with Victoria?"

"She disappeared at a concert."

"When?"

"Years ago. We all feel responsible. She was our baby..."

"You can't protect everyone."

"I know. I just—I bought her those tickets, Rissa. Me. The big brother who always spoiled her."

"It's not your fault."

She waited for him to elaborate, but he didn't. He'd been like this since they'd gotten up this morning. Was he having second thoughts? She wouldn't blame him if he did—she had a few doubts herself that this marriage was the right thing to do.

"Have you changed your mind about our wedding?" she asked.

He fiddled with the radio dial, tuning in a rock station. "No."

He turned the volume up and Three Doors Down sang about being Superman. She tried to relax against the leather seat, but she couldn't. She tried to tell herself that this marriage wasn't their kryptonite, but it felt like it.

She tried to tell herself it was the fact that she was leaving the Southeast, something she'd never done before. She tried to tell herself it was the fact that she'd left Peter with her soon-to-be in-laws. She tried to pretend it had absolutely nothing to do with the man sitting next to her.

"I've never been out of Georgia, really. I mean, I've been to Hilton Head, but that's practically Georgia, it's so close."

He didn't turn the volume down or even glance her way. She remembered last night when he'd put her hand on the top of his thigh. "You're rambling."

"Yes, I am. I wonder why?" she asked. She wanted to touch him again. Even though they had an early flight, he'd still taken time to go for a run this morning. His legs were muscled and solid. Her fingers tingled with the remembered feel of his leg under her touch.

"Nervous?" he suggested.

"I wasn't until you started acting like some darned robot this morning."

"Robot?" His tone was disinterested. He'd practically ignored her at his parents' house.

"Listen, Jake, I'm not in the mood to play word games with you. If this is what our married life is going to be like I don't think we should go through with it."

He turned the radio off and removed his sunglasses, glancing over at her. There was something unreadable in his eyes that warned her that he was not in a pleasant mood. "It's too late for that."

"No, it's not."

He didn't say anything else and Larissa knew she should have remembered the lesson she'd learned a long time ago. That she couldn't really depend on anyone but herself. Despite what he said, she knew her shoulders were strong enough to carry the burden of single-parenthood. She wanted to take Peter and her grandfather's Bayliner and take to the sea. They would find a place where the two of them could live together—maybe an island somewhere.

But she knew her son wasn't going to be happy leaving behind his new family. And Larissa could never live without her son.

"I don't want to live my mother's life, Jake," she said quietly.

"You don't have any family to disown you," he said.

Nice of him to point that out. She wrapped her arms around her waist and hugged tightly. "I have Peter."

"We have Peter," he said.

"We don't have anything except a media blitz between us."

He cursed under his breath. One of his less flattering habits was that tendency of his to curse when she made him mad. She made a mental note to lecture him on that at a later time.

He pulled the car to the side of the road and turned to face her. "I'm not sure what you want from me."

"Courtesy would be a nice start."

"I'm not being rude."

"Well, I don't understand these one-word answers."

"I can't be your best buddy, Larissa."

"Why not?"

"Because we're living together and I want that to be real. And you don't."

"It's not that I don't want it to be real."

"Then what is it?"

"What if I start believing this is real and you decide that I'm not the right woman for you to spend your life with."

"I'm not that flaky, Rissa. I know my mind."

"Right now you think you do because of Peter."

"Woman, are you trying to drive me insane?"

"No, I'm not. I just don't want to end up like my mom did."

"Alone?"

"Yeah, alone."

"Where was your dad?"

She took a deep breath and looked into Jake's eyes. There was no way she wanted to get into this conversation with him. But she wasn't prepared to spend the rest of her life or the rest of the weekend with Jake while he gave her the cold shoulder.

Taking a deep breath, she said, "I don't have one."

Eight

"No dad? I don't understand," Jake said. He rubbed the bridge of his nose with two fingers and tried to assemble everything she'd told him of her past. He knew she'd had a rough childhood and he didn't really want to be responsible for her having to relive it now. But he had to understand her.

He hadn't been able to sleep last night and his future evenings looked just as restless unless she gave up her idea of a platonic marriage. The only idea he'd had that might work was keeping a distance between them, but even that was next to impossible.

"Explain it to me," he said at last. She was seated next to him in a pretty pink dress that made her eyes seem even bluer. With her blond hair free around her shoulders she looked too feminine for him. Too soft and gentle and he was very afraid that his baser instincts would overwhelm him, despite his mother's best efforts to make him into a gentleman.

"There's not much to say. My mom trapped herself a husband, but Reilly wasn't interested in being a dad, so he refused to have any contact with me. When I was four, he ran off with his secretary, leaving us nothing."

"I'm sorry, Larissa. But I don't see how our marriage resembles your mom's. I've already told you I don't feel trapped. We were both there the night Peter was conceived."

She smiled at him—the first time she'd done so today, and though he knew he shouldn't let it, he felt that smile all the way to his soul. It made him feel bigger than he was—like a man who wasn't a disappointment to his dad. A man who hadn't spent most of his adult life dodging responsibility. A man who could be hers for the rest of his life.

"Thanks."

"You're welcome. Do you feel better now?" he asked.

She shrugged and glanced out the window of the car. Jake leaned back in the seat and thought about all Larissa had told him. He suspected she was leaving out some very important details. He realized suddenly that perhaps her own father's treatment of her had influenced her decision not to tell him about Peter.

"You kept Peter a secret because you thought I'd treat him the way your dad did you," he said.

She turned to look at him, but she didn't say anything.

Her silence confirmed his suspicion. This was why he'd never dated a woman for too long. He knew he wasn't good at building relationships.

"I'd never hurt our son," he said at last. He meant it too. Realizing that made him doubt he should continue with his custody suit. Because the one thing that would really hurt Peter was not having Larissa in his life. And though he justified his suit as insurance that Larissa could never cut him out of their lives again, he knew it was more about payback. Suddenly payback didn't seem justifiable. He'd keep it on the back burner if this marriage didn't work out.

Larissa bit her lower lip, tears glittering in her eyes. "I know that. Believe me, Jake, I wouldn't have made love with you that night if I thought you were anything like Reilly was."

He should put the car back in gear and do what Nicola had suggested this morning before they left—pretend they were actors and show the world a couple in love. Jake knew he was going to have no problem pretending to be in lust with Larissa. His real problem was going to be remembering it was a charade.

"Then what did you mean by not wanting to end up like your mom?"

"Just that Reilly resented her."

"I don't resent you," he said, drawing his finger down the side of her neck. She shivered under his touch and leaned just the tiniest bit closer to him.

He leaned down and kissed the base of her neck. She trembled under his touch, her fingers coming to hold his head. He glanced up at her. Her eyes were closed and she held him with a fierceness he knew she'd deny.

They were both masters of hiding. But he didn't intend to let her hide anymore. She didn't want a platonic relationship with him and they both knew it.

He raked his teeth down the column of her neck and she moaned deep in her throat. He felt the vibrations against his lips.

"This is crazy," she said.

"This is right," he said, pulling her more fully into his arms. She wedged her hands between them and pushed away slightly.

"What now?"

"We said we'd try to keep this nonsexual."

"God, woman, how many times are you going to bring that up? I think it's obvious we're fighting a losing battle."

"I know."

"Then why'd you bring it up?"

She took a deep breath. "Because I'm not the type of woman who is going to make a good Danforth wife."

"Why not?"

"You need someone of your own class. Someone who comes from money and is used to eating on bone china and drinking from Waterford crystal glasses."

"I don't live like that."

"No, but your family does. And they're going to realize I'm not worthy of the Danforth name."

"I'm not sure I'm worthy of the name. But it's mine

and once we're married it'll be yours. I don't want to hear any more about it from you."

"Yes, sir," she said.

"Woman," he growled at her.

She laughed. It made him feel lighter in that moment than he'd have thought possible. The more he learned of Larissa's childhood, the more he understood why she'd kept Peter a secret. Understanding wasn't the same as forgiving, though.

"Now, let's get back on the road. I don't want to miss our flight," he said, putting the car in gear.

"Want a drink?" Jake asked once they were seated on the plane in Atlanta. There hadn't been a direct flight to Vegas from Savannah.

"Yes, something strong."

"Still wigged out from the landing of our flight from Savannah?" he asked, waving the flight attendant over to them.

"I'd like to say no," she said.

He ordered two bottles of Corona. He handed her one and Larissa played with the lime and bottle while other passengers filed past them, taking their seats.

"It felt like we were on a roller coaster. I hate roller coasters," she said.

"I love 'em," he said, tilting his bottle back and taking a long drag.

Was there a better example of all that was different between them? "You would. I'm not like that."

"Like what?"

She thought about it for a minute. "Adventurous."

"I'd disagree with that. In some settings you are extremely adventurous."

"Which ones?" she said.

He leaned closer to her. His spicy cologne surrounded her and then she felt his breath brush against her cheek. "Intimate ones."

She gave him a secret smile. Every time she was convinced they were an ill-suited match, this physical spark flamed back to life. There was a bond between them that went way beyond being parents to Peter, and touched on her secret fear of depending too strongly on this man.

"Drink your beer before I decide to test that adventurous spirit," he warned.

She took a sip of her beer and threw caution to the winds. "What if I want to take that test?"

"You don't. Platonic friendship, remember?" he asked.

"Hoisted on my own petard," she said. She wondered if she'd merely issued Jake a challenge by insisting on a platonic marriage—a challenge he'd be helpless to resist. She knew him well enough to know he liked to win. Was that why she'd done it? So she could say he'd seduced her into changing her mind? So she could blame him if things went wrong?

She didn't dwell on that too closely, because it made her the worst kind of manipulator. She was only fooling herself. Jake wanted her and had made no bones about it.

She was the one attempting to play it safe…and failing miserably.

"Indeed. Changed your mind?"

Time for honesty, Larissa. "About a dozen times, but I always come back to the same decision."

"No sex?" He arched an eyebrow at her.

If she changed her mind it would make this ache deep inside her go away. For a little while, things would seem fine between them, but she suspected in the end she'd end up with a bigger ache. "Yes," she said quietly.

He finished off his beer. "In that case I'd better find something to distract me."

She took a sip of her beer and pulled the SkyMall catalogue from the pocket in front of her. Their time in the air passed quickly.

"The pilot has turned on the fasten-seat-belt sign signaling our descent into the McCarran International Airport."

Larissa nervously gripped her armrest. Once the plane landed, everything would be out of her control. Jake had worked on his laptop through most of the flight. He'd scheduled a meeting for late this afternoon with the Vegas D&D's. She was a little in awe of his business persona. It was nothing like the frat boy she'd known in their college days or the man she'd come to know since Jasmine Carmody had forced them back into each other's lives.

He put his hand over hers on the armrest and pried her fingers free. "Nervous?"

"Yes."

"Don't be. I'm right here and I won't let anything happen to you," he promised. Lifting her hand to his lips, he brushed a soft kiss against her knuckles.

She bit her lip and looked away from him and out the window. That was the problem. Jake was here and she wanted to believe it was forever. It was getting harder and harder to remember that he was here because his family had forced him to marry her to save face.

He'd been solicitous during their flight—friendlier than he'd been in the car on their way to the airport. She'd been tempted to lift the armrest and scoot as close to him as she could, to rest her head on his shoulder while he worked. She wanted to pretend for a minute that they were really going to Vegas to marry because they couldn't bear not being man and wife any longer.

But she knew the truth and that knowledge had kept the armrest firmly in place and her head on the back of the leather first-class seat.

He lifted the armrest and tugged her against his side. Leaning close to her, he whispered, "'The woods are lovely, dark and deep.'"

She glanced up at him. God, this felt too right. Too good. But for this moment, while the plane was landing, she wasn't going to pull away. She was going to stay close to the only man she'd ever trusted and repeated the words of their poem to.

Together they recited the rest of Frost's poem. The last line echoed in her head..."miles to go before I sleep." She'd felt alone on her journey for so long. But as she glanced up at Jake and saw him watching her with those brown eyes of his, she didn't feel alone anymore.

And in her heart she knew she'd never be the same. Because Jake wasn't just the right man to fix the mess Jasmine Carmody's report would create, he was the right man to fill the emptiness in her soul.

Every time he thought he had Larissa figured out, she did something that made him realize he didn't. He'd meant to keep his distance from her, but he'd been unable to. In all the years he'd known Larissa, he'd never realized how much of herself she kept from the world, and especially from him.

The one thing she'd never tried to hide was how much their son meant to her, and he had a few doubts about the wisdom of continuing with his plan to sue for full custody of Peter.

Larissa started to pull out of his arms when the plane pulled up to the gate. He stopped her with a quick kiss. She smiled up at him and he felt it in his groin. He didn't know if he could keep up the dual life that they'd decided on. Public touching and kissing, private hands-off.

Yet, she'd said again today she wasn't ready to make love with him. And he wasn't going to push her. He was going to sit back and let fate direct him. Hell, no, he wasn't. He was going to do his damnedest to make sure she came to the same conclusion he already had.

"Nicola has arranged for a reporter to meet us here."

"Jasmine Carmody?"

"No. Another one who will write up a piece about how in love we are and how circumstances kept us apart."

"What circumstances?" she asked.

"My traveling, your job. We'll be vague. The important thing is to appear totally in love."

"Totally?"

"Yes," he said. Nicola had said nothing about appearing to be in love, but Jake wanted to know what it would be like to have Larissa look at him with complete devotion.

"I'm not sure I can do this."

"Too late to back out," he said.

"I won't leave you hanging, Jake. That was just nerves."

"Would it be so hard to love me?" he asked.

She bit her lower lip and closed her eyes. They were so close she was still in his arms, but he felt a gulf open between them. He felt the space that Larissa used to protect herself from relationships open up. He felt her backing away and did the only thing he could think of to pull her back to him.

Storm her barricades. Lay siege to the fortress that was her body and win the battle. He brushed his lips back and forth over hers. "Don't fight it," he whispered.

"Fight what?" she asked, against his mouth.

"This," he said, angling his head and taking her mouth the way he wanted to take her body. With long thrusts of his tongue. Claiming every inch of her mouth with his own.

She opened for him and he felt her capitulation. This was the one place where they communicated with total honesty. Seducing her with tender pulls of her lips, he pushed his own hammering desires to the back burner and strove for patience.

He smoothed his hands down her back, bringing their chests together. Her heart hammered against his. She felt small and fragile in his arms.

Lord, she tasted better than he remembered. It felt like it had been years since he'd last held her like this. Then the dynamic of the kiss changed. Larissa lifted her hands to frame his face and tasted him with long, slow kisses.

Dammit, he was the one in control, he thought. But as she scraped the edges of her fingernails down the side of his neck, he gave up all pretense. He was putty in her hands.

Sliding his hands to her waist, he started to pull her onto his lap. He needed her over him now. He was hard and straining and he honestly didn't think he could wait another second to bury himself in her body.

"The captain has turned off the fasten-seat-belt sign, you are now free to gather your things and disembark."

Larissa jerked away from him. He cursed under his breath, dropping his head to his hands and breathing deeply to try to regain some control. He'd been ready to take her here in the damn airplane.

The other passengers began gathering their luggage and filling the aisle. There was no way he was going to be able to walk off the plane until he'd had a few minutes to forget about the incredible woman he'd just had in his lap.

He glanced over at her. She watched him with wide eyes that were full of confusion and possibly hope. She touched her lips gingerly.

"I'm not going to apologize," he said.

"Good. I'm not either."

He'd forgotten how sensual she was. Forgotten that night in Atlanta when he'd discovered that her passion for books and words extended to him as well. "I figured total lust would make better headlines than being in love."

"Good idea."

She gathered up her purse and unfastened her seat belt, preparing to stand. He put his hand on her arm, holding her in her seat.

"Aren't you ready to get off the plane?"

"No," he said.

She gave him a quizzical look. He gestured to his lap. Her eyes widened.

"I guess I do owe you an apology."

"Not on your life, Larissa."

She got that heavy-lidded look in her eyes and leaned toward him, but he held her back. "I'm an inch away from saying to hell with it and seeing if we can both squeeze into that rest room up there."

"Jake—"

He covered her lips with his fingers. "Not another word."

The last of the passengers filed by and Jake felt better under control. He picked up his briefcase and stood, keeping his hand on Larissa's elbow as they exited the plane.

She tugged her arm out from under his grip and took his hand. She slid her fingers through his. He glanced down at their joined hands and tried to not let it matter. Their holding hands shouldn't mean anything, but it did.

She trusted him. If she didn't want to admit that, it was fine with him. But he knew there was something between them now that hadn't been there before.

Nine

Larissa smoothed her hands down the sides of her simple wedding gown. She wasn't sure who had arranged for it, but there had been a small fortune in wedding gowns in the suite when Larissa had arrived. Jake had told her to pick one. He'd left her alone in the suite for the past four hours.

The hairdresser, makeup artist and photographer had arrived forty-five minutes ago and now she looked like someone she didn't recognize. Oh, God, what was she doing?

"Can I have a few minutes to myself?" she asked.

"Yes, ma'am." All three filed out of the room.

Larissa walked to the mirror staring at the woman there. A woman who was sleek and sophisticated and not at all like the woman Larissa knew herself to be.

She looked in the mirror like a woman suitable to be a Danforth wife.

She reached toward her reflection, touching the glass. This wasn't real. This was all pretend. Game face and all that.

But it felt real. It felt like the dreams she'd secretly harbored since she'd given birth to Peter. It's not real, she reminded herself again.

There was a rap on the door and Larissa went to answer it.

"Sorry, ma'am, but it's time to go upstairs for the ceremony."

She nodded. The hairdresser took the veil from her hands and placed it on her head. Tears burned the backs of her eyes. She was alone with strangers, people paid to help take care of her because she had no family of her own to help with these moments. No mother to help her with her veil. No sisters to help pick out flowers or choose bridesmaid dresses. Just her. Alone. The way she'd always been.

The chapel was small and intimate. Jake stood at the front, talking to the photographer and Artie O'Neil, the reporter that Nicola had arranged to have write about their wedding.

Larissa tried to smile. Tried to pretend that this was what she wanted. That she was marrying a man who loved her. But she felt sick.

She turned and blindly ran down the hall. She heard voices and someone calling her name, but she didn't stop. She escaped through the fire exit and paused on the stairs.

She leaned back against the wall and wrapped her arms around her waist. She was crying. Crying for things that she'd never had. Crying for the dream that now seemed so childish and ridiculous. Crying for something that she'd never realized she wanted until now.

The door opened and she felt raw, exposed.

"Rissa, what's wrong?" Jake asked softly.

She tried to swallow so she could speak, but she couldn't. She turned her head from him.

He closed the door and walked toward her. She put her hand up. "Don't."

He stopped and she tried to pull herself together. But her mind was filled with pictures of perfect families. The kind of family she'd been trying to create for Peter. What she wanted and what she would have were very different.

"Talk to me, baby. I don't know what you need."

She didn't, either, and that was the problem. How was she going to be able to explain that she wanted something she'd never had? That today, when she was standing at the back of the chapel, she realized she wanted a mother? A real mother who would have noticed her daughter and not stayed mired in her own bitterness.

"I...I'm sorry."

Jake closed the gap between them and pulled her into his arms. "About what?"

She shrugged. When he held her like this she didn't

want to leave. She wanted to believe the illusion they were presenting to the world was true. "This. Being so emotional."

Jake tipped her chin back and she stared up at him through the filmy lace of her veil. "A wedding is a big deal in a woman's life."

"What about a man's?" she asked.

"What?"

"Is this a big deal to you, Jake?" She should have kept her mouth shut, shouldn't have worried about what he was going to say, but she did. She didn't want him to answer unless he said the words her wounded heart needed to hear.

He pushed her veil up and smoothed it back away from her face. Without the barrier between them, his breath brushed her cheek and his eyes were very sincere. He leaned close to her and whispered, "You're the only woman I've ever asked to marry me. You know this is a big deal."

She sighed. She did know that. Jake was a good man. A good man who she was falling more and more in love with each moment she spent with him.

She realized suddenly that her tears had nothing to do with the family she'd never really had and everything with wanting Jake to marry her for love and not convenience.

He handed her a snowy handkerchief that bore his monogram. She wiped her face and saw the residue of the makeup she wore on it.

"I just felt so alone," she said.

"Well, you're not. We're in this together."

"Sorry I made a mess of my makeup."

"I don't care about that."

"You don't?"

"Rissa, you're the most beautiful woman I've ever seen."

Suddenly things didn't seem quite as desperate as they had earlier. "Thank you."

"You're welcome. Are you ready to get married now?"

She nodded. He gently kissed her forehead and lowered her veil once again. Then taking her hand firmly in his, he led her back to the chapel. When they exchanged vows, a part of her began to believe that Jake never would leave her.

Larissa smiled for the pictures after their wedding, and even though Jake knew that they were playacting, it felt real to him. A little too real, he thought uncomfortably. He'd always been a loner even though he'd been surrounded by siblings and cousins. There'd been a core part of himself he'd kept private. Larissa was the only person he'd ever let get a glimpse of it.

And now they were married. Jake moved away to have a few final words with the reporter.

Larissa was standing by herself. She'd clung tightly to his hand throughout the ceremony and he remembered promising her he'd help shoulder her burdens. He knew she didn't believe his words. But when he'd looked into her eyes and given her his vow, he'd realized he meant them. Legally she was his and there was a sense of rightness that accompanied that feeling.

Artie promised to send a rough draft of the article to Nicola for approval before his magazine printed it. Soon they were alone. Just him and his bride. The primitive part of Jake's soul was ready to claim her. To throw her over his shoulder and carry her upstairs and push aside her doubts. To prove to her that she'd made the correct decision when she'd pledged her life to him.

But he'd been raised with more sophistication than that. He'd arranged for them to have dinner on the rooftop of the hotel. Away from the prying eyes of any reporters.

Away from the intimacy of their suite. He crossed the chapel to her side.

"What else do we have to do tonight?" she asked nervously. He knew she hadn't liked the public part of their wedding—the pictures that would be sent to magazines and newspapers, the questions that Artie had asked and they'd answered.

"Nothing. The evening is ours."

She flushed a little and licked her lips. God, she was making all his good intentions hard to carry out.

"I've got a surprise for you."

"Really? What is it?" she asked, tilting her head to the side. He noticed she did that when she was in a contemplative mood. What was going on in her head?

He wished he understood her better. But he was honest enough to admit understanding Larissa or any woman had never been a top priority.

"A secret that I think you'll like. Now close your eyes and follow me."

"Okay."

He took her hand and led her to the elevator. He used the passkey he'd gotten from the casino manager to access the rooftop. When the doors opened, he pocketed the key and lifted Larissa into his arms. He walked to the table surrounded by candles and string lights. He set her on her feet.

"Open your eyes."

Larissa looked around at the romantic setting. A dining tent had been set up on the roof. It was draped in sheer gossamer fabric and lights twinkled from underneath it. She saw a table set for two. Beyond the dining area, the night sky was bright with the lights of the Vegas strip. But the smooth sounds of Jimmy Buffett poured from the speakers.

"Stars Fell on Alabama" was playing. It was their song. The song they'd danced to at the reunion on the night they'd made love.

Jake led her under the canopy and they were secluded from the world. She felt that she was the wrong woman in the wrong place. This was a romantic dream and not at all anything that practical Larissa Nielsen had ever experienced. But she wasn't Larissa Nielsen anymore. She was Larissa Danforth. And maybe romance was what she needed.

"Dance?" he asked.

She nodded and he pulled her into his arms. Her head fell to his shoulder and he danced her around the rooftop. "It feels like a lifetime since that night," he said.

Jimmy Buffet sang…"did it really happen?" And it was a question that Jake had asked himself many times since he'd last made love to her. The memory of it was so vivid and so real, and yet unbelievable.

"I was so nervous about dancing with you," she confessed.

"Why?"

"Because you're a good dancer and I'm not."

"I didn't notice that."

"I didn't either. Once you took me in your arms, all my worries dropped away. It was…magical."

He didn't say anything, but he'd felt the same way. It had been a magical night. A moment out of time to be treasured for always. He lowered his head and dropped nibbling kiss down the side of her neck. She sighed and tipped her head to the side to give him greater access.

He sucked lightly at the pulse beating strongly at the base of her neck. She shivered in his arms. He soothed her with languid strokes of his hands down her back.

She pushed her fingers into his hair and pulled his head down to hers. Rising on tiptoe, she kissed him. Her lips moved over his with intent, arousing in him a need that had never been sated.

He wanted to let her take the lead so that later on there'd be no question of him seducing her. But he couldn't just stand there. He stopped dancing and lifted her in his arms with his hands on her buttocks and thrust his tongue deeply into her mouth.

He craved her. He doubted that anything less than total surrender would satisfy the ache that kept growing inside him.

She pulled back, gasping for breath and watching him with wide eyes. He dropped his hands and stepped away from her, clenching his fists at his sides.

"Let's eat."

"Jake?"

"Not right now, Larissa. Food, first."

"I don't want food."

He paused and glanced over at her. "What do you want?"

"You," she said, and walked toward him purposefully.

Blood rushed through his veins, pooling in his groin as she walked closer. He staggered back and had to sit down on one of the dining chairs. He'd expected to have to woo her slowly. He had, in fact, arranged for total privacy for them on the rooftop by asking the hotel staff to wait for his request before coming upstairs.

She continued toward him, a smile spreading over her face. The music still played in the background—no longer Jimmy Buffett but some smooth-sounding classic jazz. Miles Davis. Not an artist that was his favorite but one that he knew Larissa loved.

She paused. "Miles Davis?"

He nodded.

"How'd you know?"

"Woman, you've got about fifteen different CDs of his."

"You're observant."

Only when something mattered, he thought. And Larissa mattered to him in ways he was only beginning to explore.

"I like that," she said, still moving toward him slowly.

"Good." He stood and crossed the small space between them in two strides. It had been an eternity since he'd last held her in his arms.

He'd been aroused since they'd stepped off the plane and no amount of work, exercise or cold showers had dulled it.

Her mouth opened under his and he told himself to take it slow, but slow wasn't in his programming with this woman. She was pure temptation. He slid his hands down her back, pulling the zipper of her dress down at the same time.

Her bodice loosened, and from his angle looking down at her, he could see the tops of her breasts and the barest hint of her nipples. He lowered his head, using his teeth to pull the loosened fabric away from her skin.

She wore a demure cotton bra under her wedding dress and that simple undergarment made something clench deep inside him. Her nipples stood out against the plain fabric. He ran the tip of one finger around her aroused flesh. She trembled in his arms.

He undid the front clasp of her bra and brushed the cups away. Lowering his head, he took one of her nipples in his mouth and suckled her. She gasped his name and held him to her with a strength that surprised him. He pulled back and blew lightly on her skin.

She shivered and tried to direct his attention to her other nipple, but he held back. Knowing that his control would shatter at any moment, he wanted to savor this feeling of anticipation while he still could.

Her other nipple pouted for his attention, growing harder under his stare. He lifted one hand to touch her and saw the differences between them. His hand was huge and her breast small, smooth…flawless.

He cupped her breast, rubbing her nipple with the palm of his hand. Rissa tilted her head back, her hands still clutching at his head. Her mouth opened and he heard her moan his name.

He took that other nipple in his mouth. Teased her with his tongue and then the edge of his teeth, scraping carefully against the nubby texture.

Her fingers drifted down his back and then slid around front to work on the buttons of his shirt. She took a half step back and pushed his shirt open. She growled deep in her throat and leaned forward to brush kisses against his chest.

He continued caressing her breasts until they were full and her nipples prominent. He slid his hands down her smooth skin. Everywhere he touched he wanted to linger, but tonight wasn't for extended love-making. They had been apart too long.

She bit and nibbled at his chest. His groin hardened so painfully, he could take his pulse between his legs.

He felt like her plaything. He wanted to lie back and let her have her way with him. But there was no room here.

He pulled her to him and lifted her slightly so that her nipples brushed his chest. Holding her carefully, he rotated his shoulders and rubbed against her. Blood roared in his ear. He was so hard, so full that he needed to be inside of her body now.

Impatient with the yards of satin pooling at her hips and down to her toes, he shoved them up and out of his way. He caressed the long length of her thighs. She was so soft. She moaned as he neared her center and then sighed when he brushed his fingertips across the front of her panties.

The cotton was warm and wet. He slipped one finger under the material and hesitated for a second, looking down into her eyes.

Her eyes were lidded. She bit down on her lower lip and he felt the minute movements of her hips as she tried to move his touch where she needed it.

He was beyond teasing her or prolonging their torture. He pushed her panties aside and plunged two fingers into her humid body. She squirmed against him.

He lifted her and crossed to the table in two long strides. He sank to the chair and pulled Larissa over his lap.

He turned Larissa in his arms. "What are you doing?" she asked.

"Trust me," he said.

She murmured something he didn't catch.

"Rissa?"

"Yes, Jake. I trust you."

He guided her hands to his shoulders. "Hold on."

Reaching between their bodies he freed his erection and then pushed the satin of her skirt to her waist. He held her hips in his hands. She was soft and womanly. Their naked loins pressed together and he shook under the impact.

He had to have her. Now. She was naked to the waist and he used one hand to pluck at her aroused nipples, the other testing the readiness of her desire for him. He found her wet and ready. He adjusted his hold on her hips and then entered her with one long, hard stroke.

She moaned his name and her head fell forward, leaving the curve of her neck open and vulnerable to him. He bit softly at her neck and felt the reaction all the way to his toes when she squirmed in his arms and thrust her hips toward him.

A tingling started in the base of his spine and he knew his climax was close. But he wasn't going without Larissa. He wanted her with him. He caressed her stomach and her breasts. Whispered erotic words of praise and longing in her ears.

She moved more frantically in his arms and he thrust into her deeply with each stroke. Breathing through his mouth, he tried to hold back the inevitable. He slid one hand down her abdomen, through the slick folds of her sex, finding her center. He stroked the aroused flesh. She continued to writhe in his arms no closer to her climax than before.

He circled that aroused bit of flesh between her legs with his forefinger, then tickled it very carefully with his nail. She screamed his name and tightened around him. Jake pulled one hand from her body and locked his fingers on her hips, holding her still for his thrusts. He penetrated her as deeply as he could. Suckling at the base of her neck, he came long and hard.

He held her carefully in his arms and cradled her to him.

This marriage that had started out as a media Band-Aid had just become very real. And Jake didn't know whether he liked that or not.

Ten

Aftershocks of pleasure still rocked her body. She closed her eyes and leaned fully into him. Jake held her with a strength that scared her. What had she done?

He was big and strong and more man than she'd ever known—the only man who'd ever seen the real Larissa and now she was his wife. And she wanted it to last forever. Not just until Abe Danforth won or lost his senate bid.

Forever…that elusive thing had always been just out of her grasp. She had Peter, but in her heart she knew one day he'd leave her as well. But Jake had never been hers and she had the feeling he never would need her as deeply as she needed him.

This couldn't happen again. And yet she didn't know if she'd be able to keep her hands to herself. One time wasn't enough. She still wanted him. She hadn't gotten to explore his body and relearn his shape. She doubted a lifetime would be long enough for that.

Her cheek rested on his shoulder and she never wanted to leave the circle of his arms. If only this moment could last forever.

"Well, Mrs. Danforth." Jake sounded much too pleased with himself.

He idly stroked her back and the hair on his chest tickled her nipples. She didn't want to want him again. She wanted him out of her system so she could move on with her life. A life that had been disrupted by him and the emotions he evoked in her.

"Well what?" she asked, lowering her head and nipping his pec. The muscle flexed under her mouth and she traced a random pattern with her tongue. He tasted good. Salty and masculine like only Jake did.

He cupped her jaw and tilted her face up to his. His nostrils flared with each breath he took and she knew he was reaching the point of no return. She was already there. Her center was dewy and her body ached to be taken by him again. To have him fill her until she couldn't think of anything but the pleasure he gave her.

She licked her lips, tasting him on her. He leaned down and spoke directly into her ear. "That was a nice appetizer. But I'm hungry for more of you."

Her heartbeat sped up and everything feminine in her melted. The night breeze was cool and she shivered as it brushed over her aroused body.

Her mind said to step away from him but her body ignored that advice. This was her wedding night and likely the only one she'd ever have. She'd face the consequences of this night tomorrow.

She rubbed her nipples against his chest and tugged his head down to hers. His pupils dilated and his breath came in short pants. His erection pressed urgently against her and she doubted they were going to make it off the rooftop tonight.

He thrust against her and groaned as he encountered layers of skirt. "Damn. I want you naked."

"Me, too," she said, bathing his chest with kisses. She slid off his lap and lowered herself to her knees in front of the chair. She took his hard length in her hands.

He held himself still. His hands in her hair moved in circles and his hips thrust toward her the slightest bit. She knew what he wanted. What she wanted. Taking his buttocks in her hands, she drew him forward until the tip of him brushed her lips. She breathed against him and heard him groan.

She tasted him with delicate licks, then took the tip into her mouth. He shuddered. She felt his hands tighten in her hair and he pulled her to her feet. He fastened his pants with quick, careful movements, then refastened her dress.

"We need a bed. Now."

"Yes," she said. Her voice was husky and barely recognizable to her own ears.

Scooping her up in his arms, he carried her across

the rooftop to the elevator. "There's a key card in my pants pocket."

She fished around for it, deliberately fondling him before she found the key. He staggered back against the wall and she knew she was playing with fire. He took her mouth in a kiss that demonstrated his dominance. It was deep and carnal and left her quivering in his arms. The elevator car opened and he carried her inside.

"Push the button," he ordered.

She did. The ride was mercifully short and soon they were in their suite. Jake carried her to the king-size bed and put her on her feet beside it.

His fingers made quick work of the zipper running down her back and her dress slid from her body, pooling at her feet in a sea of white satin. Jake stood there watching her. Her breasts were full and heavy, her nipples stood taut and ready for his touch. Her panties were long gone and her thigh-high hose were her only garments.

"Get on the bed," he said.

She stepped delicately out of her dress and turned slowly to crawl up the bed. She heard him growl deep in his throat and then felt his warm hand on her ankle. He tugged her flat.

"Don't move," he said.

She heard the sounds of him disrobing and then felt his naked body pressed along her back. She was completely surrounded by him. He held her like that for long minutes. His hands sweeping down her sides, his fingers reaching under her body to tweak her nipples.

He turned her over and sat back on his haunches watching her. He ran his forefinger down the center of her body. Helplessly she watched her sensitized skin grow rosy under his touch and when he skirted the curls at the apex of her thighs, she moaned softly.

He gave her a wicked smile but continued his path toward her feet. He reached her ankles and chained each one in his loose grasp. Then he slowly pushed her legs back toward her body. She felt totally exposed and vulnerable. And more turned-on than she remembered ever being.

He slid up her body; lowering his head he tasted her hot center with his lips and tongue. His hands left her ankles and he reached up to fondle both breasts.

He rubbed and pinched her nipples until her breasts felt too heavy, too full. She needed him. His mouth on her most feminine flesh was driving her toward orgasm, but she wanted Jake's body over hers. She wanted to watch his eyes as he took her and experienced a shared climax.

"Jake," she said, pulling on his hair.

"Come for me, Rissa."

"I want us to be together."

"We will…later. Please."

She couldn't deny him or her body. She rubbed her hands against his scalp and waited for his intimate touch. His breath brushed her first and then his tongue. His slid his hands down her body, gripping her hips and maneuvering her so that he had greater access to her secrets. He thrust one blunt finger into her channel and she clenched around it. He teased her with that one long finger, reaching up and pressing on a spot beneath her pubic bone. He continued to tickle the nubbin between her legs with his tongue and the twin pressures on her forced her over the edge. Her climax was intense and powerful but still she wanted more. She needed Jake.

He moved up over and held her still. He entered her with one long deep thrust. "Ah, that's it."

He penetrated her so deeply she felt they really were becoming one being. She lifted herself, tugged his head down to hers and took his mouth the way he took her body. He tore his mouth from hers as his thrusts increased. He lowered his head and suckled on one of her breasts and she felt a change come over him seconds before he flooded her with his release. Her own followed closely and she held him to her with a desperation she'd deny in the morning.

Jake ordered breakfast while Larissa showered the next morning. The night before had put to rest any doubts he had about making their marriage a real one. He wasn't sure what had changed her mind about keeping their marriage platonic, and frankly didn't care. He was starting to feel he and Larissa had a real chance at happiness, and that scared him.

But he was willing to do his duty this time. With a wry grin, he realized that duty had never felt so good. Slowly he was beginning to trust Larissa again. He understood now why she'd kept Peter a secret.

He picked up the phone and dialed Marcus's office.

It was time to stop his bid to win full custody of Peter. Marcus had handed the paternity suit off to Ted Larson, one of his co-workers who specialized in family law. Jake got Ted's voice mail. He left his name and the number at the hotel for a return call.

The bathroom door opened and Larissa walked across the room to her suitcase. She wore a hotel bathrobe and a towel turbaned on her head. She looked cute and sexy at the same time.

"Come over here, woman," he said.

She gave him a haughty look over her shoulder. "You gave enough orders last night."

He had. And she'd responded to them beautifully. "I'm ready to take them," he said.

"I'll bet you are."

She rummaged through her clothes, selecting a pretty sundress and undergarments. She headed back toward the bathroom with her clothes.

"Where are you going?" he asked.

"In there to change."

"You can change here. I'll be a good boy and keep my hands to myself."

"Well, that's kind of why I was going back in the bathroom."

"You don't want me to keep my hands to myself? No problem, Rissa." He stood up and walked toward her.

"Stop, Jake. I need to talk to you."

He didn't like the sound of that.

"About what?"

"Our intimate relations."

Sometimes you could tell Larissa was a librarian. "You mean our sex life."

"Yes. I think I gave you the wrong impression last night."

"No, you didn't, sweetheart," he said. Last night had been raw and earthy. He crossed to her and took her in his arms. "I still respect you."

"Oh, Jake. Not about that. I…I want to stick by our original agreement."

"Which one?" he asked.

She sighed and tilted her head to the side as she looked up at him. "The platonic one."

He cursed under his breath and stepped away from her. The woman was trying to drive him insane. "Why?"

"Because sex makes things complicated. I'm sorry, I should have spoken up sooner, but I wanted a wedding night to remember."

"Good. I did, too. But this doesn't have to end."

"Yes it does."

"Explain it to me," he said.

"This wasn't real. The wedding, the setting, the dress. Everything was playacting."

"It felt real to me when I took those vows that made you my wife."

She blanched and looked away from him. "Me, too."

"Baby, I'm not like your dad. I'm not going to do to Peter what he did to you."

She wrapped her arms around her waist, holding

herself so tightly that he knew he wasn't saying the right thing. Hell, he had no idea what the right words were. It was like being in virgin territory; he knew how to seduce Larissa into his bed, but he had no clue how to keep her there.

"I'm waiting to hear you say you know I won't hurt Peter."

"Of course I know that, Jake. The first time I saw you with him, I knew I'd cheated both of you out of something."

"Then what's the problem?"

"Me," she said, softly. "I'm the problem."

"You know I won't hurt you."

"What if I hurt you?"

"I'm not that fragile," he said. What kind of wimp did she think he was?

"That's what I was afraid of."

"I'm not following."

"I can't hurt you because I'm nothing more than a make-believe wife to you. You don't care for me."

"Don't put words in my mouth. I care for you more than I do any other woman."

"Right now."

"Larissa, there are no guarantees in life. You know that and so do I. I'm not sure what you think you're going to achieve by not sleeping with me."

"I'm trying to keep from falling in love with you, idiot. I don't want to be vulnerable to any man."

"I'm not just any man, Larissa. I'm your husband."

She shook her head and turned away. There was a

knock on the door and Jake didn't move to answer it. He wanted to hash this out to a conclusion, but Larissa was already retreating behind that wall of icy cool that she used to keep him out. "Room service," they both heard from the door.

"This isn't over," he warned as he exited the bedroom.

Larissa was dressed by the time Jake returned. She'd clipped up her hair and was fastening her sandals when he walked back into the room.

"In a hurry?" he asked.

"No. I just didn't want..."

"To appear weak," he said. Cursing under his breath he stalked to his suitcase and removed his clothing for the day.

"Go eat, Larissa," he said without looking at her.

She stood in the doorway. "Didn't you want to finish our conversation?"

He gave a derisive snort. "No. I don't think so. I've had enough of trying to convince you I'm respectable." He walked away from her without a backward glance.

She shivered and rubbed her hands over her arms, feeling colder and more alone than ever. She'd expected Jake to say many things when she told him she wanted to stop sleeping with him. But she hadn't anticipated the depth of his anger.

She picked at the breakfast he'd ordered for them, but could only manage drinking the coffee. The phone rang and she answered it.

"Jacob Danforth please," a male voice said.

"One moment. Can I tell him who's calling?"

"Ted Larson."

Larissa set the handset on the table and crossed their suite to the bathroom door. The shower had stopped. She rapped on the door and Jake opened it, shaving cream on his face and a white towel slung low around his lean hips.

She swallowed. His hair was damp and a bead of moisture trailed down his neck to his chest. Unconsciously she lifted her hand to catch the drop. Jake caught her hand in his and held her captive. She glanced up into his eyes.

She could read nothing in his gaze. Had she just made the biggest mistake of her life by demanding a celibate marriage with this man?

"Change your mind already?" he asked.

Sometimes it was as if he could see straight to her soul. Had she changed her mind? It would be so easy to loose herself in the web of sensuality that Jake created, but in the end, she knew she'd have a tough time moving on when he was tired of her. And Jake had never stayed with one woman too long.

She shook herself. "You have a call."

He rubbed her hand over his chest before letting it drop. She flexed her fingers, raking her nails over his skin. His towel stirred. She wanted to stay. What had she been thinking to put the brakes on this? "Take a message for me."

Her hand tingled and her body said her mind was on

the verge of insanity. She couldn't live with Jake and not be his woman. "Okay."

She pivoted on her heel, but her legs were weak and she didn't know if she was going to be able to walk away from him.

"Rissa?"

She glanced over her shoulder at him. "Yes?"

"You never answered my question."

"I'm afraid to," she said, and walked away, firmly closing the bedroom door behind her. She needed to regain her perspective. She needed to talk to her son. She missed him. She'd talked to him right before the ceremony yesterday.

She took a message from Mr. Larson and left the note on Jake's briefcase. She dialed the number to Jake's parents' house. The housekeeper answered on the third ring.

"This is Larissa Nielsen…Danforth. May I speak to Peter?"

"Just a moment, ma'am."

"Hi, Mama."

Tears burned the backs of her eyes. God, she missed him. They'd never been apart before this. "Hey, baby. I miss you."

"Me, too. I'm having so much fun here. I'm going to see some horses today."

Peter's happiness was palpable on the phone. Realizing she'd given her son something he never should have been denied made all the sacrifices worth it. She had to remember her marriage to Jake was for

Peter. It wasn't for her and it certainly wasn't for Jake. "Good."

"When will you be home?" he asked.

Larissa wasn't sure of the exact time since Jake had their tickets but he'd said sometime this evening. "Before bedtime."

"I love you, Mama."

"Love you too."

They said their goodbyes and she talked to Miranda briefly about what time to expect them. It felt weird to be discussing her son with someone else. She hung up and sat on the edge of the coffee table where she'd taken the call.

"You okay?" Jake asked from the doorway. He wore a pair of chinos and a shirt in a flattering shade of blue.

She nodded.

"Who was on the phone?"

"Ted Larson. I took his number for you. I called to check on Peter."

"How's he doing?"

"Great. They're going to see some horses today."

"That would be the stables near the house. Does he ride?"

"Jake, he's three."

"So?"

"So, he doesn't ride."

"We'll have to teach him," Jake said.

"Is this going to work?" she asked without thinking.

"Yes, Rissa, it is. I'm angry right now, but I'll get

over it and we're going to work things out," he said, and there was a promise in his voice that she trusted.

"For Peter?"

Jake crossed the room to her side and tipped her head back with his knuckle under her chin. "For us."

Then he slipped away to make his phone call. She cautioned herself not to believe him but she couldn't help it. Hope had been born and she believed they had a chance at forever.

Eleven

"Oh, no," Larissa said as they pulled to a stop in front of his town house a little before ten that night. Peter was sleeping fitfully in the back seat and Larissa had been in a quiet mood since they'd left Vegas.

"What's the matter?"

"I recognize that car," she said.

Jake waited.

"It's Jasmine Carmody. What's she doing here?"

Jake reached over and patted Larissa's hand. "Probably checking up to see if our marriage is a real one."

"Let's go to my place. We can hide out until she leaves."

"I'm not hiding from anyone. Especially a reporter."

"I guess you're right."

"Of course I am."

Jake pulled into the driveway and shut off the car. Larissa nervously twisted her fingers together. "Calm down. We're in this together."

He leaned across the seat and brushed his lips over hers. She sighed into his mouth and he hesitated, then deepened the kiss. He'd decided in the shower this morning to let Larissa set the pace for their marriage. She had too much sensuality in her to keep them apart for long. And once he'd gotten past his frustration, he'd realized she had a good point. Sex between the two of them was a convenient way to avoid talking.

Hell, he'd been the first one to use it that night in Atlanta when they'd conceived their son.

"Ready?"

"I guess."

"Chin up, Rissa. We're a team now and I don't think one determined reporter can defeat us."

She smiled at him and he felt ten feet tall. He climbed out of the truck.

"Mr. Danforth, I'm Jasmine Carmody with the *Savannah Morning News.* Can I have a few minutes of your time?" the stunning African-American woman asked.

"For what?"

"To discuss the circumstances of your recent marriage."

"What do you want to know?" Jake asked.

Larissa got out of the truck and walked around to

his side. Jake pulled her close to his side and dropped a kiss on her forehead.

"Very touching," Jasmine said. "I'm curious about something."

"What's that?" Jake asked.

"How does it feel to know you're the second generation of wealthy Southern gentlemen to be deceived by a Nielsen woman?"

Larissa stiffened under his arm.

"I didn't deceive Jake."

"Of course you didn't, Ms. Nielsen."

"It's Mrs. Danforth," Jake said. "And Larissa didn't trap me into marriage, Ms. Carmody. I trapped her."

"Do tell," Jasmine said.

"That's private and personal. I don't think we have anything further to say."

"I'm not giving up," Jasmine said. "I'm going to write this story with or without your cooperation."

"Then write this—Larissa and I have been friends for over ten years and our marriage has brought us the kind of happiness neither of us thought possible."

Jake lowered his head and kissed Larissa, hoping she'd understand from his embrace that he meant those words. Their marriage wasn't a temporary media fix, as it had started out—it was real and lasting. Because with Larissa, he'd found a place in his family. And a family of his own.

Peter stirred in the back seat of the car, coughing and crying out. Jake opened the back door and lifted out his son.

"Where's Mama?"

"Right here, sweetie," Larissa said, rubbing her hand over their son's head.

Peter squirmed in Jake's arms, leaning over toward Larissa. Jake let the boy go though he didn't want to. Peter coughed again and Larissa cradled him close to her.

"We better get him inside," Larissa said.

Jake closed the door and put his arm around Larissa. Jasmine continued to watch them and Jake had the feeling that they hadn't seen the last of her. But it didn't change the way he felt. He wasn't going to let a reporter hurt Larissa. She'd carved out a life for herself the only way she knew how.

"I didn't think she'd find out about your dad."

"Reilly Peyton isn't my dad. He was a sperm donor."

Jake laughed. She didn't sound angry with Jasmine. "You're okay that she found out."

"I'd rather she hadn't. But when you came to my defense I realized something."

Peter coughed again and Larissa rubbed his back. "I hope he's not getting sick."

"I'll call the doctor when we get inside," Jake said. He knew he should focus on Peter, but in the back of his mind her words lingered. "What'd you realize?"

"That having you by my side made all the difference in the world. Even if she prints her article—and I'm sure she will—it won't be me standing in front of Savannah society by myself. We're a family and together we'll decide what makes us Danforths. I've never really felt like I could fit in at home, either."

"Why not?"

"My father put a lot of pressure on me to be the responsible one. That eldest sibling thing, I guess. I've dropped the ball a lot, Rissa. You know I'm not perfect, but I'm not going to drop the ball this time."

"I know, Jake," she said. She reached up to touch him with her free hand.

"Let's get this little guy into his pajamas and then finish this conversation," Jake said.

"Mama?" Peter said, his breath rasping in and out. His chest was heaving with the effort to breathe.

Jake didn't like it. "Has he done that before?"

"No. Call the doctor," Larissa said. Though she tried to keep her voice calm, he saw her hands tremble.

Jake grabbed one of Larissa's laminated index cards and dialed the doctor's number. Larissa sat on the couch holding their son close and murmuring softly to him. But Peter kept struggling to breathe and Larissa finally stood up. She paced around the room with their son in her arms. Jake was suddenly afraid that now that he'd found the happiness he'd always sought, he wouldn't be allowed to keep it.

Jake got the doctor on the phone and described Peter's symptoms. Dr. Gold instructed Jake to take Peter to the hospital, saying he thought Peter might be having an acute asthma attack.

Jake got his family out of the house and into the car, his heart pounding as he raced to the hospital.

* * *

Larissa had never been so scared in her entire life. Peter was hooked up to a drip IV and a nebulizer. His entire chest heaved with each breath he tried to take.

She clung tight to her son's hand and willed him to breathe easier, but she knew that wasn't possible. Jake rested his big strong hand on her shoulder, and she sensed he was urging her to share her burden with him but she couldn't.

She wouldn't be able to relax until Peter was off this machine and breathing easier, though she appreciated having Jake and his family around her. And she knew that Peter did as well.

Tonight she'd had her first taste of what being a Danforth meant. Instead of sitting in the waiting area until it was their turn, they'd been given a private room and admitted with little trouble. Dr. Gold had seen Peter once and this was the second breathing treatment that Peter had taken.

Jake's parents had arrived and were now in the waiting area. Jake hadn't left her side the entire time. He held her hand or Peter's and made sure they were very aware of his presence.

He was a solid support for Larissa and she realized she loved him. Watching him talk quietly to their son, and handle every detail that came up in the hospital had shown her what she'd secretly been afraid to admit all along.

Jake wasn't just her husband, he was her love. She also realized, when he'd talked to his family, that Jake kept the depth of his feelings a secret. It was humbling to know she might be the only one who realized Jake was so much more than the easygoing, successful businessman that he presented to the world.

Peter finished his breathing treatment and lay back against the pillows. He looked so small. Jake tucked Mr. Bear and Peter's worn blanket up next to him. Larissa leaned down and kissed him.

"Mama? Can we say our poem?"

"We sure can, baby."

Quietly she started Frost's poem and Jake and Peter joined in. By the time they'd gotten to the last line, Peter's eyes drifted close.

Larissa turned to Jake. "I feel so helpless."

"Me too."

She felt like crying. When she'd made her decision not to tell Jake about Peter, she'd only had Reilly Peyton as an example—a man who'd never wanted to be a father. But from the first moment Jake had known about Peter, he'd proved that fatherhood was a natural part of him.

"Why are you looking at me like that?" Jake asked.

She didn't want to let him know how desperately she was coming to need him. "Like what?"

He shrugged and looked uncomfortable. "I'm not sure."

She slid off the bed and sat on his lap. Wrapping her arms around him, she held him tightly to her. God, she didn't think she'd survive if he left her.

"Thank you," she said against his lips.

"For what?" he asked, running his hands down her back and hugging her to him.

He smelled good. His cologne was spicy and woodsy, a direct contrast to the sterile scent of the hospital. "For being here. I'm so glad I didn't have to deal with this on my own."

He looked at her. His brown eyes were serious and she remembered all the promises he'd made her. Promises that she'd been afraid to believe. "That's my job now."

"Are you sure?" she asked, still afraid to accept his words.

He squeezed her tight and then tucked her head under his chin. "Hell, yes. I'm not letting either of you out of my sight."

"Oh, Jake."

Jake kissed her with a passion that she sensed concealed hidden depths. She clung to him. For the first time in her life she really needed someone by her side and it scared her. Almost as much as her fear of being left alone. She watched Peter sleeping. Each exhalation wheezed a little.

Someone cleared their throat and she glanced up to see Harold Danforth in the doorway. Jake's dad was dressed in chinos and a button-down shirt. He looked tired and tense but his face filled with love when he glanced at his sleeping grandson.

"No need to ask how things are in here," Harold said.

Jake stiffened under her. Larissa got to her feet and walked over to the hospital bed to check Peter. She rested her hand lightly on his chest to feel each breath he took. "You know me, Dad. Can't keep my hands off a pretty girl."

"I do know you, son," Harold said. There was a pride in his eyes that Larissa realized Jake didn't see.

"Your mom and I wanted to check on Peter before we went home for the night."

"He's sleeping," Jake said.

"I'll go get your mother," Harold said.

Jake cursed under his breath and pushed to his feet, joining Larissa by Peter's side. Jake settled his hand over hers on their son's chest. "God, I hope he beats this thing."

"Dr. Gold said there's a chance he could outgrow the asthma."

Jake said nothing, but Larissa felt some of her anxiety wane. She knew that with Jake by her side there was nothing they couldn't handle.

"What's up with you and your dad?"

"Nothing," Jake said, pacing across the room.

"Jake?" She turned to face him, but he wasn't paying the least bit of attention to her.

"Leave it be, Rissa."

She crossed the room to Jake and wrapped her arms around him.

"Talk to me," she said at last. She'd been so caught up in her own feelings of inadequacy that she hadn't noticed the tension between Jake and his father before.

"I don't want to get into that. You've got enough on your mind with Peter."

She tilted her head back and met his eyes. "Peter's resting now. Tell me about your dad."

"It's nothing," he said, moving away. It seemed he couldn't stand still. "I've never been able to please the old man."

She stopped his pacing with a hand on his arm. "I don't get that from him. He seems really proud of you." That was the truth. Harold had taken her aside earlier and told her when the chips were down there was no better man to have by her side than Jake.

"Yeah, right. What dad wouldn't be proud of a son who can't keep his hands off his wife while his grandson struggles to breathe?"

"I'm sure your dad understands that we need each other now."

Jake shrugged.

Larissa wasn't sure what else to say. She thought Harold was probably relieved that their marriage wasn't just for the media, but she didn't want to open that topic of conversation. "It wasn't like that. And I think your dad knows it. You should talk to him."

"I don't think so."

She raised herself on tiptoe so they were almost eye-to-eye. "Well, I do. I think you should do it. And I'm not going to stop bringing the subject up until you do."

"We've only been married two days and already you're nagging me."

For the first time since they arrived at the hospital she felt like smiling. "Start out as you mean to go on, I always say."

"Good thing I know how to keep you quiet."

"How?" she asked, smiling teasingly up at him.

"Like this," he said, lowering his head and taking her mouth in a kiss that said things he'd never say with words. That embrace said thank-you and I'll be there for you. She clung to his broad shoulders and kissed him with the same intensity.

When his parents returned to the room, he reluctantly let Larissa go. A storm raged inside him. He'd never felt so helpless as he had on the drive to the hospital. He was used to focusing on a goal and achieving it. And tonight had shown him that life with Larissa and Peter was going to be anything but predictable.

Since they'd landed back in Savannah, he'd realized that the only thing he wanted was some peace and quiet with his small family. He wanted what his folks had always had, but he didn't know that he was worthy of that kind of bond. He'd played around with women for so long that, even though Larissa made him feel things that he'd never experienced before, he wasn't sure he could be the kind of man she needed.

She moved across the room toward his mother and Jake wondered how Larissa felt about suddenly having an extended family. He wouldn't give up being a Danforth for anything, he realized.

"How's Peter doing?" his mom asked.

"Better. He's finally sleeping," Larissa said.

"I hope this attack wasn't brought on by anything at our house."

"I'm sure it wasn't, Miranda. He had a great time visiting with you."

"We enjoyed having him there. God, I miss having a little boy in the house."

Jake loved his parents, but he wanted them to go so he could hold Larissa in his lap again and keep an eye on both her and Peter. "It's been a long night."

"Yes, it has," his dad said.

"I'm thirsty. I think I'll go down to the vending machine and get a Diet Coke. Want to go with me, Miranda?" Larissa asked.

"Sure, dear. Do you want anything, Jake?"

"Coke would be great, Mom."

Larissa followed Miranda toward the door. At the entrance, she paused and looked at Jake. *Talk to your dad,* she mouthed. Bossy woman, he thought as she disappeared.

His father leaned over Peter, brushing back his hair. "He looks so much like you."

Jake crossed to the other side of the bed and leaned down over his son. "Yeah, he does."

"This takes me back. Remember that summer you broke your arm?"

"Do I. I couldn't play soccer for six weeks."

"That's right. You missed out on winning that MVP trophy you'd had your eye on."

"I got it the next year."

"You were always good at winning."

"Yes, I was."

"You okay, son?"

Jake shrugged. It didn't matter that he was over thirty and owned a successful business. He still felt like a boy in his dad's presence. His father was a man who had it all and made it look easy. Not even the disappearance of his youngest sister, Victoria, had phased Harold. He'd still held the family together and kept everyone focused on finding her. Jake didn't think he'd ever be the man his father was.

"Having a kid is a double-edged sword," his dad said suddenly.

"What do you mean?"

"Just that you do your damnedest to protect them and then out of the blue something you can't control happens." His dad reached out and touched Peter's forehead. In that moment he saw on his father's face the same vulnerability that Jake felt toward his son.

"Like with Victoria," Jake said. He'd never really gotten over the guilt he'd felt at her disappearance. And he'd never shared with his dad the responsibility he bore toward the incident.

"Yes," his dad said, running his hands through his hair. "Good news on that front. The body in the attic at Crofthaven isn't hers."

Jake felt a sense of relief at the news. No one in the family had given any credence to the theory that the body had been Victoria's. They all knew she'd disappeared in Atlanta, not in Savannah. "I never believed it was."

"Me either. God, I wish I knew where she was," Harold said. Another crack appeared in Jake's image of his dad. His old man had always appeared so capable and confident. Jake hadn't realized that underneath was a man who had as many vulnerabilities as Jake had.

"Me too. You know I've never forgiven myself for not attending the concert with her. I shouldn't have bought her those tickets."

His dad gave him a sad smile. "You never could tell her no."

That was the truth. He'd loved having younger sisters who looked up to him. Jake had always been indulgent with the women in his life. "It scares me sometimes to think that I might screw up with Peter that way."

"I wish I could tell you it ends, son."

"It doesn't?"

"No."

"How do you do it, Dad?"

"I lean on your mom. That woman is the best thing that ever happened to me. And you kids…well you're extensions of her."

Jake looked at his dad and for once didn't feel like a failure. "I hope I'm half the dad you are."

"I know you will be."

Before he could respond, the women returned with some cold soft drinks and a couple of bags of snacks.

"How's Peter?" Larissa asked.

"Still sleeping," Jake said.

Larissa crossed to his side and slipped her arm around his waist. He held her close and watched their son sleep. A moment later, he glanced across the bed at his dad.

His dad winked at him and for the first time, Jake felt like a man that his dad was proud to know.

Twelve

The next evening Peter was doing much better, but Dr. Gold wanted to keep him one more night for observation. Larissa was tired—she hadn't slept in more than twenty-four hours. She was emotionally drained. Jake's family was wonderful, but they could be a little overwhelming. Jake's sister Imogene had breezed in on her lunch break wearing a power suit and looking totally gorgeous. Larissa had felt unkempt and frumpy by comparison.

Though obviously a workaholic, Imogene had spent part of her lunch break sitting at Peter's side and reading to him. Jake's brother Toby had called and Peter had talked to him on the phone. Wes had stopped by with a new electronic game for Peter, and all and all her son had seemed as overwhelmed as she'd felt at having so many people care about them.

But they were alone now. Jake was outside talking with his dad. She wasn't sure what had happened last night, but she felt like all the superficial reasons she'd been using for keeping Jake at arm's length had disappeared. She wasn't protecting her heart, because it was too late to do so. She'd fallen in love with Jake a long time ago and now that they were married she couldn't stop her feelings from deepening.

Peter had wanted her to sleep next to him, so she'd crawled into the bed with her son. Peter slept quietly, resting his head on her arm. She bent close and listened to his breathing. It was deep and steady. Relief flooded her and she hugged his small body close.

"Hey, lady," Jake said from the doorway. "How's our boy doing?"

She glanced up at him and felt her heart jump in her chest. Damn he looked good. Tired but good. He had two days' worth of beard stubble on his cheeks and he'd never looked more attractive. Sensual awareness flooded her body. Not now, she thought—I'm doing the mom thing.

"He's resting now. We were watching SpongeBob before he fell asleep. A show that Peter informed me you said he could watch. Correct me if I'm wrong but SpongeBob wasn't on my index card of approved television shows."

"Really? I'm sure I saw it on there," Jake said with a sly grin.

Peter loved having a daddy and it was just as clear that Jake loved being one. Jake had spent just as much time as she had at the hospital. He'd played games with their son and made plans to go camping this weekend down in St. Augustine. Listening and watching the two of them had convinced Larissa that Jake was in their lives for good.

"I'm going to let it slide this time, but once he's out of the hospital we'll go back to our normal TV schedule."

"Whatever you say, Larissa," he said in the bland tone that told her he was going to do whatever he thought was best for their son. She had to admit Peter had bloomed since Jake had come into his life. Her little boy had always been quiet and reserved. But lately he'd come out of his shell.

"Why do I get the feeling you're placating me?" she asked.

He shrugged, but there was a sparkle in his eyes that told her he liked sparring with her. "I don't know. You always were a smart woman—you tell me."

She prided herself on her intelligence, which made it even harder to believe that she'd actually thought she could live with Jake and not be his lover. Now she just had to figure out a way to bring the topic up so he'd know she'd changed her mind.

"Did your parents go home?"

"Yes. Mom said they'll be back in the morning when Peter is released."

Jake stopped at the side of the bed and ran his fingertip down her bare arm. She must look a mess. She reached up to tuck a strand of hair behind her ear but Jake brushed her hand away. "Leave it alone. I like it when you don't look all tidy."

"It's safe to say I'm not tidy at this moment." She carefully pulled her arm out from under Peter's head and stood up. Jake didn't back up and they were pressed almost body to body.

"No, you're not."

"Neither are you," she said, running her hands over his rough jaw. He felt earthy against her soft fingers and she wished they were alone. She leaned up and kissed him. Jake responded with a longing that took her by surprise. The kiss was carnal and deep and when he stepped away she shivered with desire.

"Rissa, is there something you're trying to tell me here?" he asked.

"Well, maybe I am."

"I'm not going to make any more guesses where you're concerned any longer."

"I'm sorry about that last morning in Vegas. I guess I freaked out."

"Our wedding night was incredible."

"Yes, it was. I don't want that to be our only night together."

"It won't be."

"Good, then we're on the same page."

"Larissa, we're not in a meeting with the library board."

She flushed. "I know. But it's easier to talk about it in business terms."

He shook his head. "Are you saying you want to be my wife, in every sense?"

"Yes," she said softly and cuddled closer to the man she'd given her heart to.

Jake felt he'd been through the ringer. He was used to blithely skating through life. Keeping his emotions in a nice safe place that was only breached by his siblings, parents and cousins. Over the past twenty-four hours he'd come to realize that Peter and Larissa had found their way into his heart.

Peter was naturally easy to love. The boy was a blend of Jake's rambunctious go-get-'em attitude and Larissa's quiet intelligence. It was an odd combination and it awed Jake to think that part of him was going to live on through Peter after he was gone.

And he'd realized he didn't want to lose this family he'd found, the family he'd created when he was still so self-involved that he'd never noticed. The family that he knew he'd never be able to survive without.

Larissa yawned behind her hand and her shoulder slumped with fatigue. She looked as if she was about to collapse. "Why don't you take the Suburban and go home and rest?"

He liked to think that he'd helped her through this crisis. And it had been a crisis. He could handle any major problem at D&D's, but nothing had made him sweat like watching Peter struggle to breathe. It had made him realize how fragile this life was. It had reminded him of all the reasons he'd started hiding his feelings when Vicky had disappeared. Only now he knew that hiding wasn't the solution. Celebrating life and remembering the reasons why it was good were important.

"Thanks, but I think I'd better stay here in case Peter wakes up."

"Don't you trust me to take care of him?" he asked. He had to wonder. She'd scarcely left him alone with Peter since they'd been at the hospital. Her quiet strength surprised him, but it shouldn't have. Larissa was a survivor.

She closed her eyes, hiding from him. As always, she was a mystery to him.

"Of course, I do. It's just I don't..."

"You don't what?" He wondered sometimes what she saw in him. She'd always been the one person that had slipped past his guard. The one person he could tell his dreams to who didn't make him feel like an idiot. The one person he'd always wanted to impress. And he had the feeling that sometimes he came close to doing that.

"I don't want him to need someone else," she said in a rush of honesty.

He understood. Sometimes it was easier to be everything to someone than to share the responsibility. "I'm not some stranger, Rissa. I'm his dad."

"You're right. I'm still not used to trusting men in general."

"Me in particular?" he asked. Hell, he sounded like a sap. Why did it matter if she didn't trust him? Because you love her, a voice inside him said. The thought staggered him.

She pivoted to face him. He couldn't read her expression, but he didn't care anymore. Now he was concerned with hiding his own weakness from her. He'd always been the strong one and he wasn't going to let anything—not even Larissa—change that. "I trust you, Jacob Danforth, more than I've ever thought I could trust any man."

Her words went straight through him. The mantle of responsibility felt heavy on his shoulders and he vowed that he'd never do anything to make her doubt the faith she'd placed in him. God, he needed to be alone with his wife. He needed to know that his son was safe and healthy and then take his wife to bed and reaffirm the bonds they'd tentatively forged in Vegas.

"Come here, woman," he said.

"Why?"

Because I need you, he thought but didn't dare say. "Just get over here."

She gave him a flirty smile and walked across the room with slow hip-swaying steps. Each move she made seduced him. And made the barriers he'd thought he'd built around his heart crumble.

She stopped a good six inches from him. Her gaze skimmed over his body and he couldn't help it, he stood up straighter and flexed his muscles.

"Very impressive," she said.

"I know."

She laughed and he realized it had been too long

since he'd seen Larissa smiling. He promised himself that from now on she'd have lots of reasons to smile.

He reached out and dragged her close. He wanted to clutch her to his chest but forced himself to just hold her loosely instead, carefully so not to reveal the intensity of the emotions swamping him. But deep inside he knew he'd never be complete without Larissa by his side. She made him a better man and he knew that if she ever left he'd be incomplete. How was he going to keep her by his side without letting her know?

Larissa left Jake and Peter at the hospital. She felt more certain than ever that she and Jake were going to make it. That they were going to be one of those couples that succeeded despite the circumstances under which they'd started their marriage. She returned to Jake's town house on autopilot and when she entered the house she went straight to his bedroom and crawled into his bed.

Surrounded by his scent, she fell into a deep sleep. The doorbell woke her four hours later. She stumbled from the bed and shrugged into Jake's robe.

She hoped it wasn't Jasmine Carmody again. Though she'd made a kind of peace with her past, that didn't mean she wanted to discuss it with that reporter.

A quick peak through the peephole showed that it was a man she didn't recognize. She opened the door.

"Can I help you?"

"Are you Larissa Nielsen?"

"I used to be. I'm Larissa Danforth, now." God that

sounded right to her ears. She'd feared marrying into a moneyed family but she realized her fears were based on her father's attitude and her mother's marriage. Jake was so different than Reilly Peyton.

He handed her an envelope and walked away. She closed the door and reentered Jake's town house. That was strange, she thought. She went into the kitchen and put a cup of water in the microwave. She used her fingernail to open the envelope and pulled out the papers.

She skimmed them and lost feeling in her legs. Clutching the papers, she sank to the floor. Jake was suing her for full custody of Peter. He'd lied about the paternity test! He'd had it done so that he could take her baby away from her.

She pulled her knees to her chest and hugged them tight, realizing that her worst fears had been realized. She'd trusted him. And he'd betrayed her. The entire time he'd been playing a game calculated to hurt her in the worst way possible.

She staggered to her feet and went into the guest bedroom Jake had given her when they'd moved in. She took a shower and dressed with care. She didn't know what to do next but knew that she had to confront Jake. If he thought she was going to give up her son because he needed revenge on her, he had another think coming.

But she knew she'd never drag Peter through any kind of custody battle. She never wanted her son to feel as if his birth was something that brought regret to his mother and father.

When she was dressed, she got in her car and sat in the driveway while her hands stopped shaking. She leaned down on the steering wheel and tried to figure out how things could go from being close to perfect to a nightmare.

Finally she had her trembling under control and a slow anger began to build inside her. By the time she got to the hospital, she was ready to tear Jake Danforth apart. How dare he manipulate her that way? Didn't family mean anything to him? Didn't he realize how legal battles tore at a child's security?

She entered the hospital and rehearsed her words in the elevator on the way up. Then she thought about Jake's parents. Miranda had invited Larissa to call her Mom. Had she known that her son was planning to take Peter away? Had they all been in on the scheme to keep her from her son?

The elevator doors opened on Peter's floor and suddenly she was afraid to face the future. She knew that she wasn't going to be her usual levelheaded self. She knew that she was an inch away from tears and outright wailing.

She got off the elevator and walked slowly past the nurses station. It was early in the morning and the halls were filled with doctors making their rounds. She paused outside the door to Peter's room. Tucking a strand of loose hair back into her ponytail, she cautioned herself not to get emotional.

She pushed open the door and stepped inside. The room was dark except for a stream of sunlight coming through the gap in the curtains. Jake lay on the bed next to Peter. He cradled their son against his chest.

The scene looked so right. Too right. Maybe she should do the adult thing and back away. Let Jake have Peter. Jake could give him so many things that Larissa couldn't. He had a large family, plenty of money and most importantly, he loved Peter.

Tears burned the backs of her eyes and she fought to keep them from falling but couldn't. They were hot on her face and when she lifted her clammy hands to wipe them away she caught a glimpse of her wedding ring.

She felt like a fool for ever believing that Jake would have wanted her for his wife. Maybe he'd just wanted to get her out of town so that he could build his case against her.

And she'd made it so easy by falling for him. By letting him manipulate her in the most intimate way.

A sob escaped her and she knew she wasn't in any shape to confront Jake right now. She turned to leave the room. She'd wash her face and get herself together.

"Rissa?" he asked.

She steeled her heart against the compassion she heard in his voice. Before, her lonely heart had been looking for love, but now she knew the truth. Jake was using his silky words and smooth ways to lull her into complacency. She glanced over her shoulder at him. Jake sat up, easing his arm out from beneath Peter and crossing the room to her.

"Baby, what's wrong?"

"I..." She couldn't get the words out of her mouth. How could she verbalize the hurt that had come on so unexpectedly? This was her worst fear and why she'd fought so hard to keep from falling in love with Jake.

"Did that reporter bother you again? I'm going to call my lawyers and have them take action against her."

Strangely those words were the ones that made her stop crying. "Call your lawyers?"

"Yes, my lawyers."

"You're good at that, aren't you?"

"What do you mean?" he asked, his eyes narrowing.

"That I'm well aware of how you've been keeping your lawyers busy—planning to take Peter from me."

Jake cursed savagely under his breath and Larissa took a few steps from him. Crossing her arms over her chest, she looked at him the way she would an enemy.

"Larissa—"

"Don't bother lying to me now, Jake. I've got the proof in my hands."

Jake shoved his fingers through his hair. A million excuses and defenses hovered on the edge of his tongue. He knew what to say and how to dance away from her. How to keep himself emotionally safe and protected from the vulnerabilities that only this woman could make him feel.

But seeing her hurting like this, knowing he was

responsible, made him feel horrible. He didn't want to see her cry.

He pulled her into his arms. She struggled against him and he knew he only had a few seconds to say the right words. But what were they?

He caught her face in his hands and stared down at her. He rubbed the tears from her eyes and leaned close to her. God, she was so small and vulnerable. "I'm sorry."

She started to speak, but he pressed his mouth to hers, stopping her words. She smelled so good and he knew he should be concentrating on making his mistakes right. She kept her mouth tightly closed but stopped struggling to get away from him. He lifted his head.

"I was angry when you first told me about Peter."

"I know. But I thought we'd gotten past all that. Dammit, Jake. I thought we were starting a life together."

"We are, Rissa. We have started a life together." He was hedging and she knew it. But if he told her what was in his heart and she didn't return his feelings, he'd feel like a fool. Better a strong man than a fool, he thought.

"It doesn't feel like this is much of a life. I wanted a real marriage, not one based on vengeance."

"I wanted revenge," he said honestly.

"I can't let you take Peter. You can offer him much more than I can when it comes to money and family, but you can't offer him the one thing that every child needs—love and nurturing."

"What makes you so sure?" he asked.

"Because you don't know how to love."

He shuddered. Jake shoved his hands through his hair and turned away from her. Was she right? Had he forgotten all he'd learned about loving relationships in trying to keep himself insulated from the pain that came with failing? He paced to the window and rested his head against the cold glass. There were no answers in the sky or in the densely crowded parking lot below.

The only place with the answers was inside him. And losing Peter or Larissa wasn't an option. He needed them in his life.

He straightened and turned back to the woman who didn't realize she held his heart in her hands. She watched him carefully, clearly not sure what to expect next. He realized it was time to stop running and stop hiding from the emotions that scared him the most and the woman who inspired them.

"I'm not going to take Peter away from you. Hell, woman, I don't think I could live without the both of you in my life. And I certainly can't live with the knowledge that I hurt you so deeply.

"I never could have gone through with the suit. It was my back-up plan. A safe way for me to pretend I could keep you under my control."

He opened his arms and she hesitated only a second before running across the room and jumping into his arms. He held her tight and whispered all the words he was afraid to say out loud.

"You are the breath in my body, the light in my soul

and the beating of my heart. I can't survive without you. I love you."

"Oh, Jake. I love you, too."

He bent to capture her lips with his and this time she opened her mouth to his. The kiss was deep and sensual, but heavy with the promise of tomorrow. A promise Jake hadn't been able to believe in for a long time.

"Mama? Daddy?" Peter called from the bed.

Jake pocketed the legal papers Larissa had brought with her and they crossed the room to their son.

"Hey, baby. How do you feel?" Larissa asked, brushing his hair back from his forehead.

"Hungry," Peter said.

Jake laughed. His son was always hungry. "I'll go get you some food. What do you want?"

"Krispy Kremes."

"Peter, how do you know about doughnuts?" Larissa asked.

"Daddy told me about them last night and promised we could go as soon as I leave the hospital."

"Sounds like a good plan," Larissa said.

The doctor entered the room and in a short while Peter was discharged. Jake's parents arrived and Jake felt really worthy of being a Danforth for the first time since Victoria had disappeared. He realized that his coffeehouse business and his playboy lifestyle were just excuses to keep from staying still long enough to feel the guilt.

But he let go of the guilt. He knew his sister was alive somewhere and he knew that they would find her.

"Mom and Dad, will you take Peter in your car? We're going to the Krispy Kreme."

"Sure thing, son," his dad said.

Jake took Larissa's hand in his and led her to the Suburban. "What are we doing?"

"I just wanted a few minutes alone with you, Rissa."

"I thought we settled everything."

"I'm going to call Ted Larson as soon as his office opens and drop the custody suit."

"I know."

"You sound pretty confident," he said.

"Honey, you told me I was the air you breathe. I think that gives me the right."

"Am I the air you breathe?"

She leaned up and kissed his jaw. "No."

"No?"

"You're the blood in my veins."

He scooped her up in the parking lot and spun around with Larissa in his arms. Then he bent and kissed this woman who'd given him more than he ever expected to have—love and a family.

Epilogue

Jake had decided that their honeymoon in Vegas had been too short and had surprised Larissa and Peter with a two-week trip through the Southeast following Jimmy Buffett's concert tour. This was their last night before heading back to Savannah. They were in Orlando in the parking lot at the TD Waterhouse Center. Jake and Peter wore identical unbuttoned Hawaiian-print shirts and khaki board shorts under grass skirts.

They were parked next to Courtney and Jen, two college girls they'd met at the concert in Miami the day before. They were grilling chicken and making margaritas. Jake came up behind Larissa and slipped his arms around her waist. He kissed her on the neck and whispered delicious promises in her ear.

Larissa leaned back against him and looked over at

their son playing nearby. This was the life she'd been afraid to let herself dream of. But here it was nonetheless and it was so much more than she'd ever imagined.

"Mama, look," Peter said.

Their son proceeded to shake his hips and start singing fins. "Did Daddy teach you that?"

"Yes, come on, Daddy. Let's dance for her."

Peter and Jake did their hip-shaking dance for her and earned applause from the others in the parking lot. Larissa felt a sense of peace and belonging that she'd never thought to find. She closed her eyes. She realized that she was going to have to thank Jasmine Carmody for giving her the family she'd always dreamed of.

* * * * *

THE FORBIDDEN PRINCESS

Day Leclaire

To Melissa Jeglinski,
who felt my book might be Desireable.
Many thanks!

One

Merrick Montgomery studied the woman whose life he was about to destroy...and who could, ultimately, destroy his.

Alyssa Sutherland was stunning, he conceded. Sexy, even in the silver wedding dress she wore. He adjusted the binoculars to get a closer look. She sat without moving while a bevy of women fluttered around her like jewel-colored butterflies. Her features were as close to perfection as a man could desire and her figure—what he could see of it beneath the embellished gown she wore—threatened to rouse that desire to a fever pitch. Dappled sunlight touched the champagne blond of her hair, kissing it with the merest hint of rose.

He felt an inexplicable and powerful urge to fully bare her to his gaze, to see if her body mirrored the perfection of that face. Not that there was much doubt about what he'd uncover. Such was the gift nature bestowed on certain women—warm, breathtaking beauty combined with cold, avaricious natures.

Beneath her gown he'd find her flesh pale and unblemished enough to make any man forget her true nature. She'd feel soft and supple against his calloused hands. Would she be built like a goddess, her hips a lush, feminine sanctuary? Or perhaps her gown hid a smaller, more boyish figure. He'd found such women to be strong and lithe in bed. Miniature dynamos.

Goddess or dynamo, it didn't matter. She'd sold herself to Brandt von Folke, which had forced his hand.

"Merrick."

The voice whispering in his ear brought him to his senses and his mouth tightened. He'd allowed the Sutherland woman to distract him from his goal and that angered him. It had never happened before. Not once in all the years he'd been head of the Royal Security Force. But this woman... He studied her one final time, acknowledging the intensity of her allure while deliberately setting it aside as nothing more than an obstacle. Her beauty would be a problem. It wasn't easily overlooked and threatened to draw attention to his actions, something he needed to prevent at all costs.

He readjusted his binoculars, sweeping them in a slow, wide arc around the courtyard where the woman sat. It only took him a moment to find what stood between him and his goal. There were eight guards in all. Six clearly visible and two on either side of the chapel doors. He checked his watch and then sent a quick hand signal to the men who accompanied him. They would move in in ten minutes.

Once again he fixed the powerful binoculars on the Sutherland woman, tightening the focus until all he could see was the porcelain perfection of her face. She might have been lifeless for all the emotion she showed. Her eyes were downcast as though in thought, and he couldn't help but wonder what, if anything, went on behind that perfect oval mask. As he watched he caught the tiniest quiver of her mouth. Nervousness, perhaps? Second thoughts? No, not a chance. Not this woman. A prayer of thanksgiving for her coming triumph? Now that was more like it.

His mouth tightened. Pray, woman. Pray for all you're worth. Not that it would help. In a few more minutes he'd take this woman. He'd do whatever necessary to ensure that this day ended much differently from how she envisioned as she sat far below.

"It's time," Merrick announced. "No matter what, we make certain the woman doesn't marry Brandt von Folke. Understood?"

He didn't wait for agreement. His men were hand-picked. They would follow his orders without question or hesitation. His mouth curled into a hard smile. There was no doubt what would happen next. His reasons were just. His need absolute. He was doing the wrong thing for all the right reasons. He was going to kidnap another man's bride for the most noble of causes.

* * *

Alyssa Sutherland sat silently amidst a sea of chaos. It took every ounce of her self-control to keep from jumping up and shrieking at the women surrounding her to leave her alone. To give her just two minutes in which she could sit quietly and try to catch her breath. To allow her the luxury of tears or breaking down in momentary hysteria or even to close her eyes and escape into a brief, blissful fantasy where someone would come and rescue her from this nightmare. Not that there was any likelihood of that happening.

Events for the past week had moved at a breakneck pace and she hadn't found a single minute to regain her equilibrium. Not a moment to think. Not to fight. Not to negotiate or protest or plead. Or run. She'd simply been told what to do and been expected to obey without argument.

And she had, though it went against every instinct and every aspect of her personality. Unfortunately, there had been no other choice.

"Princess Alyssa, it's almost time." The woman spoke in lightly accented English. But then all the people Alyssa had met so far had spoken English as fluently as their native tongue. "You should enter the chapel now."

She spared the woman—Lady Bethany Something, she recalled—a brief glance. "It's just Alyssa. I'm not a princess."

"Yes, Your Highness."

Alyssa closed her eyes in despair. Lowering her head,

she struggled to maintain her composure. She could feel her mouth quiver, but it was beyond her ability to control it. "I need a moment," she whispered.

"I'm sorry, Your Highness. That isn't possible."

How many times in the past week had she been told the same thing? Too many to count. Always polite, always phrased with the utmost care and consideration and always the same underlying message: Not a chance in hell will you be permitted a single moment alone. You'll be guarded every single second that ticks off each endless hour of every hideous day. And yet…

They called her Princess Alyssa. They bowed and curtsied and treated her as though she were made of spun glass and was twice as fragile. Their respect wasn't a pretense. She sensed an underlying sincerity she couldn't mistake. For the first time in over a week, a spark of hope ignited. Perhaps she could work their deference to her advantage.

Taking a deep breath, she lifted her chin and fixed Lady Bethany with a steely gaze. "I need a moment alone."

Lady Bethany fluttered, casting nervous glances over her shoulder. "I don't think—"

"I'm not asking you to think. I'm telling you that I need five minutes alone before I return to the chapel. I need to…to gather my thoughts. To prepare myself for the ceremony so I don't let down my—" she swallowed, struggling to speak through the distress gripping her throat "—my husband-to-be."

Lady Bethany's fluttering grew worse. "I don't

think His Highness would approve. He ordered—requested—we remain with you at all times."

"The guard will see to my safety," Alyssa pressed, sensing victory.

"But His Highness—"

"Would agree to your making an exception on my wedding day." She infused her voice with "royal" demand. Not that she had a clue what that really meant. She could only give it her best shot and hope she hit the mark. "Why don't we send for Prince Brandt and see who's right?"

Apparently, it was the perfect tack to take. Her bluff worked. Lady Bethany blanched and stumbled back a step, dropping a hasty curtsey. "That won't be necessary, Your Highness. I'll ask the guards to escort you to the chapel when you're ready. Will five minutes be sufficient?"

Five minutes. Five short, precious minutes. How could she possibly prepare herself for what was to come in so little time? She inclined her head. "That will be fine, thank you." It would have to be.

Her bevy of ladies-in-waiting, as they'd described themselves, gathered into a hurried group, whispering in their native tongue of Verdonian—a language Alyssa didn't understand, which put her at a distinct disadvantage. Shooting quick, anxious looks over their shoulders, they withdrew into the chapel.

Drawing a deep breath, Alyssa stood and walked from the courtyard into the garden. The largest of the guards followed, putting enough distance between them that she didn't feel crowded, and positioned himself between her and the woods that bordered the garden. She crossed to the stone bench farthest from the chapel and all the prying eyes.

Earlier that morning it had rained, but now dappled sunlight filtered through the branches of the oaks, warming her chilled skin. Not long ago she'd caught a glimpse of a rainbow—a sign, her mother had always claimed, of better times to come.

"There's a pot of gold waitin' for us out there, Ally, baby," Angela Barstow had always insisted. "And one of these days, we're gonna find it."

"Not this time, Mom," Alyssa whispered.

They couldn't run away from their problems this time. No new starts. No new stepfathers. No being dragged from her bed in the middle of the night so her mother could sneak them out of whatever city they'd pitched their tent in. This time the trouble was too great to run from.

She fought against a wave of panic. She didn't have long to gain control of her emotions. The seconds were ticking by. She could sense the restless movement of her guard and attempted to dismiss him from her mind. She drew in another breath, filling her lungs with the spring air that permeated what little she'd seen of the European country of Verdonia.

If this had been any other time, if the series of events that had brought her here had been different, she would have been enchanted by the beauty she'd encountered. But she was far from enchanted. She was alone and frightened and desperate to find a way out of this nightmare.

If only she hadn't gone chasing off to save Angela from her latest catastrophe. But the express envelope begging for help, along with the prepaid airline ticket to Verdonia, had been too much to ignore. So, Alyssa had postponed the start of her latest job and flown to the rescue. She couldn't have anticipated that she'd be snatched from the airport and carried off into the wilds of Verdonia any more than she could have foreseen being forced into a marriage as a result of threats she didn't dare challenge—threats to her mother's well-being.

Somehow she'd become caught up in a political maelstrom, one she didn't understand. Her mother had tried to explain but there'd been so little time. From their frantic and painfully brief conversation, Alyssa had learned that everyone believed she was a princess of Verdonia, and that her marriage to Brandt von Folke would unite two of three warring principalities. It was a crazy mistake. Even so, she found herself at the very heart of the current turmoil. She'd simply been told her only option was to say "I do" or her mother would suffer the consequences.

"I beg your pardon, Your Highness. It's time."

Alyssa opened her eyes and stared at the burly guard hovering over her. Panic tightened her throat. "Already?"

"It's time," he repeated, though she caught a hint of sympathy in his gruff voice and kindly brown eyes.

Before she could plead for another moment of solitude,

just a few precious extra seconds, a small whine sounded in her ear, whooshing past like a starving mosquito. A strange expression drifted across the guard's face as though he, too, had heard the odd noise. He made a small strangled sound and started to lift a hand to his neck, before dropping like a stone. With an exclamation of horror, Alyssa leaped to her feet.

She managed one quick step in his direction before an iron band wrapped around her arms and waist, lifting her off the ground and up against a tall, muscular male body. At the same moment, a large, powerful hand closed over her mouth, cutting off her incipient scream. She hung in his arms for an endless moment, a rush of sensations swamping her.

His scent washed over her. It held the confusingly civilized odor of cedar and spice. But underlying the crisp, delicious scent came something far more basic and dangerous, a primal pheromone that invaded her senses at the most carnal and instinctual level. An image of a lion flashed through her mind's eye, streaking across the African veld, claws extended, teeth bared, its powerful haunches contracting as it hurdled toward its prey… toward her.

Alyssa exploded into motion, kicking and twisting. It didn't have the least impact. He controlled her with frightening ease. The warmth of his breath stirred the curls alongside her temple and his laughter rumbled against her back.

"Calm yourself, Princess," he told her. "Fighting

won't do you any good. It will simply wear you out and make my job all the easier."

His voice contained the distinctive lilt of most she'd met in Verdonia, though his was deeper and darker. Educated. The realization filtered through her terror. She struggled to control her panic and pay attention, to gather as many facts as possible in the hopes that she could somehow use the information to her advantage.

She stilled and he gave a grunt of satisfaction. Turning his head, he called out several soft words in his native language. They weren't aimed at her. She sensed others around her—not the guards—but men who worked in concert with the one who held her with such casual strength.

As soon as he'd satisfied himself that she'd given up her struggle, he melted into the shadows of the surrounding trees, carrying her from the garden outside the chapel's courtyard into the woods. She caught a glimpse of the men he'd spoken to before they were blocked from view by a stand of trees. All three were dressed in black, hooded and ominous in both appearance and size, and they moved with unmistakable purpose. What did they want? What were they planning? Dear heaven, she'd wanted a way out of the marriage, but not like this and not at the expense of her mother. Her mother! She tensed within her captor's hold, preparing to struggle again, but his grip tightened in warning.

"Don't." He lowered his head so his whisker-roughened jaw brushed her cheek. She shuddered at the delicately abrasive sensation. It might have been a lover's caress—would have been—if it hadn't come from a ruthless kidnapper. The dichotomy only further served to escalate her fear and she squirmed in reaction. "Keep struggling and I'll tie you up. Is that what you want?"

Oh, God, anything but that. Frantically, she shook her head. The movement dislodged her veil, sending it sliding over one eye. The finely tatted lace obscured her vision, increasing her terror. She'd always suffered from mild claustrophobia and the idea of being robbed of both her freedom of movement, as well as her sight, horrified her. Panic bubbled upward and she forced herself to focus on her breathing, to drag the air into her lungs bit by bit.

In the few moments it took to regain control of herself he carried her through the woods to a narrow country road. A pair of SUVs idled on the dirt shoulder, one black, the other a silver-gray. So far she'd counted four men, the one who'd spirited her off and the three from the courtyard who had yet to rejoin them. Now she heard a fifth member of her abductor's team emerge from one of the vehicles. Her heart sank. A single kidnapper, particularly one as powerful as the man who held her, made any attempt at escape next to impossible. But five against one killed all hope.

"It's time." Her abductor addressed the newest member. To Alyssa's relief he continued to speak in English, enabling her to follow the conversation. "You don't have to go through with this. You can still change your mind."

"I can't and I won't. There are...reasons."

At the sound of a woman's voice, Alyssa stiffened. From the corner of her eye she caught a flash of silver. She started to turn her head to look, but the man's grip on her tightened, preventing it.

"Quickly, Merrick," the woman murmured. Merrick! Alyssa filed the name away for future reference. "We have only moments until her disappearance is discovered."

Ripping the voluminous veil from Alyssa's head, he tossed it to the woman. "Will this work?"

"It's perfect. From what I can tell our dresses are almost identical. The veil will conceal any discrepancies."

She said something else, something in Verdonian that caused Merrick to give a short, gruff laugh. His reply was unbelievably tender and gentle. Loving. At total odds with the ruthless kidnapper who'd just abducted her. There was a soft rustle of clothing that came from the direction of the woman and then the swift fall of her footsteps faded in the direction of the chapel.

Now they were alone and Merrick continued to restrain Alyssa within the protective shadow of the woods. Releasing the arm that anchored her to his chest, he set her on the ground and spun her around to face him. Her gaze inched upward past his thickly muscled chest to his face. She shuddered. It was as though the lion she'd pictured earlier had been reborn as a man.

Dark brown hair awash with streaks of every shade from umber to desert sand fell in heavy waves to frame strong, fierce features. Arching cheekbones underscored intense eyes, the brilliant gold irises ringed in dark brown. His razor-sharp nose had been broken at some point, but it only added to the unrelenting maleness of him, edging his appearance from the realm of stunningly handsome toward dangerously intriguing. More telling, his broad mouth had a scar that hooked the left side of his upper lip and slashed toward his cheek.

This was a man who'd lived a life of dangerous pursuits. Ruthlessness blazed in his eyes and was echoed in the grim lines etched into his features. Any hint of gentleness had been carved away long ago, honing his appearance to the bare essence of a man who eschewed softness and compassion and all things temperate, who couldn't be swayed by a woman's love, and certainly didn't compromise or yield, no matter how overwhelming the odds.

He backed her against a tree trunk, holding her with only his hand clamped to her mouth and the sheer force of his personality. The rough bark bit through her gown and clawed at her back. "I'll release you if you promise not to scream. Otherwise, I pull out the duct tape. Clear?"

She gave a careful nod. One by one his fingers lifted away, his hand hovering a mere breath from her mouth. Tilting her chin she forced herself to meet his leonine gaze without flinching. She wouldn't plead, she refused to beg. But she'd demand answers before she took another step.

"Why?" She breathed the single word from between

numb lips, allowing a hint of outrage to underscore the question.

He shrugged, his black shirt pulling taut across broad, well-muscled shoulders. "You're a pawn. A pawn I intend to remove from the playing field."

Her heart pounded in her chest. How did he plan to remove her? Did he mean…by killing her? A bubble of nearly uncontrollable hysteria built inside her chest, pressing for release. "Isn't there some other way?" She forced the words past her constricted throat, despising the hint of entreaty they contained.

His expression remained unrelenting. Merciless. This wasn't a man who could be affected by a woman's tears. Nor pleading, nor demand, nor wiles. What would happen had been predetermined by him and she was helpless to change that.

"I can't allow the wedding to go on." He hesitated, and to her surprise a hint of distaste gleamed in his odd golden eyes before being ruthlessly extinguished. "I need your gown."

The demand caught her off-guard. "My what?"

"Your wedding gown. Take it off."

"But…why?"

"Wrong answer."

She shook her head. Her hair, loosened when he'd ripped the veil from her head, cascaded to her shoulders, cloaking her. "Then you won't like this one any better. I can't remove it."

She was right. He didn't like her answer. Hard furrows bracketed his mouth and tension rippled across his frame. The lion stirred. "Pay attention, Princess. Either you take it off or I do. Your choice."

For some reason his response angered her. She didn't have a clue what hidden wellspring it erupted from, or how it managed to overcome the fear that held her on the very edge of control. She simply recognized that she had two choices. She could give in to the fear and start screaming, knowing full well that once she started, she'd never be able to stop—not until he silenced her, perhaps permanently. Or she could choose to react to an impossible situation with a shred of dignity.

She looked Merrick square in the eye. "I'm telling you the truth. I can't remove my clothing. I've been sewn into my wedding gown. I gather it's the custom in this principality. So, if you're going to kill me, get it over with."

"Kill you?" Something flashed in his eyes. Surprise? Annoyance? Affront? "I have no intention of killing you. But I do need that dress. It'll draw too much attention to us. So, if you can't remove the damn thing, I will."

She heard the distinctive scrape of metal against leather and, unable to help herself, her gaze darted downward. He'd pulled a knife from a scabbard strapped to his leg. It was huge and serrated and gleamed wickedly even in the shadow of the massive oak. The breath hissed from her lungs and she discovered that she couldn't draw it in again. Darkness crept into the periphery of her vision but all she could focus on was that knife and the hand that held it—a hand that fisted around the textured grip with unmistakable competence and familiarity.

"No—"

She managed the word just as the knife descended in a sudden, swift arc, the edge biting into the bodice of her gown. For a brief instant she felt the repellent coldness of metal against the swell of her breast before it sliced downward through the silk straight to the hem. He shoved the ruined gown from her shoulders, allowing it to pool on the verdant tufts of grass at their feet.

She turned ashen, every scrap of color blanching from her skin as she struggled to suck air into her lungs.

Merrick watched her reaction with a bitter distaste for the necessity of his actions. He despised what he'd been forced to do, what he'd been forced to become because of von Folke. And yet, despite everything he'd done to her, her recovery was as swift as it was impressive. The panic and fear rapidly faded from her expression and renewed anger glittered in the intense blue of her eyes. He applauded her spirit, even as he realized it would make his job all the more difficult.

The instant her breathing stabilized, she attacked. "You son of a bitch."

He conceded the truth with a twisted smile. "So I've been told before."

She stood with her spine pressed against the rough tree trunk, her arms folded across her chest. Seeing her without her gown answered two of his earlier questions. She had, indeed, the creamy complexion he'd imagined, perfect in every regard. And she was more goddess than dynamo.

For such a petite woman her breasts were surprisingly full, overflowing the low cut demi-bra she attempted to conceal with her crossed arms. A tiny pink bow rested between the cups holding them together, though how it managed to remain tied defied explanation and tempted him beyond reason to release the pressure keeping all that bounty in place.

His gaze lowered and he almost smiled. Damned if she wasn't wearing a petticoat, no doubt another custom of the region. But then, he supposed it was necessary given the gown she'd worn. The layers of white silk and tulle belled around her, whispering in agitation in the light breeze.

His amusement faded. Time to set the tone for their relationship from this point forward. Distaste filled him again, but he forced himself to do what he knew he must. "Don't move," he ordered.

He lifted the knife again, giving her a full ten seconds to fixate on it before driving it through the voluminous skirting at her hip and deep into the tree trunk, pinning her in place. Then he reached down and snatched up the shredded wedding gown, crumpling it in his fist. Deliberately turning his back on her, he carried the gown to the silver SUV and tossed it inside. His men would dispose of it.

Merrick paused, interested to see what the Sutherland woman would do next. Her choice would determine how they spent the rest of their time together. He didn't have to wait long for his answer. Nor was he surprised by her decision. The sound of rending silk signaled her response.

Turning around, he was just in time to see her stumble free of the knife and run—as best she could given her three-inch heels—back into the woods, her petticoats fluttering behind her. To his relief, it didn't occur to her to scream. He retrieved his knife before giving chase, running in swift and silent pursuit. Her hair streamed behind her like a golden flag of surrender and her breath came in frightened pants. She'd kicked off her shoes at some point and the tear in her petticoats where she'd ripped free of the knife gave her plenty of legroom, allowing her to run more easily and making her far more fleet than he'd anticipated.

Merrick gritted his teeth. Miri's disguise would only hold up for so long. Before von Folke discovered the deception, he needed to have his princess whisked far away from here. Putting on an extra bit of speed, he closed the distance between them. He waited for her to take a couple more steps so that he could control their fall, and then he launched himself at her.

He twisted so he'd take the brunt of the landing. Hitting the earth with a thud, he skidded a foot or two in the leaf litter and tree bracken before coming to rest in a grassy section free of rocks and sticks. He wrapped one arm around her body and the other around her neck, controlling her air supply. She struggled for a brief minute before giving up the fight with a soft moan of surrender.

"You don't listen very well." He spoke close to her ear. "That's going to cost you, Princess."

"You don't understand." His choke hold prevented her from speaking above a whisper. "I have to get back to the chapel. I have to go through with the marriage. If I don't—"

"If you don't, you won't get to be Her Royal Highness, Queen of Verdonia. Is that it?"

"No! You don't understand. My mother. He has my mother."

"If your mother is anything like you, I'm sure she'll be able to fend for herself."

He released his choke hold and rolled, reversing their positions, which might have been a mistake. Seeing her splayed beneath him against the grass-sweetened earth, her tousled hair fanned around her beautiful, treacherous face was more provocative than he could have imagined. And though honor kept him from touching, he sure as hell could look.

Her petticoats belled around her, nipping in at her narrow waist. The tear in the endless layers of tulle allowed him to catch a glimpse of a lace garter and silk stockings—stockings that seemed to glisten along every endless inch of her leg. And then there was the practically nonexistent bra she wore with the tiny bow that tempted a man almost beyond endurance, begging him to tug at the ends and allow the feminine scrap to drift from her body.

Merrick's body clenched, reacting to a powerful need with frightening predictability. He was infuriated to discover that it was beyond his ability to control the automatic response. Not even a lifetime of training enabled him to overcome the temptation of this particular woman. It defied explanation.

Beneath her silver wedding gown she'd been dressed to seduce, to provoke the ultimate possession, to make a man forget everything but the desperate need to mate. She stared at him with wide aquamarine eyes and in that insane moment he saw what it would be like to have her. He saw them locked together in the most primitive dance of all. A give and take that went much further than mere sex. He saw the ultimate possession, a sharing he'd never dared allow himself with any of the women he'd had in his life. White-hot passion. Basic driving need. A mindless surrender. Blind trust—something he'd never known in all his twenty-nine years. He saw every last detail in eyes rich with promise.

And he wanted as he'd never wanted before.

He forced words past a throat gone bone dry. "Von Folke must have caught one glimpse of you and thought all his dreams had come true."

To his surprise she shuddered. "If he was attracted to me, he never showed it." She squirmed beneath him, which thrust her breasts and pelvis up against him in a provocative brush and swirl. "Please let me up."

He wanted to refuse her request, wanted it with a raging fervor that proved to him that man was still at heart a creature of wanton instinct, an unleashed animal lurking beneath a thin veneer of civilized behavior, ruled by emotions barely kept in check and not always within his ability to control. He fought with every ounce of willpower. Endless seconds ticked by before intellect finally managed to overcome base desire.

"Very well, Princess." Or maybe intellect hadn't fully won out because he found himself saying, "But I warned that running would cost you. Time to pay."

With that, he took advantage of her parted lips and dipped downward, possessing the most lush, sumptuous mouth he'd sampled in many a year.

Two

Alyssa sank beneath the powerful onslaught of Merrick's kiss. She'd never felt anything so all-consuming, so fierce and passionate. This wasn't remotely similar to what she'd experienced during her lighthearted collegiate years, untutored kisses that tasted of beer and youthful enthusiasm. Nor did it resemble the well-practiced embraces from the men she'd dated in the years since, embraces tainted with calculation and ambition.

This was an experienced man with an experienced man's skill and knowledge. A dark desire underscored his breaching of her lips and the sweeping possession of his mouth and tongue. He consumed her, igniting a fire she'd never known existed until he'd fanned it to life.

Heat pooled in the pit of her stomach, a finger of

flame scorching a path downward to the most intimate part of her and she moaned in protest. She shouldn't want this—didn't want this. And yet she remained still beneath him, offering no resistance. His fingers forked into her hair, tilting her head so he could deepen the kiss. He softened it, coaxing where before he'd subdued, tempting instead of demanding. Teasing. Enticing. Daring her to respond.

And she did respond, her blasted curiosity getting the better of her.

Her mind screamed in protest while her body softened to accommodate a taking she didn't want, yet somehow couldn't resist. Her jaw unclenched and her lips relaxed beneath his, parting to offer easier access. Maybe she surrendered so readily because it would keep him off guard and allow for the possibility of escape when he least expected it. But in her heart of hearts she knew the excuse was sheer self-deception. She couldn't explain her response to Merrick. She reacted to him in ways she hadn't with any other man, in primal ways that overrode rational thought and intellect in favor of reckless impulse and base desire.

And it horrified her even as it thrilled her.

One of his hands slid from her hair and followed the line of her throat to her shoulder before settling on her breast. That single brushing stroke branded her, marking her his in some inescapable way. He cupped her in his palm, his thumb grazing her rigid nipple through the thin layer of silk.

Her breath escaped in a soft cry of shock, the sound

absorbed by his mouth. His hand shifted, hovering above the bow that held the cups of her bra together. Before he could pluck the silk ribbons free, the urgent clatter of church bells rang through the forest while a pipe organ bellowed forth the first few triumphant notes of the wedding march prelude. The change in Merrick was instantaneous. He levered himself off Alyssa in a flash, his scar standing out bone-white against his tanned face.

"What the hell…?" With a quick shake of his head, he focused on her, the passion scoring his face dying a rapid death. "Clever, Ms. Sutherland. Very clever. You'll do whatever necessary, even seduce the enemy, to make sure you wear the crown of Verdonia, won't you?"

The breath hissed from her lungs and she glared at him as she shoved herself upright. "Seduce you? How dare—"

To her surprise, he whipped off his shirt and thrust it at her. Beneath it he wore a black stretch T-shirt that clung to his muscular form, emphasizing every hard bulge and angle. "Put this on."

"You kissed me, not the other way around," she reminded him as she thrust her arms into the over-long sleeves.

"And you fought me every inch of the way, didn't you?"

Hot color flooded her cheeks while the unpalatable truth of his accusation held her silent. She searched for a sufficiently quelling retort as her fingers fumbled with the buttons of his shirt. Not that she came up with anything. Perhaps she had so much difficulty because his distinctive scent clung to the black cotton, distracting her with his crisp, woodsy fragrance. Or perhaps it was because she kept sneaking quick glances at Merrick—or rather how Merrick filled his impressive T-shirt.

Regardless, she worked each button into each hole with a stubborn doggedness until she'd fastened her way straight to her neck. The instant she'd finished, he reached into his back pocket and to her horror pulled out a flat roll of duct tape. Before she could utter a single word of protest, he'd slapped a piece across her mouth and wound another length around her wrists.

"Note to self," he muttered, his mouth twisting into a humorless smile, "from now on, no kissing the bad guys."

She shook her head in furious denial, her angry protests stifled by the tape, though she didn't doubt for one moment that he understood the gist of what she'd attempted to impart, if not the full flavor. Standing, he lifted her with ease and slung her over his shoulder. A strong, calloused hand held her in place, gripping the backs of her thighs. She shuddered beneath the intimate contact even though it came through layers of tulle, hating herself for the sizzle of heat that vied with her terror at her predicament.

Within minutes he'd retraced the path they'd taken in her desperate flight through the forest, carrying her with long, swift strides to the SUV that idled on the side of the road. Opening the back door, he tipped her onto the floor.

"Keep silent and still," he instructed. "Don't make me take more drastic measures than I have already. Nod if you understand, Princess."

She fought a silent inner battle for five full seconds. With no choice but to acquiesce, she jerked her head up and down. Satisfied, he tossed a blanket loosely over her and closed the door. An instant later the driver's door opened and he climbed in. Without wasting another moment he put the car into gear, driving swiftly from the scene of her capture.

They continued for what seemed like hours, the route twisting and turning, the roads rough and bumpy. She could tell that many were either dirt or gravel. As the sun crept lower and lower in the sky, she worried endlessly about what was happening back at the chapel.

It hadn't been difficult for her to figure out that the woman who'd been part of Merrick's group had taken Alyssa's place. But how long would the woman's disguise work? Even more imperative—why had Alyssa been kidnapped and what did Merrick plan to do with her? Clearly, Verdonia had political problems in which she'd somehow become embroiled. Her abduction must be related to those problems.

Of even more concern was what Prince Brandt had done when he'd discovered the switch in brides. Had he taken his fury out on her mother? Was her mother safe? Although the prince hadn't leveled any specific threat against her when she'd been brought to his palace, the implication had been loud and clear. If Alyssa didn't marry him, her mother would meet with an unfortunate accident.

She closed her eyes, fighting her tears. So now what? She had to find a means of escape, that much was obvious, though even if she succeeded in freeing herself, how could she rescue her mother? The worrisome questions swirled through her mind, increasing her fear and desperation while offering no practical solutions.

During the interminable journey, a single goal formed, burning in the forefront of her mind, and she latched onto it with unwavering determination. She had to escape and return to Prince Brandt, no matter what that entailed. But how? Slowly, an idea grew through her fear and worry.

There was little question that her abductor was attracted to her, even if he fought hard to resist that attraction. She'd seen the desire in those extraordinary eyes of his, the hunger that had risen unbidden to score his face when his hand hovered over the tiny pink ribbon holding her bra in place. It had been strong enough an attraction for him to act on, despite the circumstances and the clear need for haste. Assuming nothing better presented itself, she could attempt to seduce him in order to free herself, no matter how distasteful she found the prospect. Then, once she'd returned to Prince Brandt, she'd marry him if doing so ensured her mother's safety.

It was a frightening plan, one that just a short week ago would never have occurred to her. But she hadn't come up with a better idea, and right now time was her enemy.

She wriggled in place, the floor of the SUV uncomfortable. Unable to stand it for another moment, she inched onto the backseat, shoving the blanket under her head as a pillow. Over the next several minutes, she surreptitiously peeled the duct tape off her mouth, wincing as the glue left her sensitive skin raw and chapped.

She took several slow, deep breaths, gathering her courage to speak. "You have to take me back," she finally called to Merrick.

He didn't seem surprised to hear her speak. But then, if he'd wanted to permanently confine her, he would have wrapped the duct tape around her head instead of slapping a short strip across her mouth. And he'd have taped her wrists behind her instead of in front of her. She grimaced, wishing she'd thought of that a couple of hours ago.

"You aren't going back."

She sat upright. "Why not? Why have you abducted me?"

"Lie down," he snapped. "Keep out of sight or I'll gag you again."

She stretched out along the backseat, unwilling to put his threat to the test. Not that anyone driving by could have seen her. Twilight was full upon them. "You don't understand. I have to go back. It's a matter of life or death."

"Very melodramatic, Princess." He made a sharp turn

that almost sent her plummeting to the floor again. "But my reasons for taking you are equally imperative."

"Please." She choked on the word, despising the need to beg. But she'd do whatever necessary if it meant getting to her mother. "I'm not being melodramatic."

"This is not the time for that particular discussion." The SUV came to a sudden halt and this time she did roll onto the floor, landing on her hands and knees. "Welcome to your new home."

Before Alyssa could get up, Merrick opened the door and lifted her out, setting her on her feet. She shook her hair from her face and forced herself to confront him. Shoeless, wearing little more than his shirt and a rumpled petticoat, she'd never felt more vulnerable in her life. Not that she'd allow that to undermine her determination. "You have to listen to me. There's more than a marriage at stake here."

"I know far better than you what's at stake," he bit out, holding her in place with a hand on her arm. "This is my country, Princess. You come here and upset the political balance. All I'm doing is resetting that balance by removing you from the equation."

"I didn't choose to come back here," she argued. "And I don't care about your country's political problems. I only care about—"

She broke off at his expression and if his grip hadn't tightened just then, she'd have fallen back a step. In the little light that remained she could see a fierce anger turn his eyes to burnished gold, warning that she should have selected her words more judiciously. He leaned in, huge and intimidating, his comment little more than a whisper in the sultry night air.

"Interesting that you care so little for Verdonia when you're intent on becoming her queen. But somehow I'm not surprised. Your type sells herself for fame and fortune. Money and attention, that's all you care about. The throne. The crown. The jewels." He emphasized his point by flicking her earlobe with his index finger where a heavy amethyst and diamond earring hung. The pair were a gift Prince Brandt had insisted she wear for their wedding. "You have no concern for the people or their problems, only for yourself."

His comments threw her. They didn't make a bit of sense, but instinct warned she'd do well to listen rather than question or argue. He released her arm and assisted her toward a small house set beneath a stand of towering pines, steadying her as she picked her way around a scattering of stones gleefully intent on torturing her bare feet. The structure was a pretty A-frame, what she could see of it through the gathering darkness. The roofline and shutters were decorated with gingerbread trim painted a crisp white that stood in sharp relief against the charcoal stain of the siding. High above, a balcony jutted out from the second level and no doubt offered a spectacular view of the surrounding area.

"Where are we?" she asked.

He paused by the front door and removed a set of keys from his pocket. "In Avernos, on the border of Celestia."

A fat lot of help that was. Maybe if she knew where

Avernos or Celestia were, she'd have a clue. But she didn't. The names weren't the least bit familiar. "Why are we here? Why did you abduct me? What are you going to do with me?" So much for listening rather than peppering him with questions.

He shoved the front door open without replying and ushered her inside, flipping on an overhead light. She looked around, filled with a reluctant curiosity. Directly in front of her a staircase led to the second level. To her left she caught a glimpse of a great room complete with a stone fireplace and wall-to-wall shelving overflowing with books. A dining room occupied the right side of the house and she could see a doorway leading to a kitchen at the far end.

Merrick gestured toward the kitchen. "Let's get something to eat."

"I'd rather not."

"No?" He lifted an eyebrow. "We could pick up where we left off earlier, if you'd prefer."

An image of them in the woods flashed through her mind, of his mouth on hers. Of his hands on her. Of heated desire and helpless surrender. Her throat went dry and she moistened her lips in response. Lord, she could still taste his distinctive flavor. Worse, she felt a craving to taste it again. "No kissing the bad guys, remember?"

A grin slashed across his face, changing his appearance. Where before he'd been harsh and remote, his features were now rearranged into an expression she found quite stunning. A tug of forbidden desire swept over her, causing her to stumble backward. He must have noticed her awareness of him, or at the very least sensed the shimmer of sexual tension humming between them, because his smile grew.

"You sure?"

"Positive."

She tugged at the tape that restrained her hands. What a fool she was, she conceded bitterly. She'd wasted endless time in the car imagining herself capable of seducing this man. It had seemed reasonable at the time, even straightforward. But she'd never bothered to consider how she'd set about accomplishing such an impossible task. Should she simply touch him, drape her taped arms around his neck? Would that even be sufficient to provoke him to make the next move, or would she have to push it further still? Was she supposed to initiate a kiss or just offer her mouth for his possession?

None of those issues had been addressed when she'd come up with her idiotic plan. And even if she enticed him to kiss her again, what would be her next step? Did she allow him to fondle her, to remove the shirt he'd given her and untie the little bow that held her bra in place? She shivered as her imagination took it one step further—the final, terrifying step. Did she let him make love to her? And once she had him focused on her sexually, how did that help her get away? It would only work if she knocked him out, or something.

Standing in front of him, confronting all that innate masculine strength and power forced her to concede how futile her plan was, not to mention foolhardy. For one thing, she suspected he'd instantly figure out what she was up to, which wouldn't be beneficial to her overall health and well-being. And for another, her reaction to him warned that he'd have more success seducing her than the other way around. How could she keep her wits about her when every time she came within arm's length of him her body sizzled with desperate heat?

Her mouth tightened. Just because her body responded to him in such an unwelcome way didn't mean she had to act on that response. If seducing him wouldn't work, she'd have to remain alert to other possibilities.

"Well, Princess?" he prompted. "I assume your silence means you'd prefer to eat."

"If the choice is food or picking up where we left off, then yes, I prefer to eat." He laughed at her dry tone, the sound deep and dangerous and far too attractive for her peace of mind. "Will you at least explain why you're doing this?" she asked.

He dismissed her question with a shrug. Planting his hand at the base of her spine, he guided her in the direction of the kitchen. "You know why. Don't play games with me, Princess."

"Games?" She turned on him in outrage. "Let me assure you I don't consider any part of this a game."

Once in the kitchen, he pointed to one of two chairs tucked beneath a small butcher-block table that had been positioned beside a wide picture window. In the final glow of twilight, she could just make out a fenced garden overrun with flowers, weeds, and to one side, a collection of indeterminate vegetables.

"Sit, Princess. It's pointless to keep up this pretence of ignorance."

"I wish it were a pretence. I wish all of this was."

Feeling the rising panic, she took a deep breath, striving for calm. Pulling out the chair he'd indicated, she curled up in it, drawing her knees against her chest beneath the voluminous petticoats. Her pink-tipped toes peeked through the rips in her stockings and she studied the smudges of dirt marring them as she considered how best to get through to Merrick. If she didn't get answers soon, she wouldn't have the necessary information to plan her escape, an escape that—second by second—became increasingly more important if she were to save her mother.

"Why does everyone keep calling me Princess Alyssa?" she asked. "I'm not a princess."

Merrick paused in the act of removing a selection of meats, cheeses and fruit from the refrigerator and turned to study her. "You're Princess Alyssa, Duchess of Celestia."

"No. I'm Alyssa Sutherland, soon to be Assistant VP of Human Relations for Bank International."

He ignored her attempt at humor. "You left Verdonia when you were just over a year old." He placed the selection of food in front of her, along with a crusty loaf of bread and several bottles of sparkling water. "Your mother, an American college student who'd met the prince while on vacation, married and divorced him in the span of two short years. A bit of a scandal at the time. Apparently living the life of a princess wasn't the fairy tale she'd envisioned. After the divorce, she took you back to the United States, leaving your father and your older half brother behind."

Alyssa hesitated. "She told me some of that years ago. But my father wasn't a prince any more than I'm a princess."

"It would appear your mother neglected to mention a few pertinent details about your background."

For the first time a twinge of doubt assailed her. What had her mother said in the few minutes they'd been permitted to speak? She'd been incoherent, tearfully apologizing for tricking Alyssa into coming to Verdonia and for not finding a way to warn her about the mess she'd managed to entangle them in.

There had also been something about how she'd fled the country twenty years earlier, never suspecting Alyssa would be expected to assume her brother's responsibilities—a brother she hadn't even known existed. The one thing that had been abundantly clear was that in order to keep her mother safe, Alyssa would have to marry Prince Brandt.

She tried again. "Everyone thinks I'm a princess. I assure you, I'm not. This is all some hideous mistake."

He saluted her with a sardonic smile. "Am I supposed to believe your story and let you go? Good try, but it won't work."

"No, I thought you'd realize that you have the wrong

person and help me figure out what's going on." Her feet hit the floor with a small thud. "I'm telling you there's been a mistake. I'm no more a princess than I am this Duchess of Celdonia."

"Celestia. Verdonia is the country, Celestia is one of her three principalities. And there's no mistake." He tilted his head to one side. "Fair warning, this tactic isn't going to work."

"It's not a tactic." Frustration edged her words. "I don't know what's going on."

"Enough!"

Something in the roughly stated word had her swallowing nervously. "Fine." She waited a beat and then whispered, "He has my mother, Merrick. He's holding her hostage. That's why I agreed to marry him."

Merrick stifled a groan. It was her tone more than anything else that stopped him in his tracks; the soft, American-accented voice was filled with fear and anguish. He vaguely recalled her mentioning her mother while they were in the woods, but he'd assumed it had been another ploy to gain her release. He kept his expression implacable as he joined her at the table but inside he was filled with rage at von Folke's ruthlessness. "Regrettable."

"I have to know what's going on. Please." Her mouth worked for a moment. "Can you explain it to me so I understand?"

"Eat. You'll need your strength."

He fought a brief inner battle while she picked at the meal he'd provided, weighing his belief that she was in on von Folke's plan against the possibility that she was an innocent victim in all this. If she were telling the truth, it was only fair that he explain the situation. Honor demanded as much.

He left her long enough to fetch a map from the great room. When he returned, he spread it across the table, anchoring the corners with the bottles of water. Next, he removed a fillet knife from a butcher block on the kitchen counter and after first slicing the duct tape binding her wrists so she had more freedom to eat, he used it to trace the outline of the country.

"This is Verdonia. It's divided into three principalities."

She studied it with all apparent interest as she massaged her wrists. "Where are we?"

He shook his head. "Not a chance, Princess."

"In general. You said we were on the border of Celestia and…and—"

He tapped the upper portion of the map. "We're just inside the border of Avernos. Mountainous and riddled with amethyst mines. The gems provide the economic backbone of Verdonia. This principality's ruled by von Folke." He broke off a chunk of bread and ate it before shifting the knife downward to the very bottom of the map. "The most southern principality is Verdon, the financial heart of Verdonia."

She glanced at him. "And the principality in the middle?"

He outlined the S-shaped bit of land that curled between the northern and southern principalities, cupping each in turn. "Celestia. Traditionally the artisans who work the amethyst have come from this principality. Until ten days ago, your half brother ruled here."

She leaned forward and was forced to shove a tumble of unruly curls behind one ear in order to get a better look. In the few hours since he'd first seen her, she'd been transformed from regal princess to rumpled seductress, both of whom appealed far more than he cared to admit. His awareness of her disturbed him. It was one thing to take her, but committing such a dishonorable act, even for honorable reasons, had been the most difficult decision he'd ever made. But to compound it by lusting after von Folke's intended bride.... Touching her, making love to her.... Damn it to hell!

He shoved a plate of cheese in her direction and didn't say anything further until she'd helped herself to some. She nibbled at it with a marked lack of enthusiasm before cracking the seal on one of the bottles of water. Tipping back her head, she took a long drink, unwittingly revealing the creamy line of skin that ran the length of her neck.

The memory of how she'd looked in the forest earlier rose unbidden to his mind. She'd lain sprawled in a lush pocket of ripe grass and summer leaves, like a sacrifice to the heathen gods of old, the scent of her lightly perfumed skin mingling with the odor of rich, fertile soil. Dappled sunlight had gilded her creamy skin, while the mystery of womankind had gleamed in eyes the color of aquamarines, tempting him to plumb its many secrets. And he'd wanted her. Wanted her more than he'd wanted any other woman. If it hadn't been for the church bells…

His mouth tightened. He'd come close to sacrificing both honor and duty in that moment. Too close.

She eyed him quizzically. "You haven't explained what's happened to my brother. How's he involved in all this?"

He didn't see any benefit in withholding the information. "My sources inform me he was paid a lot of money by von Folke to abdicate his position," he replied. "When that happened, the title fell to you. Where before you were Princess Alyssa, now you're also duchess of Celestia. Or you will be once church and state make it official."

Alarm flashed across her face. "I don't want the position."

"Don't you?"

He could tell his skepticism annoyed her, but she impressed him by holding on to her temper, though she spoke with a clipped edge to her voice. "Even assuming all of this is true, why would Prince Brandt have paid my brother to abdicate?"

"Two weeks ago the king of Verdonia died."

"Oh. I'm sorry." She hesitated briefly. "I don't mean to sound crass, but what has his death got to do with any of this?"

"Verdonia has a rather unusual system for replacing their monarchs. It calls for the people to vote in an election, choosing from the eligible royals from each principality."

"And there are three eligible royals?"

"Were three," he corrected. "With your brother's abdication we're down to two. There's Prince Lander, duke of Verdon—"

"That's...that's the southernmost principality, right? The one that governs the finances?"

"Correct. And the other contender for the throne is von Folke. If you were over twenty-five at the time of the election, you'd be eligible to rule, as well."

"Wait a minute. Are you saying that if my twenty-fifth birthday had fallen a few minutes sooner, I'd be a contender for the throne? Me?" If she were feigning shock, it was a stellar performance. "No. No, thank you. I have no interest in ruling Verdonia."

He shot her a sharp look. "Interesting that you're so quick to refuse when marrying von Folke will accomplish precisely that."

She stared at him, narrow-eyed, for a long, silent moment. "How?"

He stabbed the knife into the paper heart of Celestia, driving the point deep into the butcher-block table. "The popular vote, remember?"

He only had to wait an instant for comprehension to dawn. Her brows drew together. "If I really am a princess and duchess of Celestia and I marry Prince Brandt..." Her breath caught. "He'd win the popular vote of the entire country, wouldn't he?"

"Yes. To be honest, it's a brilliant plan. The principality of Avernos—von Folke's people—would vote in his favor. And with Celestia's princess married to von Folke—that's you—honor and loyalty would force the citizens of Celestia to vote for him, as well. Verdon would fall to Lander, but it wouldn't matter because von Folke would walk away with a two-thirds win."

"Which you want to prevent from happening." It wasn't a question, but closer to an accusation. "Why?"

He studied her grimly. "I'll do whatever it takes to ensure a fair election. I'm honor bound to protect all of Verdonia, not just any one principality."

"Isn't who becomes king up to the people of your country to decide?" she argued.

He leaned in, crowding her. "Von Folke is the one who chose to tip the balance. He upset the natural order of things—with your help. I'm merely righting that wrong."

Apprehension flashed across her face before she managed to regain control. "By getting rid of me?"

He offered a humorless smile. "In a manner of speaking. The election is in a little more than four months. Once it's over, you'll be free to marry whomever you wish."

It took her several seconds to process his words. The instant she had, her breath escaped in a horrified hiss and she shook her head. "You can't be serious. Four months? No! I won't let you keep me here that long."

"And just how are you planning to stop me?"

"Like this!"

He had to admit, she surprised him, something that

hadn't happened since he'd first begun his training as a callow youth. She fisted her hands around the filet knife embedded in the table and yanked it free, thrusting the razor-sharp tip toward his throat. She paused just shy of cutting him.

"My mother doesn't have four months. You're taking me back to Prince Brandt right now."

Even with a knife at his throat, he couldn't help marveling. God, she was beautiful. Vibrant. Infuriated. Infuriating. He deliberately leaned closer until the razor-sharp point pricked the base of his throat. "Listen up, Princess. Nothing you say or do will convince me to return you to him. There's only one place I'm willing to take you."

She glared at him for a split second before her gaze shifted downward to where the knife had nicked him. She shuddered at the sight of the blood she'd drawn. "And where is that?"

"My bed, of course." In one easy move he knocked her hand aside, sending the knife clattering against the wall and then to the floor. Before she could do more than utter a soft cry of protest, he swept her into his arms and lifted her high against his chest. "Consider it your home for the next four months."

Three

Merrick wasn't the least bit surprised that Alyssa fought him, though this time she struggled even more fiercely than when he'd initially abducted her.

"Stop it, Alyssa. You'll only hurt yourself waging a battle you can't win."

"I don't care. I'll fight you until my last breath." She clipped him with her fist. "I won't let you do this."

"I'm afraid you can't stop me."

He carried her from the kitchen to the steps leading to the bedroom and took them with swift efficiency, despite his struggling armful. Depositing Alyssa on her feet at the top of the stairs, he reached around her and thrust open the door on one side of the landing. Instantly she tried to skitter away. He gathered her back up and held her wriggling body tight against his. Damn, but he needed to put some distance between them. She'd become far too great a distraction, something he didn't need when tomorrow promised to be even more challenging than today.

"I don't want to hurt you, Princess," he warned. "But you will do as I say when I say it, or you'll spend the next four months tied to a bedpost."

"You can't honestly believe that I won't fight, that I'll just let you—" She clamped her mouth shut, unable to utter the hideous words.

"You'll sleep in my bed for however long we're together." He captured her chin and tipped it upward, forcing her to look at him. "Allow me to emphasize the word sleep."

She stared at him, her eyes wide and dilated. "Not… not—"

"No. Not," he repeated calmly. "Just sleep. Tomorrow's going to be a long day. I'd like to close my eyes for a few hours between now and then and I need to make certain you won't try anything foolish. Like escape."

"Why did you make me think—" Her voice broke and she waved her hand in an impatient gesture. "You know."

"Because you had a knife at my throat and I was angry." Even though the confession came hard, he didn't shy away from taking full responsibility. He let that sink in before adding, "But I wasn't lying, Alyssa. You will be sharing my bed for the next four months, though what happens in that bed is up to you."

She reared back as if he'd struck her. "Nothing will happen there!"

He didn't bother arguing. Time would prove her right or wrong more readily than anything he could say. Turning her to face the open doorway, he gave her a gentle shove toward it. Under other circumstances her expression of surprise and confusion when she found herself standing outside a bathroom would have been amusing.

"Get cleaned up. Shower if you wish. You can also help yourself to any of the toiletries you find. There's a robe hanging on the back of the door. Put it on before you leave the bathroom."

She bristled. "And if I don't?"

He deliberately chose to misunderstand. "Come to bed naked. I won't object."

"I meant, what if I don't come out at all?" Her fighting spirit had clearly been revitalized. "I'll...I'll sleep in the bathtub."

"You can try, but since the door has no lock you won't be very successful." He checked his watch. "You have thirty minutes. Use it wisely. When your time is up, I'm coming in after you."

"You wouldn't!" The response was an automatic one. Even she realized as much, because she shook her head. "Of course you would. But then, raiding the bathroom while I'm in the shower would be the least of the offenses you've committed against me, wouldn't it?"

He simply looked at her. Men rarely opposed him;

women never did. And those few men who dared balk at his orders only did so once. But then, they knew who he was. Alyssa's unwavering defiance impressed the hell out of him. Even as she acquiesced to his demand, her expression and posture warned that she did so under protest.

When he remained mute, frustration vied with her anger. "You're a total bastard, you know that, Merrick?"

"Yes, as a matter of fact, I do."

Actually, the term was mild. As commander of the Royal Security Force, his life was comprised of making impossible decisions that had dire effects on the people with whom he came into contact. Worse, he had to live with the ramifications of his decisions. He didn't doubt for a minute that the actions he'd taken today, and would continue to take over the next four months, would produce the most painful results to date.

With a look of utter contempt, Alyssa turned her back on him and slammed the door in his face. He took it without flinching.

Score one for the princess.

She emerged from the bathroom thirty minutes later, timing it to the very last second, and he straightened from where he'd been lounging against the hallway wall. Despite her earlier threat, she wore the bathrobe he'd left for her and had washed her hair, which hung down her back in damp, heavy curls. Her face was scrubbed clean and to his consternation she looked all of twelve. Or she would have if it hadn't been for the womanly curves that turned floor-length terry cloth into a garment every bit as seductive as the scraps of silk and lace she'd been wearing earlier. How she managed it he couldn't begin to guess, but it guaranteed him a near sleepless night.

She stalked to the bedroom doorway, only a slight hitch in her stride betraying that she wasn't as amenable about the night ahead as she pretended. He followed, watching in exasperation as she crossed to a chair on the far side of the room and curled up in it.

He shut the bedroom door and locked it, steeling himself for yet another pitched battle. "Get in the bed, Alyssa."

"No, thanks. I'm good here."

"I can't allow that. I need to sleep and I won't be able to if I'm constantly watching to make sure you stay put."

She snuggled deeper into the chair, burrowing in for the duration. "You won't get much rest, anyway. I'm…I'm a very restless sleeper. I toss and turn all night long."

He almost smiled at the blatant lie. Or he would have if she hadn't been right about one unfortunate fact. It didn't appear he'd be getting much sleep. But it wouldn't have anything to do with her restlessness. "I'll manage." He pointed toward the double bed. "Get in."

She took several deep breaths before obeying. Leaving the safety of the chair, she approached the four-poster with all the caution of a mouse sneaking up on a baited trap and stood beside the bed for several long moments. Just when he was on the verge of picking her up and tossing her in, she pulled back the covers and slid between the sheets, curling up in as minute a ball as possible on the very edge of the mattress.

Hell. The next few hours were going to be some of the most difficult of his life. He circled the bed and yanked his black ops T-shirt over his head, tossing it onto the chair she'd abandoned. His boots came next, hitting the floor with a distinctive thud before he released his belt buckle and unzipped his trousers. He saw her stiffen at the distinctive rasp of the zipper and he could hear the nervous intake and exhalation of her breath.

Stripped down to his boxers, Merrick joined Alyssa in bed. She made a pathetically small mound on the farthest side of the mattress, no doubt attempting to remain as still and inconspicuous as possible in the hopes he'd leave her alone. Releasing his breath in a sigh, he hooked his arm around her and tucked her close, spooning her back against his chest. She remained stiff as a board, refusing to accommodate the alignment of curve to angle.

As for thinking she was pathetic, he was forced to hastily revise his opinion. Though she didn't struggle, somehow the dainty, fragile woman he held within his arms had managed to transform herself into hardened steel, gouging bony elbows into the few vulnerable parts of his body. Steel-tipped fingers dug into the arm anchoring her in place, and even her heels and toes had became lethal weapons. The only place she remained soft and cushioned was her backside, though he didn't doubt she would change that if she could. But at least it offered some small shielding against the rest of her anatomy.

"Do you have to touch me?" she whispered, squirming. "Isn't it enough that I'm in the same bed with you?"

Dear God, if she didn't hold still there'd be hell to pay. "It's necessary," he explained with impressive patience. "This way if you attempt to escape, I'll know. And I'll stop you."

Her breath trembled from her lungs. "I won't attempt to escape."

"Yes, you will. You think your mother needs you. So you'll continue to try to get away, just as I'll continue to stop you."

She shifted again and he stifled a groan, only half succeeding. "There's nothing I can do about it," she snapped. "I did warn you. I'm not used to sleeping like this."

"Tonight would have found you in some man's bed sleeping just like this, whether it was with von Folke or with me." Though with von Folke there would have been a lot more involved than talking and sleeping. He'd have wanted to consummate their union in order to make the marriage legally binding as per Verdonian law. For some reason the mere idea of anyone else putting his hands on Alyssa roused Merrick to a white-hot fury. "Or are you forgetting this would have been your wedding night?"

He didn't know what prompted him to ask the question, but to his surprise she shuddered. "I had forgotten," she confessed. Then her voice dropped to a whisper so soft, he barely caught it. "Being with him... It would have been far worse."

He didn't cut her any slack. "If that's how you felt, you should have refused to marry him. I doubt he'd have hurt your mother."

Her elbow clipped him in the gut and this time he suspected it was deliberate. "You didn't see his expression. I did. Prince Brandt will do whatever it takes to get me to the altar."

"If it means winning the throne, you're right. He'll say whatever he must to force your agreement. But even a man like von Folke has lines he won't cross. I suspect murder is one of them."

"People cross lines all the time when they're desperate." Her voice held a note of cool conviction. "One of my stepfathers was an auditor and I worked for him the summer between high school and college. That's how I became interested in finance in the first place. I could always sense when someone had been cooking the books. You can almost smell their desperation. If I were auditing Prince Brandt, I'd be checking his accounts very carefully."

Interesting. "Are you saying he's embezzling money?"

"No. I'm saying he's desperate. I have no idea why. But I can sense it, even though he's working really hard to keep a lid on things. Whether it's related to finances or not, I can't tell."

She fell silent after that, leaving Merrick free to sift through her observations. Something was up. Too bad he couldn't be certain what. He didn't doubt that von Folke would go to almost any extent to wear the crown. Avarice. Power. Prominence. All were substantial motivators. But why would a man be desperate to become king? Desperation implied a driving need rather than a burning desire. Why would a man need to be king?

He'd already checked von Folke out. Maybe it was time to dig a little deeper. A full profile, he decided, including—he smiled—any books that might have been cooked.

Alyssa had finally settled, for which he was eternally grateful. Moonlight crept through the doors leading out onto the balcony and slipped into bed with them, frosting their entwined forms with silver. The crown of her head rested beneath his chin and silken strands of her hair snagged along his whisker-roughened jawline. He inhaled, filling his lungs with the odor of the herbal shampoo she'd used. He could also catch a hint of a lighter, more irresistible aroma, though whether it came from her soap or the natural scent of her body, he couldn't be sure. Either way, the fragrant perfume soaked into his pores, permeating his senses in a way he knew would forever be a part of him.

"That woman who was with you earlier," she said, catching him by surprise. "What were you saying to each other? The part in Verdonian, I mean."

He lifted onto his elbow and drew her head to one side so he could look at her. The moonlight muted her vibrant coloring, turning her hair to silver and darkening her eyes to black. Her features took on a pearly glow, given depth and definition by the charcoal shadows sinking into the gentle planes and angles of her face. Watching her closely, he bit out a swift comment in Verdonian. She responded by staring at him in utter bewilderment.

"You don't speak the language, do you?" He shook his head in disbelief. "You come here expecting to be our queen and you can't even speak to your people in their native tongue?"

"Why should I?" she retorted indignantly. "I didn't know I was part Verdonian until last week."

"I would think if you were going to rule a country you might want to communicate with your subjects. What would you do if English wasn't our second language?"

"If I'd known that's what was going to happen to me, I would have learned Verdonian." Exasperation edged her words. "What did you say to me? How do you know I wasn't pretending I didn't understand? You think I'm pretending about everything else."

"Because my comment was unforgivably coarse." Unable to resist, he stroked his thumb along the sweeping arch of her cheekbone. "If you'd understood, you'd have reacted." Slapped him, most likely.

"Oh." She rolled away from him, not protesting this time when he spooned her into their earlier position. "You still haven't answered my question. What did she say to make you laugh?"

"She called me a bear cub. It can also mean a stuffed animal."

"A teddy bear?"

"A teddy bear. Yes."

Silence descended for several more minutes, though he wasn't the least bit surprised when she spoke again. "That woman—the one who called you a teddy bear—she took my place, didn't she?"

"That was the plan."

"Who is she?"

"My sister, Miri."

Alyssa turned her head again, this time of her own volition, and gazed at him in confusion. "Aren't you worried about what Prince Brandt will do to her when he discovers the deception?"

"Yes." He was incredibly worried.

"Then why did you let her do it?"

He hadn't wanted to but she'd insisted, threatening to reveal his plans if he didn't allow her to participate in the abduction. "It was necessary," Merrick limited himself to saying.

"She mentioned there were reasons for what she did," Alyssa said slowly. She settled onto her back. "Were they the same reasons you have? To make sure the elections are fair?"

He hesitated. He'd assumed that'd been what Miri had meant at the time, but since then he'd had several long hours to reconsider her words. Something in her tone had disturbed him, though he'd been unable to pinpoint what. With anyone else, he'd have managed it, had been trained to do precisely that. But his feelings for Miri interfered with his training, clouding his logic with emotion.

He narrowed his gaze on Alyssa. She'd proven herself a shrewd judge of character when it came to von Folke. Perhaps she'd picked up on whatever he'd missed. "Something's bothering you about what Miri said. What?"

Alyssa shrugged and her robe parted to reveal the soft skin of her throat and shoulders. "Her comment sounded…personal."

Personal. The longer he thought about it, the more certain he became that Alyssa was correct. He could see it now—the quiet despair in Miri's green eyes, the stalwart determination in her stance, the way she'd flinched when von Folke's name had been mentioned in connection with Alyssa's. Hell. Why hadn't he seen it before? He should have. Another concern to contemplate during the endless hours of the night.

"Go to sleep," he told Alyssa. He needed to think without distraction—and she'd already proven herself a huge one. "Tomorrow is going to be difficult enough as it is."

"Why?"

He sighed. "You ask a lot of questions, Princess."

"Yes, I do. And here's one more…" She rolled over to face him and her subtle perfume invaded his senses once again, threatening his sanity. "Are you certain you want to go through with this?"

It wasn't the first time the question had been posed,

and Merrick didn't hesitate in his response. "The future of Verdonia depends on it."

She moistened her lips, choosing her words with care. "Eventually you'll be caught. You realize that, don't you? What will happen to you when you are? Will you be sent to prison?"

"Maybe. Or banished. It depends on who catches me."

"But if you send me back—"

So. She'd found a new angle of attack, one he cut off without compunction. "Enough, Alyssa. Prison or banishment, I'll deal with the consequences when they occur."

"What about Prince Brandt? What will he do to you? You said there were lines he wouldn't cross. Are you willing to bet your life on that?"

"He won't be pleased that I've taken away his best chance at the throne." That had to be the understatement of the century. "Not that it matters. Whatever occurs as a result of my actions is an acceptable penalty."

"You can't be serious."

"I'm quite serious." He lifted an eyebrow. "Don't tell me you're worried about me?"

"Of course not." But he caught the flicker of concern that gave lie to her claim. The temptation to touch her became too much and he stroked his hand along the curve of her cheek and down the length of her neck. She shivered beneath the caress.

"Don't," she whispered.

He spoke without volition, drawn to tell her the truth

regardless of the consequences. "I'm honor bound to protect Verdonia from you."

"Am I such a threat?"

"A threat to my country." His mouth twisted into a ghost of a smile. "But a far worse threat to my honor."

As though to prove it, he lowered his head and captured her lips. They were every bit as soft and lush as he remembered, honey sweet and welcoming. A half-hearted protest slid from her mouth to his and he absorbed it, wanting to absorb all of her in every way possible.

How could she have been willing to give herself to von Folke? Didn't she realize it was criminal? More criminal than his abduction of her, and he told her as much with sharp, swift kisses. Then he sank back between her lips, reacquainting himself with every warm inch within.

He knew her mouth now. Laid claim to it. Drank from it. Possessed it, just as he planned to possess her. She went boneless in his arms, a surrendering that was every bit as wrong as it was overwhelmingly right.

The instant he released her mouth she whispered his name and it shivered between them into the velvety silence of the night. "You promised," she said.

"What did I promise?"

"That you wouldn't."

"Wouldn't what?"

Her head moved restlessly on the pillow. "I can't remember."

"Neither can I." Nor did he want to.

He found her mouth again and there was no more talking. Lips clung, then parted before unerringly finding each other again. Hands brushed, tangled, then released. Sweet murmurs filled the room, broken words that shouldn't have any meaning, but somehow spoke volumes.

Desire fired his blood, filling his heart and mind, crowding out rational thought. He needed more. Wanted the woman in his arms as he'd never wanted anything before. Clothes impeded him, taunting him, as they came between him and the warm, soft skin he so desperately craved. Skin that teased him with an irresistible perfume that had burrowed deep into his subconscious.

He found the belt that kept Alyssa from him. The knot fought his efforts to release it. And then it gave up the struggle, just as the woman had. He parted the coarse terrycloth and found the silken flesh within, soft and fragrant and burning hot.

"I swear, I'll make this good for you."

But the second he'd said the words, he knew he'd lost her. She stiffened within his arms and the desperate heat that had burned in her eyes only moments before faded, replaced with horrified distress. The princess had awoken from her enchantment and discovered she wasn't with Prince Charming. Far from it.

Her breath came in short, ragged gasps. "I want you to stop."

Desire rode Merrick hard and it took every ounce of effort to pull back from the edge. "Easy, Princess. I've stopped."

But his assurances had little effect. Panic held her in its grip and wouldn't let go gently. "You claim you're honor bound to protect all of Verdonia. Doesn't that protection extend to me, as well?" she demanded. "Or does your code of honor allow you to rape helpless women?"

She couldn't have chosen a more effective insult. He tamped down on his anger with only limited success. "It wouldn't be rape, and you damn well know it."

"Maybe not. But it wouldn't be honorable, either. Not when I'm being held prisoner. And not when you can't be certain I haven't given in because I fear the consequences if I don't."

He swore, long and violently. He'd never had his honor called into question. Not ever. Even so, he knew she was right, which disgusted him all the more. If matters weren't so desperate, he'd never have abducted her in the first place. He told her there were lines a man didn't cross. But hadn't he just stepped over one of them? Hell, he'd run full tilt over it, which bothered him more than he was willing to admit. Honor was everything to him, as was duty. He'd had a lifetime's training in each and in one fell swoop, had destroyed both. But no matter how far he'd sunk, forcing himself on a woman was unimaginable.

Sweeping the edges of her robe closed, he secured the belt, making certain every inch of her was covered, from neck to ankle. "Turn over," he ordered. "No more talking."

And no more touching. He needed every remaining

hour to recharge his batteries because he could predict exactly what sort of trouble the morning would bring.

Eventually his prediction was proven all too correct. At dawn the next day Merrick awoke—as he was certain he would—with guns pointed at his head.

Four

Alyssa stirred, switching from soft, sweet dreams to heart-pounding alertness in a single breath. She didn't understand what caused the sudden burst of fear. She only knew that it slapped through her, causing her pulse to race and a bitter metallic burn to scald her tongue. She started to speak but Merrick's arm tightened in clear warning and she fell silent.

"Don't move, sweetheart." Merrick whispered the instruction, his mouth nuzzled close to her ear. "I'll protect you. Just do exactly what I say. And…trust me."

Trust him? Of course she trusted him. The thought was immediate, instinctive and totally wrong. In the next instant, her brain kicked into gear and she remembered who he was, what he'd done. How his actions had put her mother's life in jeopardy. And she remembered a lifetime of her mother's warnings—never trust a man. They'll always betray you. No, she didn't trust him. Not in the least.

"Squeeze my hand if you're ready."

With no other choice, she did as he instructed and he shifted her within his arms, just the gentlest of movements, as if they were lovers easing into a more comfortable position. And then he seemed to explode. One instant she was held in the sweetest of embraces and the next she found herself cocooned in pillows with her face pressed against Merrick's broad back.

He'd somehow grown during the night, turning into a human wall. It was the only explanation for how he'd become twice as tall and broad as he'd been just hours ago. The muscles across his back were roped into taut steely cables, contracting smoothly in preparation for... for what, she wasn't quite certain, other than it would undoubtedly be violent. She dared one quick peek around her human Stonehenge and stopped breathing.

There were six of them. Each wore the sort of black special ops gear that her abductors had the previous day. And each held an assault rifle pointed directly at Merrick's head. She shuddered. Not good. Not good at all. She could sense Merrick's compulsion to act, which would have only one horrific outcome. She needed to put an end to their little standoff, and fast, before matters escalated out of control. Without giving herself time to consider, she rolled out from behind him and scrambled to the far side of the mattress.

One of the gunmen caught her by the shoulders

and dragged her from the bed, his grip painfully tight. "Ouch! Let go of me. I'm surrendering, you idiot. See?" She held her palms up and out. "This means surrender."

Merrick hadn't moved from his crouched position on the bed. He simply cut his eyes toward the man who held her and said, "Take your hands off her."

He issued the order in a soft voice, barely above a whisper. But something in the tone had the ability to liquefy bone. Everyone froze for a brief instant and the man she'd been grappling with released her. Amazing. Then the leader of the group barked out an order and she was once again wrapped up in a crushing hold. Worse, Merrick received the brunt of the leader's displeasure, taking a fist to the jaw.

She cried out in protest, not that anyone listened to her. The assailants pulled Merrick from the bed. It required four of them to secure him and she took a vicious pleasure in that. If they didn't have guns, she suspected that even six to one odds would bring into question the outcome of this little sortie. She'd have put every last penny she owned on Merrick. Unfortunately, guns were an issue and he must have realized as much because he stopped struggling.

He stood immobile a short distance from her, topping the four men surrounding him by a good three or four inches. She'd heard the term "noble savage" before but until that moment she'd never fully appreciated the meaning. Dressed in black boxers and endless muscle, he exuded elemental male at its finest and most noble.

But the expression on his face read pure savage. He addressed the leader of the assailants in Verdonian, a man she suddenly recognized as Tolken, von Folke's right-hand man. Her heart sank. Not assailants, she realized, but a rescue party.

"Yes, old friend, I know what's at stake," Tolken replied in English, apparently in response to Merrick's question. "And it's the only reason you're still alive."

Merrick's eyes filled with fierce conviction. "This is wrong, Tolk. You know that. Our people should be free to choose who they want for their king, not have it orchestrated for them. How many times did we discuss that very issue in university?"

"Silence!"

The order came from one of the men holding Merrick, who followed with a fist to the gut. Not that it had much impact, Alyssa realized, biting back a cry of protest. Lord, the man must have steel-belted abs. Tolken rapped out a reprimand and the man who'd hit Merrick stepped back, looking sullen.

"You'll have to excuse his manners," Tolken said. "He's understandably upset. You took something that didn't belong to you and there is a price to be paid for that. Consider those two blows a down payment."

It was too much. Alyssa fought the man restraining her. Or did he think he was protecting her? Not that it mattered. She didn't like being held by him any better than she liked the attack on Merrick. "He's unarmed. You have no right to hit him."

It was pointless to struggle, but she didn't care. She

wanted their attention on her. It never occurred to her to wonder why she'd be so intent on protecting her abductor. She only knew she didn't want him harmed. She kicked at her captor, her heels pounding against vulnerable knees and ankles while she sharpened her fingernails on defenseless skin.

The recipient of her attack must have had enough of her antics. He gripped her wrists in one hand and lifted his other, planning to backhand her. "Stop, you fool!" Tolken commanded, furious. "Have you lost your mind? That's Princess Alyssa, the duchess of Celestia."

Merrick didn't wait to see whether the order was obeyed. Though his arms were pinioned, his legs were free and he put them to good use, lashing out with his foot and knocking the man to the floor. It earned him another fist. Dropping to his knees, he shook his hair from his face and fixed his gaze on Tolken.

"If your man touches her, or even attempts to touch her again, he's dead."

Once again, the words were barely above a whisper, and once again they had an immediate effect on the rescue party. It was subtle, but more noticeable this time, perhaps because she was in a better position to observe. Every one of them stiffened, including Tolken, coming to attention the way subordinates do in the presence of a superior.

As soon as Merrick saw he had their full attention, he added, "And if I don't succeed in killing him, von Folke will."

Tolken hesitated only a moment. She could see the

inner battle he fought played out in the souring of his expression. Part of him wanting to defy Merrick's demand, to establish who was in control. The other part recognized the validity of those two simple threats. With a harsh curse, he barked out another order, this one in Verdonian, an order that had the man holding her scurrying from the room. They must not have considered her much of a threat because no one else attempted to secure her. It was a reasonable assessment. She wasn't a threat…at least not in a physical sense.

Merrick maintained eye contact with Tolken, not sparing her so much as a glance. "She won't go with you until she knows her mother's safe."

She didn't miss a beat. "He's right. I'm not leaving here until I talk to her."

Tolken dismissed her with barely a glance. "You will leave when we tell you. As for your mother, Prince Brandt will allow you to speak to her when he sees fit."

"Your Highness," she retorted icily.

The man frowned. "What?"

"You will address me as Your Highness, or as ma'am. But don't you ever again speak to me in that dismissive tone. Not if you value your current position."

Shock slid across Tolken's face, followed by a wash of mottled red. His hands collapsed into fists—fists itching to wrap around her neck if she didn't miss her guess. No doubt Merrick could sympathize. As though aware of his regard, she spared him a brief glance and he gave the barest nod.

"Get my mother on the phone. Now."

"I can't do that, Your Highness," Tolken said through gritted teeth.

Folding her arms across her chest, she dropped to the edge of the mattress. "Then I'm not going anywhere." One of his men took a step toward her and she shot him a warning look, deciding to follow Merrick's lead. "Don't even think about it. I may not have the power to stop you right now, but as Prince Brandt's wife, I plan to have a long and vindictive memory. If you dare put your hands on me again, I'll make you pay. And I'll make sure it's both inventive and painful."

To her surprise the man believed her. He stopped in his tracks glancing helplessly from her to Tolken. Behind him Merrick's lips twitched, forcing her to struggle at maintaining her "ice princess" demeanor. Damn the man. Didn't he understand how difficult she found all this? They had guns, for crying out loud. Prince Brandt held her mother hostage. And she'd been abducted—twice in two days. It wasn't a game and it sure as hell wasn't amusing, no matter how absurd the situation had become.

The stalemate lasted for endless seconds before Tolken caved. Plunging a hand into his pocket, he yanked out a cell phone and placed a call. Alyssa was fairly certain he spoke directly to Prince Brandt. They conversed for several minutes in Verdonian before he handed her the phone.

"Ally? Baby, is that you?"

Static sounded in her ear, but Alyssa could still make

out her mother's distinctive voice and it brought tears to her eyes. "Hi, Mom. Are you okay?"

"What's going on?" Fear rippled through her question. "What's happened? Why is everyone so angry? Where are you?"

"Everything's fine, Mom." She used her most soothing tone, one that came naturally whenever she spoke to her mother. After all, she'd had a lifetime's worth of experience calming her, reassuring her, taking care of her the best she knew how. "I'll be there soon. I promise." Before she could say more, Tolken yanked the phone from her hand. "I wasn't finished," she protested.

"Don't push your luck, Your Highness. We've done as you asked. Now you will come with us without any further argument or discussion." He put the phone to his ear and spoke for another moment before breaking the connection. Thrusting the phone into his pocket, he addressed his men. "Our top priority is retrieving the princess and ensuring her safe return to His Highness."

Alyssa struggled to maintain her composure while they spoke around her, referring to her as though she were a package. A possession. That's all she'd been since the moment she'd stepped foot in this blasted country and she was getting darned sick and tired of it.

"What about the commander?" one of the men asked, nodding toward Merrick.

Alyssa sat up straighter. Commander? Commander of what? Not that she had the opportunity to ask, not while they were busy determining Merrick's fate. She shot him an apprehensive glance. He didn't seem the least concerned. She remembered comparing him to a lion when she'd caught her first glimpse of him. Perhaps she'd been mistaken. He was more of a leopard than a lion, she decided, all lean muscle built for power and speed. There was also a ruthlessness about him, she associated more with leopards than lions, a deadly intent. A crouching watchfulness that preceded explosive action.

His eyes glittered a hard, winter-bright gold, watchful and determined. Whether these men knew it or not, they'd already lost. This man didn't fail, no matter how huge the odds or how dangerous the mission. She took a fierce pleasure in the knowledge before realizing that should Merrick succeed, she would lose. He'd prevent her from returning to her mother by any and all means at his disposal. How was it possible that every instinct urged her to trust him when it put her mother's life in jeopardy?

But no matter how hard she tried to picture him as the enemy, what she recalled most strongly were his arms wrapped tight around her and his hands and mouth offering the most intense pleasure she'd ever experienced. "Trust me," he'd said. She wanted to. God help her, she wanted to. And perhaps she would, if it weren't for her mother.

Tolken had reached his decision and he confronted Merrick. "I know you, old friend. It's too risky to bring you back on the helicopter with us. We'll secure you here on the premises." He stabbed a finger at three of the four remaining guards. "You will remain behind and guard him. He can be retrieved later and dealt with at that point. You will make sure he doesn't escape. His Highness will be most disappointed if you fail to do so."

"Prepare to be disappointed," Merrick murmured. "I won't be here when you return."

One of the men still surrounding Merrick raised his hand, but a single glance at Alyssa had him thinking better of it. Still, it prompted her to sweep to her feet. "Enough! I won't have a man beaten in my presence. In fact, you will keep your hands off him until he's turned over to Prince Brandt. Is that clear?" She didn't dare wait for a response since she didn't know how much longer she could maintain her bluff of future retribution. She turned to Tolken. "I need clothing, including shoes."

"Of course, Your Highness." He looked discomfited. "I—"

"Closet and dresser," Merrick said. "You'll find everything you need."

Tolken signaled his men to secure Merrick and leave. Alarmed, Alyssa took a swift step in his direction, only to stop short when she realized the inappropriateness of her actions. She stared at him in dismay, bewildered when he returned her gaze with one of calm confidence. A half smile hooked the corner of his mouth, his scar giving him a mischievous appearance that sat at odds with his warrior nature.

She didn't understand it. They were going to take

him away now. They'd tie him up while they returned her to Prince Brandt. Once on the prince's turf Merrick would be punished, severely, she suspected. And there was nothing she could do about it, nothing at all, not if she wanted to protect her mother.

She should hate Merrick for what he'd done, but she didn't. For some strange reason, she wanted to protect him every bit as much as she wanted to protect her mother. How could that be? He'd abducted her. Stripped her. Bound and gagged her. He thought she was motivated by greed and ambition. He'd taken her captive. Forced her to share a bed with him. Held her in his arms. Kissed her until she couldn't see straight. Touched her in ways no man had ever touched her. She ought to congratulate Tolken and his storm troopers. Offer profuse thanks. Instead, she wished them all a swift journey straight to hell.

The man who'd been sent away earlier appeared in the doorway. "Sir, the helicopter's arrived. We can depart at any time."

Tolken jerked his head in Merrick's direction. "Take him," he instructed. "See if there's a root cellar and secure him there. The rest of you wait for me by the car."

Without another word, they escorted Merrick from the room, the men filing out one by one until only Tolken remained. Yanking open the closet door, he removed the slacks and blouse and tossed them to Alyssa. "I'll be waiting outside the door to escort you to the helicopter as soon as you're dressed." He paused in front of her.

"And I believe these belong to you. A wedding gift from His Highness, weren't they?"

He opened his hand and held out the amethyst and diamond earrings Prince Brandt had given her the day before. Had it only been yesterday? Good grief. She vaguely recalled leaving the earrings in the bathroom when she'd showered. Color tinted her cheeks at the hint of reprimand in Tolken's voice. But what did he expect? For her to wear them to bed…with Merrick? The ludicrousness of the whole sorry mess struck her and hysterical laughter vied with embarrassment.

Lifting her chin, she regarded him with as much composure as she could manage. "Thanks." She accepted the earrings and, since he continued to stand there and wait, put them on.

He gave a nod of approval and stepped into the hallway. The instant the door closed, she crossed to the small dresser shoved against one of the walls and checked the drawers. Sure enough, she found underclothes with the tags still on them. Had Merrick chosen them, or had his sister, Miri? Not that it mattered.

The plain cotton underpants and matching bra fit reasonably well, though the bra felt a trifle snug. To her relief, they'd gotten the size of the blouse right, the soft taupe a color she often chose to wear. The plain slacks, several shades darker than the blouse, also fit well, if a little loose at the waist. She suspected the clothes had been chosen for their simplicity and in the hopes that the wearer wouldn't attract any undue attention. Understandable, if regrettable. Had the circumstances been different, she'd have wanted to attract as much attention as possible. Next, she found a pair of sandals in the closet. They were a tad large, but the various straps and buckles could be tightened to compensate.

Glancing in the mirror, she groaned. No wonder Tolken had treated her with so little respect. She looked like a woman who'd made a rambunctious night of it. Checking the rest of the drawers, she lucked onto a comb and used the remaining few minutes taming the curls billowing around her face. That's what came from going to bed with wet hair.

Finished, she opened the door, surprised to discover that Tolken wasn't waiting for her after all, but another man stood in his place. "Where's your boss?" she asked.

"I'm to escort you to the helicopter," he replied.

"What about Merrick?"

He didn't answer, but jerked his head toward the steps. She preceded him down and crossed to the front door. She managed a swift glance toward both the kitchen and the great room before she exited the house, but didn't see anyone. Perhaps they'd found that root cellar Tolken had referred to and were busy tying up Merrick. It was a depressing thought.

Outside, more men stood around the vehicle waiting to transport her to the helicopter. As soon as she settled inside they drove a short distance to a narrow valley tucked between the mountains. A large black chopper squatted in the middle. Off to one side a half dozen men were lounging on the ground in a small group while another half dozen stood guard, their weapons at the ready. She didn't have time to do more than glance at the contingent before being helped into the helicopter. Tolken had brought far more men than she'd realized. Clearly, Prince Brandt wasn't taking any chances. He wanted her back and would use every resource available to ensure it.

She glanced up to thank the man who'd assisted her onboard and stared at Merrick in utter disbelief. "What? How…?"

He smiled, taking far too much enjoyment in her astonishment. "I had men surrounding the house. They liberated me."

She fought to make sense of it all. "But, that means…. You knew Tolken would find me?"

"I had a pretty good idea. I had my men stationed, ready for that possibility."

"It was all a setup?" she demanded. "You knew in advance that Tolken and his men would raid the house? You knew we'd wake up with guns pointed at our heads?" At his nod of confirmation, the full impact of his admission struck and unbridled fury took over. "How could you put yourself at risk like that? If one of those idiots had been a little more trigger-happy you could have died! How could you be so foolish?"

He gave her an odd look. "And you," he pointed out. "I put you at risk, as well."

She waved that aside. "They wouldn't have hurt me. Prince Brandt would have had their heads if I'd been harmed. But you… Damn it, Merrick. I'm sure they considered you expendable. Those men were out for blood. Yours, if I'm not mistaken. They—" Her voice broke. "They beat you."

He dismissed that with a casual shrug. "Fortunately for us Tolken had them well under control, a fact I was counting on since we'd both been trained by the same man—a man who abhorred unnecessary bloodshed." He held out his hand. "Now, if you don't mind, hand over your earrings."

The change of subject baffled her. "Why?"

"Tolken found you thanks to them." He hesitated. "You'll be pleased to know they've also helped prove your innocence."

Too much had happened in too short a time. She didn't understand anything anymore. When he made a move toward her, she held up her hands. "Stop. Just stop a minute and explain it to me in short, easy-to-digest monosyllabic words. Use sentences and paragraphs only if there's no other option."

He assisted her into one of the seats. Tucking her hair out of the way, he proceeded to strip her of the earrings. He held them up. "Von Folke gave these to you?"

She nodded. "As a wedding gift."

"They have a tracking device embedded in them." He allowed that to sink in before adding, "It confirms the story you've been telling me about being forced to marry von Folke. He wouldn't have needed to plant a tracking device on you if you'd chosen to marry him of your own free will. It only would have been necessary if he'd been concerned that you might try to run."

Outrage left her breathless. "That's how Tolken found us? I was…I was bugged?"

"Yes."

"And you knew they'd come for me?"

He shrugged. "Suspected. Hoped." Crossing to the open doorway of the helicopter, he tossed the earrings to one of his men. "If Tolk came after you, I could secure him and his men long enough for us to disappear. It worked. Now you and I will head out and Tolken will return to von Folke empty-handed."

"But, isn't this his helicopter?"

Merrick grinned. "Kind of him to lend it to us for our escape, isn't it?"

"But, isn't it bugged or…or have some sort of tracking device on it, too?"

"It is and it does. Too bad it's been disabled or he'd know where we were going." Turning, he signaled the pilot. "Now, if you'll fasten your seat belt, Princess, we'll take off."

The blades began to whip around. "Please don't do this." She had to shout to be heard over the growing roar of the engines and blades. "Please. Just let me go with Tolken."

"Sorry, Princess. I can't. I'm afraid you're stuck with me for the duration."

The noise grew too loud to allow for further conversation. After a few minutes, the chopper lifted off and banked to the south. They climbed over the ridge of mountains separating Avernos from Celestia, a feature Alyssa remembered seeing on the map the previous evening. It didn't take long until they were on the other side and she caught her breath at the beauty of the rolling green hills spread before them. Rain clouds drifted off and the sun broke through, sending a rainbow spearing toward earth. She'd been born there, she marveled. She'd come from this place.

Eventually, the helicopter set down in another field, bordered by a dirt road. A car was parked off to one side along the grassy verge. As soon as she and Merrick had exited the craft, the chopper departed, winging northward once again.

"You had this all carefully planned, didn't you?" she asked as soon as the noise had faded enough to speak.

"It's my job to plan carefully."

Alyssa planted herself in front of the man who'd abducted her for the second day in a row, facing him with a fierceness born of equal parts exhaustion and anger. "Who are you?" she demanded. "I mean, really."

"We were never formally introduced, were we?"

She folded her arms across her chest. "No. This might be a good time."

He surprised her by sketching an elegant little bow. "Merrick Montgomery, at your service, Princess."

Not only a leopard, but a graceful one with old-world manners. She didn't want to notice such things. She wanted him to be rotten and evil so she could focus on escape, instead of being distracted by how he looked and moved, spoke and smelled. And kissed. Those kisses had been the ultimate distraction.

"This is ridiculous," she muttered.

He nodded in agreement. "Bordering on the bizarre."

"You still haven't told me what you do. How did you become caught up in all this?"

"I'm commander of Verdonia's Royal Security Force." At her blank look, he clarified, "It's the security contingent for the country as a whole, rather than any one principality."

"Like the army or something?"

"Or something. A specialized armed forces."

That explained Tolken and his men's demeanor toward Merrick, as though they were subordinates addressing a superior. It also explained their apprehension. What the hell had she become involved in? And how could she get herself and her mother out of it? "Well, Commander, would you mind explaining to me how snatching an innocent woman is part of your job description?"

"It's my job to see to the safety and protection of my country and its citizens. That includes you and your mother, something I'll deal with before much longer." He started across the field toward the car. He didn't even check to see if she followed, though considering she had nowhere else to go, it was a bit of a no-brainer. "Now let's start at the beginning, Alyssa. How and why did you come to Verdonia?"

He spoke English with a near perfect accent. But it still held a gentle lilt most noticeable when he said her name. Was there nothing about the man she could despise? "I was about to start a new job."

He nodded. "Assistant Vice President of Human Relations for Bank International in New York City."

"Do you remember my saying that, or did you have me investigated?"

"Both."

Did they have a dossier on her? She found the idea unnerving. Did he know about all her jobs? About how, since college, she'd bounced across the country, from position to position, always looking for the "perfect" one? The perfect place to finally, finally put down roots? Did he know about her mother's background, as well? Oh God.

"My mother—Angela Barstow—sent me an express envelope. It contained a brief note begging me to help her out of a jam she'd gotten herself into. And she sent an airline ticket." Alyssa shrugged. "What could I do? I flew out to help."

"This jam, as you call it—what was it?"

Alyssa frowned. "She didn't say. She and my current stepfather recently broke up and she often runs away after—" She broke off, aware she'd said too much. "She thought an extended trip to Europe might give her time to get over him. I don't know why she returned to Verdonia. Maybe she got it in her head to visit my half brother for some reason. Perhaps she wanted to visit my father's grave."

Merrick swiveled to face her. "Is it possible she set you up deliberately? Could she be working with von Folke?"

Five

Alyssa glared at Merrick. "My mother working with von Folke? Not a chance," she retorted without hesitation. "She's the least devious woman I know. She's... helpless. That's why I need to get to her as soon as possible."

With a noncommittal nod, he continued on to a white sedan and opened the passenger door. "That's not going to happen, Princess. You're going to have to trust me when I say that von Folke won't do anything to harm her."

Instead of climbing in the car, she slammed the door shut. "I'm supposed to trust you?" she demanded. "How can you even suggest such a thing? What have you done to inspire my trust?"

"Not a damn thing." Merrick dropped his hands to

Alyssa's shoulders. "Since you haven't known me long enough to trust me, consider this.... Tolken and his men know I've taken you against your will. I made that clear to them. They also know that you were willing to return to von Folke. Hell, you were eager to. The fact that you weren't able to isn't your fault and everyone will recognize that fact. There's no advantage to hurting your mother. It won't help his cause."

It made sense, but she didn't dare risk her mother's life based on Merrick's brand of logic. "You can't be certain. Not a hundred percent certain," she argued.

"I can, and I am. Right now von Folke has a certain level of sympathy. Someone has stolen his bride and that has the potential for swinging votes his way—assuming he makes that information public knowledge. I'm betting he'll keep it quiet for the time being. There are too many variables beyond his control to risk any sort of general announcement."

"What variables?"

Merrick ticked off on his fingers. "If it comes out that you were forced to the altar, his credibility is called into question. If we make it public that von Folke's holding your mother in order to ensure your compliance. If the point is made that by forcing you to marry him, he would win the throne. All of these variables are out of his control and of substantial risk to him. No, he'll remain silent. Instead, he'll send men after us in the hopes of recapturing you without creating an uproar."

"Aren't you concerned about that?"

"We have a few advantages of our own. Tolken is..."

He frowned, seeming to struggle for the right words. “You have state law enforcement in your country, do you not?”

“Yes. Local police. State troopers.”

“Tolken is like that. As von Folke’s right-hand man, he enforces the peace within the principality of Avernos. You also have law enforcement that supercedes the state level?”

“Of course. Federal agencies.”

“I am the equivalent of that. It would be frowned upon for Tolken to come into Celestia and attempt to enforce the law. When he comes—and he will—it’ll be on tiptoe, whereas I only have to tiptoe if it’s to my advantage.”

“Okay, I get it. Commander tops the principality police.” She returned to the issue that worried her the most. “I still don’t see how that guarantees my mother’s safety.”

“The only way von Folke succeeds is if you’re willing to marry him. If you return and discover your mother’s been harmed, I can’t see you agreeing to cooperate with his plans. It’s in his best interest to keep your mother healthy.”

“And if he decides his plan is a bust?” she protested. “Don’t you think he’ll want to get rid of everyone who knows what he attempted?”

“Including you and me?” He gave it a moment’s consideration. “All the more reason to stay well away from him until after the election.”

"At which point he can take his anger out on my mother."

He fought to hang on to his patience. "I'll find a way to free your mother."

"How?" she demanded.

"Again, you'll have to trust me."

She wanted to. She wanted to more than she cared to admit. Every instinct she possessed urged her to allow him to take control of the situation, to yield to his superior strength and conviction. But she didn't dare. "I can't," she said at last.

"Why?"

She hesitated, not certain she wanted to reveal such personal information. But something in his eyes held her, demanding the truth. And she found herself telling him, opening herself in a way she hadn't with any other man. "I spent a lifetime watching my mother run from one bad situation—and man—straight into the arms of another. Each time she trusted the new man in her life and gave up all her power and control, allowing her new husband to dictate how and what and when and why. And each one betrayed that trust, leaving her worse off than she'd been before."

"Hell, Princess." He was seriously taken aback. "How many stepfathers have you had?"

She waved his question aside. "That's not important."

"I disagree. I think it may be very important."

She shook her head, refusing to betray her mother. "The bottom line is that long ago I promised myself I'd never repeat the same mistakes she made. I'd stand on my own two feet. Control my own life. Make my own decisions. And the main decision would be to never allow any man to tell me what to do or how to live my life."

"And now you have a man doing just that." He blew out a harsh breath. "Tough break."

"It has been. Until now." She paced away from the car, gazing toward the mountains that bordered Prince Brandt's principality. "So far I've lived my life my way. I haven't let any man control me. I'm tired of playing the victim. One way or another, I'm going to take control again, to determine my own fate."

"Good for you. In four months, you can get right back to doing that."

She spun to face him. "Not in four months. Right now. I'm going to find a way to rescue my mother. You can either help or get out of the way. But I'm not going into hiding for the next four months and leave my mother to Prince Brandt's mercy. You can't guard me every second. Sooner or later I'll find an opportunity to escape and I intend to seize it with both hands."

"Thanks for the warning. I'll make sure I don't give you that opportunity." He opened the car door again. "Please. Get in."

"And if I refuse?"

"I'd rather you didn't."

"But if I do?"

His expression remained adamant. She could no more

move him than the mountains at her back. "I plan to succeed," he stated.

"No matter who gets sacrificed?"

He didn't answer. He didn't have to. "Please. Get in the car." He waited until she'd reluctantly complied before leaning in to fasten her seatbelt. "In case it hasn't occurred to you, if you'd married von Folke you'd have given up even more control than you have with me. He'd have seen to that. This solution may not be much better. But it is better."

She had no response to that.

"And, Princess?"

"What?" she whispered.

His expression softened. "Welcome home."

Alyssa turned her head and stared out the front windshield while Merrick watched in concern. She'd done a fair job at concealing her thoughts from him, but her mouth quivered ever so slightly. He remembered her looking just like that when he'd studied her through the binoculars the day before. At the time he'd thought of her as a lifeless doll, that betraying quiver a result of either nerves or triumph. He knew better now. She might be trying to hide the fact, but he could tell that being in Celestia, knowing her roots were here, had made an impact.

She flicked a swift glance in his direction and then away again. "Where are we going?"

"I have a place nearby where we can spend the night. We can't stay there longer than a day. Tolken may figure out where we are." He grimaced. "It depends on how good his memory is."

"What is this place?"

"A farm that belongs to my grandparents. The place is vacant while they visit my brother in Mt. Roche. That's the capital city of Verdonia."

"So you have both a brother, as well as your sister, Miri. What's his name?"

He hesitated. Would she recognize it? He couldn't afford to take the risk. "It's not important." Before she could comment, he changed the subject. "You're not going to like this next part," he informed her.

"Really?" She lifted an eyebrow. "And which part up to now have I liked?"

Score another point for the princess. "For the rest of the time we're together we'll be sharing a bed, the same as last night."

"No," she rejected the plan. "I can't do that. Not again."

"Why?" Fool. He knew damn well why. They'd only spent one night in bed together and he hadn't been able to keep his hands off her even for the space of those few hours. How was he supposed to succeed in leaving her untouched for weeks…months? "Was it because of that kiss?"

Her gaze jerked up to meet his and he read the answer without her saying a word. Her eyes were an incredible shade of blue, startling in their intensity, even more so with memories of the previous night darkening the color. Her lips parted and he could hear the quickening of her breath. He leaned closer, drawn to that mouth, that amazing, lush mouth. He'd never sampled anything like it, anything so addictive, so intoxicating. He wanted more. He wanted to drink her down until all he could taste was her, until his hands knew her body more intimately than his own, until the air filling his lungs was saturated with her scent and the sound of her voice became the only music his ears could comprehend.

The confines of the car seemed to close in around them, shrinking until only the two of them existed. He reached for her, cupping her head in his hands. Her hair slid through his fingers, the curls knotting around them, anchoring him in place. Not that he wanted to go anywhere. He leaned in until their lips brushed. Parted. Brushed again, harder this time. Sealed. She moaned, a rich, helpless sound that rumbled deep in her throat, like a cat's purr. She didn't even seem to realize she'd made it, a fact he found unbelievably erotic.

Her hands slipped to his chest and she gathered up fistfuls of his shirt. For an instant she relaxed into the embrace, welcoming his touch. Her head nestled into the crook of his shoulder and wayward strands of silky hair clung to his jaw, giving off the faintest aroma of exotic flowers mixed with tangy citrus. And then she released his shirt and her arms encircled him. He could feel her urgency, one that fed his.

Her kiss was filled with a desperate passion, as though snatching life-giving sustenance before the onslaught of a drought. She consumed him with abandonment, greedily drinking in everything he had to offer.

And that's all it took to set him off. The combustion was as violent as it was immediate, a flash fire sweeping through him and igniting the overwhelming compulsion to make this woman his on every possible level. He pushed her against the door, angling her mouth for a deeper kiss. Their tongues joined in a sweet, hot duel. Tangling. Warring. Caressing.

This was wrong. Oh, so wrong. Not that he gave a damn. If they'd been anywhere other than in a two-seater with a stick shift threatening mayhem between them, he'd have taken her right there against the door and to hell with the consequences. The only thing that stopped him was the expression in her eyes. A fierce conflict raged in them, physical desire in a pitched battle with rationality. Want clashing with common sense.

He couldn't say how long they teetered on the knife's edge, caught between a mindless, delicious fall into insanity and the far less satisfying retreat toward reason. He could take her, could have her body and use it until he was sated. But it wouldn't be enough. He didn't want just her body. He wanted far more, he suddenly realized. And he wouldn't be satisfied until he had every piece of her. If that happened here and now, so much the better. He could convince her that what had started out as an abduction had become something else altogether. Personal. Vital. Necessary to both of them. Still, he forced himself to make it a fair fight and eased back a scant inch.

She accepted the out he offered and pulled back,

gasping for air, staring at him with glazed, bewildered eyes. "Why does this keep happening?"

"Because I'm irresistible?"

She disengaged herself from his embrace and the curls wrapped around his fingers tightened in protest before reluctantly setting him free. "Every time you touch me I come undone." She glanced down at herself and the breath hissed from her lungs. She plucked at her blouse. "Look at me. This is exactly what I'm talking about. How did you manage to do that?"

To his amusement, half the buttons were unfastened. "I don't know how that happened. I thought I'd been cupping your head the entire time."

She fumbled with the buttons. "You have to stop trying to seduce me. It's not fair. It's only supposed to work in reverse. Not in…in… Not this way."

Her comment intrigued him. "You mean, it's acceptable if you seduce me?" He could only come up with one reason why she'd attempt that. The corner of his mouth kicked upward. "You think seducing me will give you an opportunity to escape?"

"If that's what it takes, then yes," she snapped. "Not that I'd have succeeded."

"You might have." He opened his arms. "I'm willing to let you give it a try if you want."

"Oh, ha ha. Very funny. But I've already thought it through. It wouldn't work."

"Why not?" He was genuinely curious.

"Simple. What happens after I seduce you?"

"I go deaf and blind?"

Her mouth twitched before she managed to suppress it. "If I thought you would, I might be willing. Because the only way I'd manage to give you the slip would be if you really did go deaf and blind. And even then, I'd need a three-day head start."

He snagged another of her wayward curls and twined it around his finger again, forcing her to look at him. "If I ever get you in my bed for real, if I ever make love to you—proper love to you—I'd never let you go, Princess. I'd keep you wrapped up so tight you wouldn't know where you ended and I began."

She jerked back. It was too much too soon and she reacted with a feminine alarm as old as time. The female preparing to flee from the pursuing male. The scent of want mingled with the fear of domination. As badly as she needed to retreat, it didn't come close to how badly he wanted to give chase. Every instinct he possessed urged him to take her. Now. To forge a bond before she escaped.

She must have read his intent because her hand groped for the door handle, clinging to it as though it were a life raft. "I think we should go now." She spoke with an authority that didn't quite ring true. Moistening her lips, she tried again. "But I have a condition of my own before we do."

He buried a smile. He could guess what that condition would be. "Which is?"

"You don't kiss me again. No touching. No sexual overtures. I need to feel safe."

His amusement died, replaced with regret. Is that

what he did to her? Made her feel unsafe? But then, how could it be otherwise? He'd abducted the woman. Tied her up. Forced himself on her—even if she had responded with a passion that blew him away. And he'd been unable to resolve the issue with her mother, something that left her frantic with worry.

"You are safe," he informed her gently. "You have my word."

"Fine. Then we can go."

"As soon as you fasten your seatbelt."

She groaned. "I didn't realize I'd unfastened it. Buttons. Seatbelts. You're a regular magician, aren't you?"

"If I were, I wouldn't bother with buttons and seatbelts. Anyone can unfasten those." He turned the key in the ignition. "I'd find it far more interesting to unfasten you from the inside out."

She didn't reply, but confusion warred with alarm. Leaving her to consider his words, he shifted the car into gear and drove to the farm. He gave her time to explore, keeping his distance so she had an opportunity to come to terms with her situation without his breathing down her neck. Dusk had settled around them when they met in the kitchen for their evening dinner.

"Who's taking care of the farm while your grandparents are away?" Alyssa asked toward the end of the meal.

Had she hoped for rescue from that direction? If so, she'd be sorely disappointed. "There are caretakers who live not far away. I warned them I'd be here tonight."

Merrick topped off her glass of homemade buckthorn wine, a wine his grandparents only served to their most honored guests. Much to his relief, Alyssa had been effusive with her praise of the exotic brew, taking to the unusual flavor as though born to it. "They won't interfere," he added pointedly.

She accepted the information with a stoic nod. "I've been wondering... What happens to Celestia when I return home? Who will inherit it after me?"

"No one."

She frowned and genuine concern lit her eyes. "Didn't my father have any relatives? Distant cousins or a twice-removed niece or nephew or something? The succession can't just end with my brother."

"No." He waited a beat. "But it can and does end with you."

Her frown deepened. "Then, what happens to Celestia?"

He took a sip of the golden wine before replying. "According to law, it'll be divided in half and absorbed by the other two principalities. One portion will go to Avernos, the other to Verdon."

Her distress wasn't feigned. "That seems so wrong."

He shrugged. "It's within your power to prevent."

She started shaking her head before he even finished his sentence. "I can't. My home is in New York. I have an apartment. Responsibilities. I start a new job in another two—"

He winced as she broke off. He could tell she'd only

just realized that being held by him for the next four months put more things at risk than just her mother. No doubt she'd lose her job, as well. She'd been thrust into a situation not of her choosing, her entire life turned upside down courtesy of the political upheaval in Verdonia. And there was nothing he could do to change that. At least, not until he could figure out what was behind von Folke's desperate maneuvering.

As much as he regretted the sacrifices her abduction created, he didn't for one minute regret her presence in Verdonia. In the short time they'd been together he'd come to realize that she belonged here. More, he realized she belonged with him.

Now all he had to do was convince her of that.

One look was sufficient to warn it would take a hell of a lot of convincing. Alyssa stood, her smile strained, darkness eclipsing the brilliance of her eyes. "I think it's time for me to turn in," she announced in a painfully polite voice. When he would have stood, as well, she held up a hand. "Could you give me a few minutes? I need some time to myself. I promise I won't try to escape."

"Of course. I'll get our luggage from the car."

"We have luggage?" She laughed, the sound heartbreaking. "You do plan ahead, don't you? At least, for most things."

She left the kitchen and a few minutes later he heard her enter the bedroom. The door closed with a gentle click, leaving Merrick swearing beneath his breath. Damn it to hell. He'd never meant for this to happen.

The decision that had seemed so obvious and clear cut a week ago had become complicated beyond belief now that he'd executed it. What he needed was time to think, to review his options, as well as review possible alternatives he hadn't previously considered.

Exiting the house, he removed the luggage and delivered it to Alyssa before retreating to the kitchen. He sat in one of the ladder-back chairs, remembering the summers he and his brother had spent here. Little had changed since then. The heart oak kitchen table remained the same, with only a burn mark from one of his grandfather William's cigars to mar the scoured surface. He could still recall his grandmother scolding her husband for his inattentiveness and the way he'd reduced her to breathless laughter by apologizing with a smacking kiss. The wide plank flooring was just as spotless now as then, as were the whitewashed walls. And every appliance had been polished to a satin sheen.

He poured himself a final glass of wine and carried it out to the front porch to William's rocker. His "thinking chair" as he'd often referred to it. Sipping the wine, Merrick allowed the minutes to ease by. The consequences of his actions weighed heavily, the potential outcomes haunting him. He'd forsaken all he'd held dear, all he'd spent a lifetime creating. Had he made the right decision? Was his purpose just and honorable? Or had he subconsciously allowed personal aspirations to guide his choices?

After two full hours of contemplation, he still didn't

have an answer. Giving it up as a lost cause, he returned to the bedroom, groping his way in the dark. After a quick shower, he climbed into bed. If he'd been any sort of a gentleman, he'd have left Alyssa alone. But he couldn't. He needed her. He slid an arm beneath her and tucked her close. He heard her breath sigh into the night as she settled into his embrace.

"I'm sorry," he murmured. "I didn't intend for you to lose your job or to put your mother in harm's way. If I could change any of it, I would."

"You can change it. You choose not to."

He couldn't deny the accusation. "True. Will they hold your job for you?"

"Doubtful. Not for four months." She spoke dispassionately, but he heard the underlying ripple of pain and anger.

"The outcome would have been the same even if I hadn't abducted you. You realize that, don't you?" She stilled in his arms. Apparently that hadn't occurred to her. He gave her the hard, cold truth—at least the truth as he saw it. "If I hadn't interfered you'd now be married to von Folke and your job would still have been sacrificed. This way you'll be free in four months, free to return home and pursue your career once again. I suspect von Folke would have kept you tied to him for a year or two. Possibly longer."

"I…I hadn't thought of that." She fell silent for a long moment. "I don't know what I'm going to do…after."

"You could stay in Verdonia."

Her laugh held a bitter edge. “Pretend to be Princess Alyssa, duchess of Celestia?”

“You are Princess Alyssa, duchess of Celestia. You have degrees in psychology and business administration, with experience in international finance. Your education is tailor-made for the position,” he argued.

“I don’t belong here.”

“You could.”

She fell silent for a long time. Then, “Was he your friend?”

The switch in topic caught him by surprise. “Who?” But he already knew.

“Tolken. You sounded...” She paused to consider. “You sounded familiar with each other. More than familiar. Friends. No, more like friends turned enemies.”

She continued to amaze him with her insight. “Yes, he was my friend. He was my best friend.”

“Until yesterday?”

He exhaled. “Until I put my hands on you. The friendship ended in that moment.”

“So much sacrificed by so many,” she murmured.

He found the reminder tortuous. “Sleep, Princess. Tomorrow’s a long day.”

“Where are we going?”

“We need to keep moving. But at least you’ll see more of your land.”

She twisted within his arms. “Not my land.”

“Deny it if you will. But you belong to Celestia every bit as much as she belongs to you.”

"And who do you belong to?"

"No one. Nothing. At least, not anymore."

It was a painful truth to face. Though his roots sank deep into the rich Verdonian soil, they didn't run deep enough to survive this. Von Folke would see to it that he paid dearly for his actions. At the very least, he'd be expelled from Verdonia, a pariah to his people. More likely he'd be imprisoned.

"What will you do?" she asked.

"Finish what I started."

"And then?"

"Face the consequences." After all, he had no other choice. Not anymore.

The next day, Merrick made tracks southward toward Glynith, the capital city of Celestia. He had to work hard to maintain a low profile. He was a public figure and easily recognized. But either Alyssa didn't pick up on the deference they offered him or she put it down to his being the commander of the Royal Security Force.

He'd arranged for several safe houses, though the first they headed for wasn't far from the Celestian capital. He'd debated just driving up into the hills and staying at the anonymous cabin he'd rented there. But he preferred a place that offered more avenues of escape while he waited for von Folke's next move.

He soon discovered that the worst part of the abduction wasn't the wait, but the endless nights. How he ever thought he could spend four full months sleeping with Alyssa, wrapped so tightly together that every luscious inch of her body was pressed against every hard-as-tempered-steel inch of him, he didn't know. After just one week exhaustion rode him almost as hard as shameless desire. Not that she noticed.

The instant he crawled into bed with her and tugged her close, she fell into a deep, abandoned sleep, accepting his embrace as though they belonged in each other's arms. It was almost as if they were two parts of a whole, separate and adrift from dawn until dusk, complete only at night, where within the velvety darkness it felt safe to express emotions they kept well hidden in the harshness of daylight.

To his relief, she didn't follow through on her threat to take off the first chance that presented itself, not that he gave her the opportunity. He guarded her every second of every day. But by the end of their eighth day together, Merrick was sick of staring at the four walls of their rooms and twitching from the effort of keeping his hands off Alyssa, neither of which boded well for the endless weeks ahead of them. She must have felt something similar, because when he suggested a short excursion through the capital city, she leaped at the offer, promising the world in exchange for the chance to be outside.

Driving through the busy streets of Glynith, he pointed out key landmarks, including the royal residence. "Not as impressive as the one in Verdon or Avernos," he observed. "But it serves its purpose."

"It's huge," she replied faintly. "It's so strange to think that my mother once lived there."

He regarded her in amusement. "So did you."

"And I had a father and a brother I can't even remember. I wish…" She swiveled in her seat. "Did you know them? What were they like?"

"I never met your father, but he was considered a good man, committed to Celestia and her people. He came from farm stock, like my grandparents, and loved the land."

Bittersweet emotion swept across her expression. "And my brother?"

"Also a good man. I find it hard to believe that he'd have taken money to abdicate. Perhaps von Folke brought other pressures to bear."

"I can't imagine living your entire life in one place." And yet, he heard an intense longing quivering in her voice. How different would her life have been if she'd grown up here? Had put down roots here? Did she ever wonder? "What about Miri? Has there been any news?"

His mouth compressed. "None. Tolk doesn't have her or he'd have said something when he found us."

"But you can't be sure."

"He wouldn't harm Miri." There wasn't a shred of doubt in his mind. "But, the few times I've called home, no one's heard from her."

And the fear and concern were tearing him apart. What had Alyssa said about so much sacrificed by so many? Here was another sacrifice—one laid firmly at his feet. His noble intentions seemed far less noble all of the sudden. He had so many to protect, so much at stake—more than his future, or Alyssa's new job, or even the safety of Miri and Angela Barstow. There was an entire country to consider. And until he found out what secret von Folke concealed and why he'd become so desperate to gain the throne, Merrick had to put the welfare of the country ahead of the few. He'd put out feelers, but so far he hadn't discovered anything pertinent.

Neither of them wanted to return to their rooms after the drive and Merrick decided to take one more risk and allow them a brief walk through one of the commercial sections near their apartment. A local jewelers window held Alyssa's attention the longest, and she returned a second time on their way back to their rental.

"My favorite is this one." Alyssa pointed to a deep purplish-blue amethyst with flashes of brilliant red at its center.

Merrick smiled. "You have excellent taste. That particular stone is called a Verdonia Royal. The color is unique to our country and quite rare, like a Siberian amethyst, only with more blue than red. The most common are these ones," he said and indicated a pinkish-lavender stone. "The Celestia Blush. Outside of Verdonia this color is often called a 'Rose de France' but our name has historic significance, so we tend to use it rather than the other."

"And this ring?" She pointed to the centerpiece of the display. "I love it."

They'd caught the eye of the proprietor who waved them in. Before Merrick could stop her, Alyssa opened the door and entered the shop. Hell. Adjusting his sunglasses, he settled the American-styled ball cap he'd recently acquired lower on his forehead and prayed he looked as much like a tourist as Alyssa. Then, he followed her in.

It was too much to hope that the store owner wouldn't recognize him, but the instant he did, Merrick gave a single shake of his head without alerting Alyssa. The owner, a man named Marston, nodded in silent understanding, clearly willing to cooperate if Merrick wished to remain anonymous. Satisfied, he leaned against a nearby counter and watched the two interact.

"Every once in a while the mines cough up a few of the Royals," Marston explained as he slid the ring on Alyssa's finger. It fit perfectly. "They're highly prized and only used in the best pieces. Like this ring."

"It's beautiful. Is this white gold or platinum?"

"The ring is platinum." He spared Merrick a brief glance and after receiving a nod, rolled into a more fulsome description. "The antique Edwardian setting features a three-carat Royal as its center stone and a blue diamond and Blush on either side, each perfectly balanced, and weighing in at 2.1 carats apiece. The broad gallery is bead set with .44 carats of European cut diamonds. Finished with fully mille-grained edges, the pierced openwork gives this ring an unsurpassed elegance." He blinked up at Alyssa through wire-rimmed glasses. "Would you like to know what the ring says?"

Alyssa lifted an eyebrow. "The ring says something? Tell me. I'd love to know."

"Our finest pieces are always designed to express a particular sentiment. In this case, the Verdonia Royal symbolizes the union of soul mates. Aside from the unique color, that's why it's so highly prized and so rare. It's considered very bad luck to give or accept one if it's not for true love. But this ring also has a diamond and a Blush. The diamond represents many different things, but mainly strength, love, and eternity. As for the Blush, it was used in olden days to seal agreements and contracts." He pointed to the pattern formed by the pierced openwork of the ring. "And then, see this?"

Alyssa examined the banding more closely. "Why does that pattern seem so familiar?"

Merrick took a look and smiled. "Because it's the shape of Celestia. Historically, Celestia has always been the fulcrum between Verdon and Avernos, unifying the two opposing forces into one country."

Alyssa exclaimed in delight. "So, the pattern represents the unification of the three separate stones into one, right?"

Marston nodded. "Very astute. The designer named it Fairytale because that's what the ring is. It's a fairy tale with a happily-ever-after ending all in one. Soul mates united in an unbreakable bond of eternal love. That's what it means."

"It's an incredible piece," Alyssa marveled. "I don't think I've ever seen anything like it."

Marston grimaced. "Unfortunately we haven't been

able to purchase any stones of this caliber for years. Even the Blushes have become rare. The problem has grown worse over the last few months. Rumor has it that the amethyst supply is drying up." He threw Merrick a hopeful look. "Perhaps you could shed some light on the source of the problem? Are the mines played out, as some have suggested? Or is it simply a means to drive the international price up by creating an artificial shortage?"

Merrick shook his head. "I can't answer that. I wish I could. But I can assure you that we're aware of the problem and it's being looked into very carefully."

A small sound came from the doorway between the retail section of the shop and the back room. An older woman stood there, wide-eyed. "Your Highness," she said with a gasp and swept him a deep curtsey. "We're honored to have you in our store."

Alyssa stiffened. "Your Highness?" she repeated sharply.

The woman offered an understanding smile. "I can tell from your accent that you're an American, so perhaps you don't recognize His Highness. This is Prince Merrick."

"No." Alyssa took a swift step backward. "He's commander of Verdonia's Royal Security Force."

The woman nodded. "That's right. The commander is Prince Merrick Montgomery. His older brother, Prince Lander, could very well be our next king." Her gaze flitted back and forth between the two and a hint of uncertainty crept into her voice. "I'm sorry. Have I said something wrong?"

"I believe His Highness is incognito, my dear," Marston explained gently.

Before the woman could do more than stammer out an apology, Alyssa slipped the ring from her finger and carefully returned it to the velvet tray. Then turning on her heel, she darted from the store.

Six

Alyssa flew out of the jewelry shop and down the street that led deeper into the commercial district. Instinct was driving her and she simply acted, determined to get as far away from Merrick as quickly as possible. To lose herself in the twisting jumble of avenues that spidered out in all directions.

She'd been deceived. Merrick had deceived her. The thought echoed the painful tattooing of her heart and pounding beat of her racing footsteps. That woman had called him "Your Highness." She'd said that Merrick was a Montgomery, that he and Prince Lander were brothers. And who just happened to be Prince Brandt von Folke's rival for the throne of Verdonia? Prince Lander.

All Merrick's fine talk about wanting the best for

his country had been nothing but a lie. Everything he'd done had been to benefit his brother. He'd had an ulterior motive for preventing her marriage, right from the start. If she'd gone through with the wedding, Celestia and Avernos would have voted for Prince Brandt and he'd be king. By stopping the ceremony, Merrick's brother still had a shot at the throne. So much for the better good of Verdonia. More like the better good of the Montgomerys.

She kept up a rapid jog, taking turns at random, forced to slow to a brisk walk when she developed a stitch in her side. The breath heaved in and out of her lungs. How could she have been so stupid? She'd seen the respect with which people treated Merrick. Had caught the casual familiarity with which he referred to Prince Brandt. His air of authority. The way von Folke's men had reacted to him. It simply hadn't occurred to her that it was anything more than the appropriate deference offered to the commander of the Royal Security Force. Now that she knew better, she needed to get away.

Ahead of her she saw a uniformed officer. Was he the local authority? If so, perhaps he could help her reach the American embassy. Before she'd taken more than a single step in his direction, a heavy arm encircled her waist, yanking her against a hard, masculine body—a very familiar hard, masculine body. At the same time a hand whipped across her mouth, cutting off her incipient shriek.

"Not a word," Merrick murmured close to her ear.

He pulled her backward into a pitch-black alleyway.

Up ahead the officer paused to speak to someone, and when the man turned his face into the glow from an overhead streetlight, she realized it was Tolken. She stiffened within Merrick's hold.

"I see you recognize our friend." Merrick's voice was a mere whisper of sound. "It appears Tolk's given up tiptoeing and is being a little more aggressive in his search. That tells me it's time for us to find a new hiding place." His grasp tightened. "Pay attention, Princess. When I tell you to move, you move. Nod if you understand and agree."

A tear escaped before she could prevent it, plopping onto the hand he kept locked over her mouth. His reaction to that single drop of moisture was subtle, but confined within such a close embrace, she felt him stiffen and heard the slight hiss of breath escaping his lungs. It sounded like a sigh of regret. No sooner had the thought entered her head than she rejected it. No. That wasn't possible. People as ruthless as Merrick didn't experience regret.

"You haven't responded, Princess. I'd hate to do this the hard way. Now, will you obey me?"

She nodded in agreement, yet even then, his hold didn't slacken. He maneuvered them backward, deeper into the alley. How he could see, she didn't have a clue. But somehow he managed to avoid the obstacles blocking their path. A few yards further on they reached the opposite end of the alley, which opened onto a dimly lit side street.

"I'm going to uncover your mouth. If you make a

single sound, I promise you'll regret it. When I release you, we're going to head back to where I parked the car. We maintain a brisk pace. We walk with purpose, but don't run. Two lovers eager to return home. Clear?"

She nodded again and he removed his hand, ready to silence her again if she so much as breathed wrong. When she simply stood there, he tucked her distinctive hair beneath her blouse and lifted the collar. Sliding his arm from her waist to her shoulders, he tucked her close against him so she was almost concealed from curious eyes and urged her onto the sidewalk. He kept to back streets, emerging close to the jewelry shop. Another block and they reached the parking lot where he'd left the car. The entire way she didn't dare make a sound. But the instant she'd slipped into the passenger seat, she turned on him.

"You lied to me, you bastard. You didn't tell me you were Prince Lander's brother!"

Without a word, he started the engine and thrust the car into gear.

"Don't you have anything to say?" she demanded.

"Not here and not now."

They sped past their apartment without pausing and she twisted in her seat, watching it vanish behind them. "Where...where are we going? Why aren't we returning to the apartment?"

"Too risky. We're moving on. I have another safe house that's not too far from here. We'll spend the night there before heading into the hills."

"But our clothes—"

"Are replaceable. Everything we need I have on me."

She fell silent at that, too upset and emotionally drained to do more than stare out the side window. There was so much she wanted to say in reply, but words failed her. Perhaps it was due to the exhaustion dogging her. More likely it was because she knew if she tried to speak again she'd end up in tears. The drive seemed endless as they darted up and down narrow, winding streets, at times backtracking and circling. After an hour he'd satisfied himself that they weren't being followed and pulled into a drive that lead up a steep embankment. At the crest of the hill stood a large house with an impressive view of the city.

As soon as they were ensconced inside, he walked her through the place, checking windows and doors as he went. Checking escape routes, she supposed. The home was beautifully appointed, far superior to the apartment they'd shared.

"Whose place is this?" she roused herself enough to ask.

"No one I know personally. No one Tolk can trace to me."

"He found us sooner than you expected, didn't he?"

"Yes."

She could tell that fact had him worried and she couldn't decide if the knowledge brought her a certain level of satisfaction, or if she joined him in his concern. They returned to the living area and Merrick crossed to a well-appointed wet bar.

"We need to talk," he announced, pouring drinks.

"What's the point? You lied. End of discussion."

"You deserve an explanation." He handed her a snifter half-filled with amber liquid. "Here. You look like you could use this."

She cupped the glass in her hands and inhaled the rich, nutty scent as she gazed at him across the wide brim of the cut crystal snifter. "Is brandy the official antidote for betrayal?" she asked.

"You'll have to let me know."

She lifted the glass. "In that case…to trust," she said and took a healthy swallow.

"I apologize, Alyssa. I should have told you who I am."

Her mouth curved in a bitter smile. "And who are you, exactly?"

"Exactly who Marston's wife claimed I was. Merrick Montgomery."

"Don't you mean Prince Merrick? Younger brother of Prince Lander, duke of Verdon." She lifted an eyebrow. "Do I have that right?"

"Yes."

"The same Prince Lander who's competing with Prince Brandt for the throne?"

A muscle jerked in his cheek. "Yes," he said again.

"It would seem your antidote isn't working." She swirled the brandy around the balloon of the snifter. "I still feel betrayed."

"I'm sorry."

"I believed you," she whispered. He didn't say

anything and she took another gulp of brandy, choking as the aged wine took a bite out of the back of her throat. "I actually believed you had an altruistic motive for what you were doing. But instead every last action has been to ensure your brother becomes king. What a fool I am. You'd think I'd have learned from my mother's mistakes. Never trust a man, especially one with an agenda."

His anger flashed, hot and potent, causing her to stumble back a step. "Do you think I haven't questioned my own motives?" He tossed back his brandy, as well, though he handled it far better than she had. "That I haven't worried that they might be less than pure?"

She turned her back on him and strode to the French doors that accessed a large balcony. Thrusting them open, she stepped outside. Glynith stretched out far below, the glittering lights of the various buildings turning the city into a virtual fairyland, filling her with a yearning she didn't understand.

She sensed Merrick's approach and spoke without turning around. "You may have questioned your motives, but it sure as hell didn't stop you from abducting me."

"No, it didn't." He dropped his snifter onto a small table at one end of the balcony, the fragile crystal ringing in protest. "Because it all boiled down to one vital consideration. What was best for Verdonia."

"And your brother's the best choice, is that it?"

"No."

She turned her head, startled to discover Merrick standing almost on top of her. She fought to conceal how everything about him affected her. Profoundly. The deep roughness of his voice. His musky scent. Even the size and shape of his hands captivated her on the most basic, primitive level. Her gaze lifted to the sensuous curve of his mouth. His distinctive scar hooked his lip into a half smile. She could still remember how that scar felt beneath her own mouth and she drew a deep breath, forcing herself to ignore everything but getting through the next few moments.

"If your brother isn't the best choice, then why did you abduct me?"

He took the brandy from her hand and set her glass on the table alongside his. "The best choice is whomever the people of Verdonia choose in the upcoming election. But it's their call. Not von Folke's. Not Lander's. Not mine or yours. It's for all of Verdonia to determine. That's what I'm fighting for."

She hated that his words made sense, that they struck a chord that resonated deep within. He stood for a deeply rooted community, for individuals joined together in purpose. It was something she'd longed for all her life. Instead, she'd always hovered on the outside, her nose pressed to the proverbial glass. "And now? What happens next? Do we continue our four-month pilgrimage?"

"That's no longer possible. Trust is a two-way street, Alyssa. Neither of us trusts the other. So, it's time to take more drastic action."

She swallowed, wishing she had more of that brandy. "I'm afraid to ask what that might be."

"I always had a plan B. I just hoped not to have to use

it." His mouth curved in an ironic smile. "We're going to marry."

It took two tries to catch her breath sufficiently to speak. "We're what?"

"Going to get married."

She shook her head. "You've lost your mind."

"Think about it, Alyssa. If I marry you, von Folke can't."

"You've hit on the perfect solution. The perfect way," she marveled, then added furiously, "the perfect way to get my mother killed."

"If we marry, he can't use you as a pawn. You're free. We'll wait a decent interval and then divorce. As for your mother—" he scrubbed a hand across his jaw "—if you marry me, I'll leave immediately afterward to rescue her."

That stopped her. "Are you serious?"

"Dead serious."

"You…you would do that?"

"I would have done it already if I'd believed she were in any real danger." He cocked an eyebrow. "Do we have an agreement? Will you marry me?"

She wished she had time to think it through, to give it more than two seconds' worth of consideration. But she was out of both options and time. She snatched a quick breath and took the plunge. "Yes. I'll marry you."

"Excellent." His satisfaction at her response vied with some other emotion, one she hesitated to put a name to. One that held a frightening element of the personal attached to it. "Then I suggest we seal our bargain."

The words hung between them for an endless moment. The driving thunder of her pulse matched the harsh give and take of his breath. He took a step in her direction, closing the scant few inches separating them. Resolve darkened his eyes and he reached for her, mating their bodies, locking them together in a fit that could only be described as sheer perfection.

There was nothing tentative about his taking, it came lightning fast and deliciously accurate. He knew precisely how to touch her, how to kiss her, how to steal every thought from her head except the burning need for gratification. Desire struck, a sharp, lustful craving that demanded satisfaction. He plundered her mouth, initiating the sweetest of duels.

She surrendered without hesitation. No. Not a surrender. A battle for supremacy. Then not a battle at all, but a giving, one to the other. His tongue tangled with hers, teasing, playing, demanding. His hands followed the length of her spine, his fingers splaying across the curve of her buttocks, fitting her into his palms. He lifted her, pulling her tight against him. She could feel his arousal pressing against her belly and it ignited her own desire, intensifying it. Spurring it to unbearable heights.

She forked her fingers deep into his hair, tilting his head to a more accessible angle. Catching his bottom lip between her teeth, she tugged urgently, before falling into his kiss again. Time and place vanished. All that remained was the harsh sound of breathing, the rustle of clothing, the slide of flesh against flesh. More than anything she wanted him to hike up her skirt and rip through the modest layer of cotton that kept her from him. To drive into her and give her the relief she craved. She'd been alone all her life. Endless, empty days and nights. A life of running from, but never to. She wanted to stop running. To fill that emptiness, fill it in the most basic, carnal way possible. If her mouth hadn't been otherwise occupied, she would have asked for it, demanded it. Begged.

And it was that image—of her pleading to be taken on the balcony of a stranger's home as mindless lust overrode common sense—that acted like a splash of cold water. She shuddered. What the hell was she doing? How could she have been so foolish? Worse, how could she have compromised herself with such ease and so little thought? Had she learned nothing from her mother's example? From Merrick's betrayal? She untangled herself from their embrace, ashamed that she couldn't resist snatching a final, hungry kiss before pushing at his shoulders.

"No more." The words were as much plea as demand. "This is a mistake and I've made enough mistakes in my life without compounding them."

She could see him debate whether or not to push, to take advantage of her momentary weakness. To her relief, he contented himself with feathering a final kiss across her mouth before releasing her. "Consider our bargain sealed."

She moistened her swollen lips with the tip of her tongue. His taste lingered, unsettling her, and she struggled to come up with a way out of the agreement she'd been foolish enough to enter. "About that—"

He lifted an eyebrow, clearly amused. "Going to break your word already?"

She was tempted. Sorely tempted. She'd gotten herself caught in a dangerous situation, one she should have walked away from the minute she'd sensed the trap. But she'd have done anything, agreed to anything, if it meant saving her mother. Now she'd struck a deal with the devil and she didn't doubt for a minute that he'd hold her to it.

"Don't worry, I'll stick. You just make sure you play by the rules from now on."

His grin slashed through the dark. "I'm not here to play by them, Princess. My job is to make them up as we go along."

He'd gotten her with that one and she turned away without another word. She stalked back into the living room, his soft laughter following her, tripping through her, rousing emotions she'd thought were long dead. She wasn't here for romance, she reminded herself. She was here bargaining for her mother's safety. Falling in love wasn't part of the plan. Nor was falling in lust. Regaining control of her life was the end goal and she'd be smart to remember it.

It took her a few minutes to remember where the bedroom was located and once she'd found it, she shut herself inside, praying Merrick would give her time before joining her. Closing her eyes in helpless despair, she leaned against the door and forced herself to admit the truth. She wanted to be swept away by his touch, to drown beneath his kisses. To sink into the powerful surge of his lovemaking before floating on the glorious tide of release that would surely follow. Why? Why did she react to him? Why this man over all the others she'd met in recent years?

She wandered through the darkened room, caught in the restless ebb and flow of her own emotions. Eventually she found herself standing beside the huge bed. Images flashed through her mind. Male and female, naked. Darkness and light, intertwined on a bed of silk. The first tentative strokes. Gentle. Tender. Soft, urgent cries of need. The slow give and take of the mating ritual. A sweet loving.

Loving.

She spun away from the bed. What in the world was wrong with her? No. Not loving. Sex was one thing. Love, something entirely different. She could use one, enjoy it, without being imprisoned by the other. She lowered her head, dragging in air. Damn it! A single crazed kiss and her hormones were all stirred up and desperate for release. What had happened to her self-control? What had happened to her focus and determination?

She had one single goal—to rescue her mother and return home—and she'd do well to remember that.

"What the hell do you think you're doing?"

Merrick winced as he opened the door a little wider to allow his brother, Lander, access to the safe house.

"I don't know what you're talking about." That seemed the smartest response, at least until he had time to find out how much big brother knew.

"I'm talking about the abduction of Princess Alyssa Sutherland."

Damn. Apparently he knew a lot. Too much, in fact. "Who talked?"

"Miri." Lander brushed past him and paced across the living room, as large and aggressive as ever, the embodiment of his nickname—the Lion of Mt. Roche. "She's on the Caribbean island of Mazoné, probably because she knows our mother will wring her neck when she finds out what the pair of you have been up to."

"Thank God she's—" Safe. Merrick bit off the word. Probably not the best thing to say to an overly protective older brother. "I'll deal with Mother."

"Good luck with that." He faced Merrick, his arms folded across his chest. "Now where is the princess? She's going back to Avernos right now, even if I have to take her there myself."

Merrick swore beneath his breath. "She's asleep and she's not going anywhere. In fact, you don't want her going anywhere. If you return Alyssa to von Folke, you'll lose the election."

Lander cut him off with a cutting sweep of his hand. "Then I lose the election."

"Don't interfere," Merrick warned. "Alyssa and I are getting married. End of discussion. When we do, it'll put paid to von Folke's scheme and the election will be based on merit rather than regional loyalty."

Lander appeared skeptical. "I can't believe Princess Alyssa is agreeable to such a drastic solution."

"Trust me. When it comes down to a choice between me and von Folke, she's agreeable."

"You swear she's willing?" Lander pressed. "You're not forcing her the way Brandt was?"

Merrick fought back a wave of indignation. "Hell no, I'm not forcing her. I'm not von Folke." Though he couldn't in all honesty claim she was a hundred percent willing. Amenable, perhaps. If he stretched it. "We reached an agreement. She marries me in exchange for my rescuing her mother."

"Son of a—von Folke again?"

"Yes." Merrick took a step in the direction of the door. "You need to go. I don't want anyone to find out we've been in communication."

Lander speared his fingers through his brown and gold mane of hair and glared with hazel eyes that were more green than gold. "I'm not going to be able to talk you out of this craziness, am I?"

Merrick shook his head. "Not a chance."

"Do you realize all you're sacrificing?" Lander asked urgently. "You don't have to do this. Not for me."

"Yes, I know precisely what I'm sacrificing. And yes, I have to do this. By tomorrow it'll be a done deal." He offered a crooked smile. "Just so you know, I consider it well worth the consequences."

Lander cleared his throat. "Thanks."

Merrick executed a slight bow. "My pleasure and my duty, Your Highness."

"Oh, knock it off," his brother said in embarrassment. "Here, I have something for you." He pulled out a computer CD in a plastic case and handed it over. "You requested a set of blueprints to von Folke's palace. I offered to play courier."

Merrick frowned in concern. "You shouldn't have brought these any more than you should be here. I'm trying to keep you out of this. I want you to have plausible deniability."

"You're kidding yourself if you think that's possible. I could shout deniability from dawn until dusk, and no one would believe it. You're my brother. The assumption will be that I'm in on the abduction and any other actions you take from here on." His face settled into grim lines. "Not that I care. We're not the ones who set this game in motion. Von Folke will have a tough time crying foul play when it's revealed that he's been cheating from the start. Was he really forcing her to marry him? You're certain?"

"Positive. Once Alyssa found out he was holding her mother, she didn't feel she had a choice other than to go through with the ceremony. If I hadn't taken action, they'd be married by now." Merrick gestured toward a small study off the living room. "Come on. There's a computer in there. Let's take a look at what's on the disk."

Lander followed him, leaning against the desk to watch. "I've been going over the situation ever since I found out about von Folke's plan," he said while they waited for the computer to boot up. "I can't figure why he'd pull such a stunt. It's out of character for him."

"I have a feeling it's connected with the amethyst supply drying up. I can't help wondering if something's happened with the mines."

Lander shook his head. "Why would he keep a problem with the mines a secret?"

Merrick considered the various possibilities. "I'm not sure. For political leverage? If it became common knowledge that the mines were tapped out and he hadn't given the country adequate warning, there'd be hell to pay come the election." He slipped the CD into its slot and pulled up the menu. "Okay. Let's see if we can figure the best way for me to get into the palace, nab Alyssa's mother and get out again with our skins intact."

Lander traced his finger along an underground passageway that ran between the interior courtyard of the palace and the chapel. "What about taking this route? You could slip in through the woods near the chapel, take the passageway to the palace and be right on top of them before they knew what hit them."

"Assuming he hasn't blocked it off."

"Hmm. If he has, you'll have to approach from this side." Lander gestured toward the south entrance. "Trickier."

Merrick began jotting down notes, sketching out the bare bones of a plan. "I'll send one of my men in tonight to see which is the most viable choice."

Lander straightened. "So, when's the wedding?"

"What? Oh. Tomorrow."

"We could just...make her disappear for a few months. You don't have to go to the extreme of marrying her."

Merrick tossed aside his pen and stood. "Too risky. She could escape. Von Folke could find her. The variables are endless. Marriage is the only way to make certain he doesn't get his hands on her and finish what he started."

Lander shot his brother a hard look. "Does she know the marriage will have to be consummated in order for it to be legal in Verdonia?"

"It hasn't come up," Merrick answered shortly.

"You're not going to tell her, are you?"

"It won't be an issue."

Lander stared in disbelief. "Are you sleeping with her already?"

Merrick bristled. "That's none of your business."

"I think it is. Damn it! You don't need me to tell you how inappropriate that is. Do you have feelings for this woman? You can't be thinking of turning this into a real marriage."

"Don't be ridiculous," Merrick snapped. "My concern—my only concern—is for Verdonia. Marrying Alyssa is a means to an end, nothing more."

Lander's eyes narrowed. "That had to be the biggest load of crap I've ever heard. You can stand there and tell me you don't care about this woman, but I'm your brother. I know when you're lying, even when it's to yourself."

Anger swept through Merrick, possibly because

Lander's comment hit a little too close to home. "There's more than a relationship at stake. More than even an election. With Alyssa's brother, Erik, abdicating, the principality is in desperate need of its princess. If Alyssa doesn't stay, it means the end of Celestia. I intend to keep that from happening."

"Or maybe you want a justifiable excuse for taking her to bed," Lander suggested dryly.

Merrick didn't have an answer to that. As much as he wanted to deny it, he couldn't. Not totally. Lander was right. In order for their marriage to be considered legal, it had to be consummated. If von Folke suspected there was a loophole somewhere, he could still cause trouble. But the marriage also gave Merrick the excuse he needed to make love to Alyssa. Once they were husband and wife, he wouldn't have any other choice if he wanted the ceremony to be legally binding. Nor would she. Still, he hoped she'd choose to remain in Verdonia and accept her rightful position. Celestia needed her. It wouldn't survive without her.

The real question was…was he making the decision to marry her for the better good of Verdonia? Or was his true motivation something far less honorable?

Seven

The morning of Alyssa's wedding dawned clear and warm, filled with the scent of springtime yielding to summer. The marriage had been planned for early evening when the church would be closed to parishioners and Alyssa couldn't help but remember preparing for a far different ceremony just two short weeks ago. On that occasion she'd been terrified and alone. She'd also feared her bridegroom, been sick with worry about her mother and unsuccessful at discovering a way out of her predicament.

This time she felt far differently, a fact that left her uncertain and confused. She should hate Merrick for twisting her arm to get her to the altar. After all, he was no better than Prince Brandt, right? But no matter how hard she tried to convince herself of that fact, it didn't quite work. Merrick wasn't Brandt and never would be. Although his motives weren't pure, they were noble.

From the moment he'd announced his plan to marry her, events had screamed by at breakneck speed. He'd chosen the venue and had a gown, veil and shoes delivered by one of his men. Even a set of wedding bands had shown up. She didn't bother contesting any of his plans. How could she? It would have been like attempting to derail a runaway train with a toothpick.

As the afternoon deepened, she dressed in the gown he'd selected, a simple three-quarter length ivory silk with a wide, sweeping skirt and fitted bodice. A hip-length mantilla veil looked stunning with it, which she chose to carry, rather than wear and risk damaging on the drive.

The chapel Merrick had chosen was glorious—small, intimate, reverent. The floors were flagstone, worn smooth from years of faithful usage. Stained glass lit the interior with a rainbow of glowing light. The pews and altar were lovingly polished to a high sheen, and the faintest hint of beeswax and lemon complimented the scent of the flowers and candles.

Once again Alyssa was struck with how differently she reacted to everything in comparison to last time. Nervousness gripped her, an excited fluttering deep in the pit of her stomach. Not fear. She remembered that sensation all too clearly. Could it be...anticipation?

She shook her head. No. That wasn't possible. She didn't want to marry Merrick. She'd agreed for one reason and one reason only—to save her mother. She'd made a bargain, one she'd honor no matter what. But it wasn't a bargain she anticipated with any degree of excitement. It couldn't be.

"This is for you." One of the staff members at the church handed Alyssa a hand-tied bridal bouquet, a medley of herbs, ivy and curling sticks and twigs. "It's a traditional bouquet. The herbs are to ward off evil spirits and endow the bride with fertility. The birch twigs are for protection and wisdom, the holly branches represent holiness. And the ivy is to ensure fidelity."

Alyssa ran a finger along the sprigs of lavender. "And this?"

"The national flower. It promises a marriage filled with luck and love."

It was a sweet gesture, if a pointless one. Or so she thought until she joined Merrick in front of the altar. She didn't think she'd ever seen him look more handsome and the sight of him stirred emotions she shouldn't be experiencing. The final glorious rays of sunlight warmed the chapel, filling it with a rainbow of color as soft as a prayer.

Taking both her hands in his, Merrick bent and kissed her. "It'll all work out," he whispered. "I swear it."

His words affected her more deeply than she cared to let on, filling her with a desperate yearning. What would have happened if they'd met under different circumstances? If she'd grown up here and met him as part of her royal duties? Would she have fallen in love with him? Would they have been celebrating a real wedding instead of this charade? Or would they have settled for a brief, intense affair before going their separate ways? The fact that she couldn't answer any of those questions left her nerves jangling.

Afterward, she didn't recall much of the ceremony. From the instant Merrick touched her and their eyes connected, time slowed. She didn't remember looking away, not once, but allowed herself to be held by his fierce golden stare, empowered by it. The one moment that burned itself into her memory was when he repeated his vows, his voice strong and sure, and slipped the wedding ring onto her finger.

She caught her breath at the beauty of the platinum band he'd chosen, a circlet studded with alternating diamonds, Verdonia Royals and Celestia Blushes. Before she could say a word, he bent and took her mouth in an endless kiss. It was in that timeless moment that she realized her feelings for Merrick had undergone a radical change.

And that she was in serious trouble.

Alyssa had no idea what happened immediately after the ceremony. A part of her retreated, stunned by the realization she'd made when Merrick kissed her. She'd allowed feelings for him to slip beneath her guard. She cared about him.

She didn't know when or why it had happened. She didn't even know how it was possible after all they'd been through. She simply felt…harmony. A rightness. A belonging. A wild passion that went deeper than anything she'd ever felt for any other man. She burned with it, bled from it. Was consumed by it. And, ultimately, she turned from it, refusing to deal with the consequences of those emotions.

They returned to the house tucked into the hills overlooking Glynith, where she'd first agreed to marry him. Silence reigned, neither willing—or able?—to speak. She entered the darkened room and stood in the middle of the living area, still dressed in her wedding finery. She removed her veil, meticulously folded it and set it on the back of the couch. And that's when all her doubts came storming back.

"What have we done?" Alyssa murmured.

"You're just wondering that now?"

She spared Merrick a quick glance, alarmed to discover him in the process of stripping off his suit. "What are you doing?"

"Getting comfortable." He tossed his jacket aside and approached. "Would you like help getting out of your wedding gown?"

She took a quick step backward. "And then what?" She couldn't believe she'd asked the question, despite the fact that it been plaguing her for the past hour or more. "I mean—"

"I know what you meant," he replied mildly.

"I'm sorry." He maintained his distance, but he was still too close for comfort. Everything about him overwhelmed her, filled her with a sense of risk. "I guess I'm not handling this well."

His eyes grew watchful. "Then chances are you aren't going to handle this next part any better." A predatory smile edged his mouth. "After we get out of our clothes, I plan to make you my wife in every sense of the word, even if it's for only one night."

Oh God. He'd said it. He'd actually said the words. Part of her trembled with anticipation, the other with apprehension. Apprehension won. "Not a chance."

"I think there's every chance. You want me as much as I want you." He stepped closer. Too close. "We've shared a bed every night for almost two weeks and it's been sheer torture. Do you deny it?"

"We're attracted to each other," she began, but the expression darkening his face had her faltering. "Okay, fine. I want you. Are you satisfied?" Maybe that accounted for the feelings she'd experienced during the ceremony. Simple desire. Not caring. Not an emotional connection. Lust. It was the only possible explanation.

"There's only one way we'll both be satisfied and you damn well know it. Or are you afraid?" His eyes narrowed. "Is that it, Princess? Are you afraid to take the final step, afraid of what will happen if you do?"

Her chin shot up. "Where do you want it? Here? On the table over there, maybe?" She scuffed a toe in the carpet. "This looks soft enough. Maybe you'd prefer it down and dirty."

She'd pushed him too far. She saw the crack in his self-control, watched as it fragmented and splintered. Before she could do more than take a single stumbling step backward, he snatched her high in his arms. "Personally, I prefer the comfort of a bed."

"Merrick, wait—"

"I've waited as long as I intend to. Tonight we finish it."

Without another word, he carried her down the short hallway and into the bedroom. The skirt of her gown flowed over his arm and trailed behind, a fluttering flag of virginal surrender. Striding to the center of the darkened room, he set her down. She took a quick, desperate look around. Even unlit, she could tell the bedroom was extremely masculine—too masculine. She wanted lightness and femininity and romance—a playful fantasy that softened the harsh reality. This…this was pure male. Unbridled male. Sharp and potent and darkly dangerous. Just like Merrick. She spun around, intent on escape and plowed directly into him.

"Shh," he soothed, gathering her close. "Easy."

"I've changed my mind. I can't." She shot an uneasy look in the direction of the bed. "I just can't."

"Let's see if I can help you with that." He caught her left hand in his and ran his thumb across her wedding band. It gleamed in the subdued lighting. "We made promises tonight. Do you remember them?"

"I promised…" Her chin wobbled. "I promised to love. To honor and cherish."

"As did I." His voice deepened, turning to gravel. "Don't you understand? This ring symbolizes the first chapter in a book you've set aside before even beginning. Don't leave it unread. What's happened so far is no more than the prologue. And then what, Princess? Where does the tale go from there?"

Her breathing grew harsh, labored. "Nowhere."

"That's not true and you know it. It can go anywhere you want. We create the story. We determine the direction. We can even start over if you want and rewrite the beginning." He lifted her hand and kissed her ring. "Or we can move in a new direction. Start fresh on a new page. The choice is yours."

"What about your choices?" She laced her fingers with his, turning their locked hands into the moonlight streaming through the windows. His wedding band splintered the gentle glow, shooting off sparks of silver and gold. "What happens to you when this is all over?"

He hesitated for the briefest moment. "My choices are more limited."

"What do you mean?"

"This can only have one ending for me. Von Folke will see to that."

Alyssa's vision blurred. "You mean jail."

"Most likely." He brushed her cheek with his thumb, erasing the tears she hadn't been able to control. A cloud drifted across the moon, casting their rings into shadows. The glitter dimmed, then winked out. A prediction of their future? "Look at me, Alyssa."

She did as he demanded and saw the calm certainty in his gaze. "I'm not afraid to make love to you." The truth came tumbling out. "I'm afraid of what will happen afterward. What it'll do to us. How it'll change us."

"Trust me."

Those two simple words hung between them. And

then the clouds passed and moonbeams once again pierced the dimness, stabbing the room with tines of silver. He stepped back from her into one of the shards, the moon's gilding leeching him of all color. Only the blacks and whites and grays remained, shades of darkness and light, of ambiguity and clarity.

Without a word, he unbuttoned his shirt and shrugged it off his shoulders. It dropped into shadow. Holding her with his gaze, he unzipped his trousers, the metallic sound harsh and grating in the silence of the room. His trousers parted and her mouth went dry. She could barely think above the fierce pounding of her heart. In one fluid motion, he stripped away the last of his clothing before drawing himself to his full height. Totally nude, sculpted by the moonlight, he made for an impressive sight. He stood motionless, allowing her to look her fill.

He had one of the most spectacular physiques she'd ever seen. His shoulders and arms were powerfully masculine, able to bear the heaviest of weights. And yet it struck her that those same arms would also be gentle enough to cradle a helpless infant. The dichotomy moved her more deeply than she thought possible. Her gaze dipped lower, to a chest lightly furred with crisp brown hair just deep enough to sink her fingers into. A narrow line speared downward, like spilled ink, splitting washboard abs on its path to his groin. He was fully aroused, yet made no effort to act on that arousal.

"Why are you doing this?" she whispered.

"So you can see you have nothing to fear." His gaze grew tender. "Whatever you want, it's yours."

"Just tonight." She choked on the words. "It can only be for tonight. You know that, don't you?"

"Then it's just for tonight." He stepped from the light into darkness, finding her where the gloom held her ensnared. "But when tomorrow comes, you may discover that one night isn't enough."

She wanted what he offered, but fear and uncertainty froze her in place. "Tomorrow doesn't belong to us. You've already warned me about that. Von Folke—"

"Will be dealt with. And who knows, perhaps it'll all work out." He planted his feet and spread his arms wide, an oak of a man—strong and sturdy and protective. His heart and soul was rooted deep in the soil of Verdonia, a fact she envied more than she could have believed possible. "Just come with me. Stay with me. Take a chance."

His words sang with endless promise, bewitching her, offering to turn dreams into reality. She gave in to their enchantment. She stepped into his arms and fell from darkness into light.

Alyssa slid her hands across Merrick's chest in a quiet prelude to their mating dance. For the first few minutes they barely touched, just a tentative brush of hands. A whisper of a kiss. Lips joining. Clinging. Parting. Then rejoining. The soft exhalation of desire across heated skin.

This time she was the one wearing too many clothes and she fought to curb her impatience. She didn't want anything separating them, nothing that would prevent them from touching flesh to flesh. And yet, this wasn't an occasion to hurry. She wanted to linger over each and every step, to sear into her memory every moment as it happened.

He found the cloth buttons holding her gown in place, and one by one released them. She lifted her arms, savoring the drag of flesh-warmed silk followed by the cool sweep of air. Her slip came next, skating down her hips to pool at her feet. He dropped to his knees, lifting first one foot free, then the other, leaving her standing in nothing but a bra and thong. Sliding his hands around her thighs, he held her steady as he trailed feather-light kisses from knee to thigh, wandering ever higher until he'd reached the shadowed apex.

His breath was warm through the triangle of silk that concealed her. Hooking his fingers into the elastic band at her hips, he tugged. Her panties drifted downward, seeming to vanish of their own volition. And then he took her, his kiss the most intimate she'd ever received. She threw back her head and dug her fingers into his hair, her throat working frantically.

"Easy, Princess," Merrick murmured against her. "We have all the time in the world."

"Okay. Fine. I just—" She shuddered. "I need to finish getting naked. I need to finish getting naked right now. And then I need you naked on top of me. Or under. I'm not particular."

She felt his smile against her heated flesh. "I can help with that."

All of a sudden she didn't want to savor each moment. She wanted to seize every last one, burn through each second in a swift, glorious blaze. She couldn't handle slow, let alone leisurely. Fast and desperate appealed far more.

"Hurry." He slid his hands from her thighs upward, cupping her, and she practically danced in place. "No, I mean it. Hurry!"

But he didn't hurry. Instead, he parted her with his thumbs and blew ever so gently, a mere whisper of sensation before he kissed her again. And that was all it took. She exploded in his arms, unraveling helplessly. A keening wail built in her throat, trapped there for an endless moment before escaping. She hung, suspended in paradise until finally her knees gave out and she collapsed into his waiting arms.

Merrick swept her up, carried her to the bed and spread her across a velvet-soft bedspread. "Why?" Alyssa demanded.

He didn't pretend to misunderstand. "It gave you pleasure." His hand slid behind her back and released her bra. "And that gave me pleasure."

"In that case, prepare yourself," she warned him as he tossed the scrap of silk outside the oasis of the bed. "Your pleasure quotient is about to go through the roof. I'm going to see to that."

Rising to her knees, she slid her arms around his neck and kissed him, a hard, urgent, open-mouthed kiss. To her amazement, desire flamed again, thrumming through her with stunning urgency. It was as though the past several minutes had never happened, as though this was the first time they'd touched, the first time they'd kissed, the first time they'd shared a moment of intimacy. She pressed closer and wrapped herself around him. It was like sliding into a pool of molten heat.

Merrick groaned. "You're killing me, Princess."

"I don't want to kill you, not unless it's to love you to death."

He tipped her onto her back. "I think I can live with that."

Her quick laugh must have provided him with a beacon to her mouth because he honed in on her parted lips with pinpoint accuracy. Sealing them with his own, he drank her in. First fast and needy, then slow and tender, before haste consumed them in a frantic burst of uncontrollable hunger. He snatched a final swift kiss and began sampling her as though she were a buffet of delicacies spread out for his tasting pleasure. Her shoulders. Her neck. Followed by the painfully sensitive tips of her breasts. He ignored her urgent pleas, feasted there while his hands took over, touching, probing, teasing, wallowing in a banquet of tactile indulgence.

The tension grew within her again. Desperate. Demanding. Frenzied. An explosion building toward a new eruption. She shoved at his shoulders, forcing him to give ground. Stabbing her fingers into his hair, she pulled him back to her mouth, consumed him in one fierce, biting kiss before wriggling her hands between them. She found him, fully aroused, steel wrapped in velvet. Scissoring her legs around him, she pulled him inward. Took him. Absorbed him.

Loved him.

He surged to the very core of her, hard and heavy, almost painfully so. She could feel him trying to hold back, to ease his passage into her body and she arched, her muscles drawn taut.

"Don't stop." The breath burned in and out of her lungs. "Even if it kills me. Even if it kills you. Just don't ever stop."

He moved then, mating their bodies in a primal give and take, stroking to the harmony of their own private song. Fire burst all around them, flames licking at her skin, burning through her blood, gnawing at her bones. She could see the brilliance of it, hear its angry crackle, feel the heat exploding within. A scream built, clawing at her throat. She could sense the release approach, more powerful than anything she'd felt before. It slammed into her, the power of it smashing through every barrier. She flew apart, disintegrating into pieces so small they could never be gathered up again.

From a great distance she heard a voice. The voice of her soul mate. "Alyssa." That single word whispered through the air, barely audible. And yet, it did the impossible.

It brought her home.

Merrick woke to complete darkness, uncertain what had disturbed him. It only took an instant to realize what it was. His arms were empty and his bed cold. He sat up, searching the darkness for Alyssa.

The curtains by the balcony stirred, alerting him to her whereabouts. Tossing aside the tangled sheet, he padded nude across the room. The French door to the balcony stood ajar and he stepped outside into the soft, dewy air. He found Alyssa there, leaning against the railing, the bathrobe she'd wrapped around herself fluttering in the breeze. She gazed out at the city where the full moon dipped low in the sky. Its silvery life's blood flowed across Celestia, a river of light pouring across her homeland.

He knew the instant she became aware of him. Without a word, she untied the robe and allowed it to slip off her shoulders. He came up behind her and slid his arms around her waist, tugging her close. Flesh slid against flesh, warm and vibrant and life-affirming. Alyssa twisted in his arms, grasping his shoulders. Cupping her bottom, he lifted her and in one easy thrust, sheathed himself in her heat. Turning, he braced her against the French door.

Then slowly, ever so slowly, he moved with her to a rhythm only the two of them could hear. She arched in reaction, drawing his hands to her breasts, tilting her head back against the cool glass in silent ecstasy. The moonlight painted her with a loving brush, turning her skin luminescent. She glowed with an unearthly passion, a passion that pierced him to the soul. Consumed him. Threatened to destroy him. They clung to each other, riding to the edge, teetering there, poised on the brink of an endless fall. She gathered him up with moonlit eyes, before leaning in and pressing her lips to his ear.

"You're right," she whispered. "One night's not enough."

And then she exploded in his arms.

Eight

Merrick woke early the next morning. Pre-dawn light eased into the room, gilding his wife in a soft, rosy glow.

His wife.

Just the thought filled him with pure masculine possessiveness. Alyssa was his woman, joined to him in every way possible. When he'd first suggested marriage, it had been with the thought of forming an alliance. A contract. He'd wanted her, he couldn't deny that. But it had been a purely physical want, nothing more. He'd intended for their wedding night to consummate their contract, to close all legal loopholes. Now he wasn't as certain of his motivations.

He closed his eyes. Damn. What was he going to do? Their relationship didn't have a hope in hell of succeeding. Too many factors interfered. Little things such as he lived in Verdonia and she in the States. He'd abducted her and put her mother at risk. Most problematic of all, he was headed for prison, she for a new job in New York City. Not the most promising foundation for a successful marriage.

The early morning light strengthened, a warning that time was passing. As much as he hated the idea, he should leave. He'd made a promise to his wife, a promise to rescue her mother immediately after their marriage, and come hell or high water, he'd honor that promise.

Yet as urgently as he needed to head out, he gave himself a few final minutes to study the sleeping face of his wife. From the first, he'd found her beauty startling. In an aesthetic sense, it was. But in the weeks he'd known her, he'd found her character even more beautiful, giving depth and dimension to the physical.

He leaned over and kissed her, lingering, slipping within. She moaned, her mouth softening, parting, responding even in her sleep. Her eyes flickered opened, reflecting the sunlight, the color deepening to the sultry blue of a warm summer sky.

"Good morning." Dreams still clung to her voice, filling it with a delicious huskiness. "You're awake early."

"Good morning, wife," he greeted her with a slow smile. "Welcome to our first day of married life."

Unable to resist, he lowered his head and kissed her again. Cupping the nape of her neck, he nudged her into a deeper embrace. Her arms encircled him and after a long moment, she pulled back just long enough to look at him. He thought she was going to speak, but instead she slid her fingers into his hair and tugged his head back down to hers. He didn't need any further encouragement. He gave in to her, gave everything. Not that he had any choice. Half measures weren't part of his nature. But he was honor bound, bound to obligations he could no longer postpone.

He swept unruly curls from her face. "It's time for me to leave."

"Leave?" The hint of sleepy passion ebbed from her voice. "Where are we going?"

"To Avernos."

"Avernos?"

He didn't know whether to laugh or groan at her look of utter bewilderment. He wished he could take credit for her having forgotten, that he could believe she'd been so enthralled by their lovemaking that it had driven every other thought from her head. But he knew the more likely cause was exhaustion. He hated to remind her, to put their relationship back onto a business footing, especially after the night of passion they'd shared.

"Your mother, remember?" When she continued to stare blankly, he added, "Our bargain?"

"Our— Oh, good Lord!" A deep blush blossomed across her cheekbones and she shot him a chagrined look. "One kiss and you drive every intelligent thought out of my head," she admitted.

Her embarrassed honesty had him fighting back a grin of sheer masculine delight. She had forgotten and it hadn't been due to exhaustion. At least he could take comfort in that much when he left. "I've made arrangements for you to stay with some of my men. They'll protect you while I'm gone."

It took a second for his words to sink in. The minute they did, she bolted upright in the bed. The sheet dropped to her waist, and she snatched it up again, tucking it beneath her arms.

"You're leaving without me? No way. I'm coming, too."

He shook his head before she'd even gotten the words out. "Too risky. It'll be faster and easier for me to slip in, grab your mother and slip out again on my own."

"She won't go with you unless I'm there," Alyssa argued. "You'll need me to convince her."

How should he phrase this? "I'll convince her the same way I convinced you."

He should have chosen a more diplomatic way of wording his explanation, perhaps something in the nature of a flat-out lie. Rage lit her eyes. "You're going to abduct my mother?" she demanded in disbelief. "You're going to terrorize her the way you did me? That's just great. Brilliant plan, Prince Charming."

He gritted his teeth. "I may not have any other choice."

"You can't do that. She's not like me. She doesn't get angry in scary situations. She'll be terrified."

"Only until I get her clear of the area." Didn't she understand? He'd been trained for this, damn it! He knew what he was doing. "I'll explain everything to her then."

"Please, Merrick. Don't do this. There's only one of you. You're one man against all of Prince Brandt's forces. Against a royally ticked off Tolken, in case you've forgotten. And you'll be abducting a struggling uncooperative woman who will be crying and screaming the entire way. Somehow I don't think that's going to work. Unless, of course, you plan on holding a knife to her throat." Her eyes widened in sudden alarm. "Oh my God. Is that your plan? To use a knife on my mother?"

Hell. Didn't she know him better than that by now? "Of course it isn't. If it'll help satisfy you, I'll arrange to bring a few men with me. But I still can't risk taking you."

"Can't risk…? And just what am I supposed to do when you're captured?" she protested. "Spend the rest of my life hiding out with your men?"

Morning had fully broken and brilliant light flooded through the window, washing over her. It struck her jeweled wedding band and splintered, shooting miniature rainbows of color in every direction. A conflicting combination of pleasure and sorrow surged through him. The ring looked right on her finger, as though it belonged. It was a declaration, a promise, a pledge for the future. His jaw firmed. A future they'd see together, no matter what it took.

She stood, struggling to wrap herself in the length of

soft Egyptian cotton sheet. "It only makes sense to bring me with you," she argued as she worked the knot.

Merrick snagged a pair of jeans from his overnight bag. "Maybe to you. Not to me."

"But we're married." She thrust a tumble of curls from her eyes. "There's nothing Prince Brandt can do anymore. You've stopped him."

"You don't know the man. There's plenty von Folke can—and will—do."

She folded her arms across her chest and the knotted sheet slipped a tantalizing inch. "Then he can and he will, whether I'm with you or not."

"I can't risk that. I can't risk you," he corrected.

"Right back at you, husband."

Husband. She'd called him husband. He approached and grasped the ends of the loosened sheet. With quick, economical movements he retied it. "Lyssa. Princess." He smiled. "Wife. You have to trust me."

"I do. It's just—"

"No, not just. No debate." He cupped her face, forcing her to look at him. "Yes or no. Do you trust me?"

Her mouth quivered. "You have no idea what you're asking."

"I know precisely what I'm asking. And you haven't answered my question." He feathered a kiss across her mouth. "Listen to your heart. What does it tell you?"

The answer he wanted hovered on her lips and glowed in the sudden softening of her eyes. The events of the life she'd shared with her mother had forced her to erect self-protective barriers, to regard others with deep suspicion. To distrust. But now those barriers trembled, their foundation shifting and he knew that he was close to breaching them.

"Merrick—"

His cell phone rang before Alyssa could say anything further. He was tempted to let it ring, to force her to answer his question. But only a limited number of people knew where they were. And they'd been told to contact him only in case of an emergency. He crossed the room and snatched up the receiver. "Montgomery."

"They've found you," his man informed him, a hint of urgency underscoring his words. "Von Folke's man, Tolken. He's on his way to the safe house. Please, Your Highness, you must leave immediately."

"What? What's happened?" Alyssa demanded the instant he cut the connection.

"Tolken. He's on his way here." Merrick grabbed the overnight bag and dumped the contents onto the bed. "Get dressed. Fast."

She didn't waste time talking. Ripping off the sheet, she started throwing on clothes. In less than a minute she was ready to go. Merrick spared precious extra seconds rolling up her wedding gown and stuffing it into the bag.

"What are you doing?" she asked. "We have to hurry."

"We're not leaving your wedding dress."

"Sentiment?"

He spared her a brief look. "Don't get misty-eyed on me. I don't want to leave any evidence behind of our marriage. No point in giving them an edge." At her stricken look, he added. "Okay, so maybe there's a little bit of sentiment involved. Grab your veil and head for the car. I need to clean out the study."

In under five minutes they were on the road and racing away from Glynith. He deliberately headed north toward Avernos, hoping Tolken would expect them to travel south to Verdon since it was Montgomery-controlled.

"What now?" Alyssa asked.

"I'll arrange to rendezvous with one of my men and pick up the equipment I'll need to rescue your mother. He'll take you with him to another safe house. With a bit of luck your mother and I will join you there within twenty-four hours."

"Let me come with you." She spoke urgently and he suspected tears weren't far off. "I can help."

"No, you can't."

A quick glance confirmed the tears—tears she seemed determined to keep from falling. "We're married now, Merrick. If we approach Prince Brandt with that fact, maybe he'll let us take Mom home without any hassle."

"I have no intention of approaching von Folke, let alone confronting him about our marriage. If I had my way we wouldn't come within a hundred miles of the man." He shot her a concerned look. "I'd keep you a solid thousand miles away, if I could."

She managed a smile, though he could tell it took an effort. She fell silent after that and two hours later they reached the rendezvous spot. To his frustration, his man wasn't there. Nor did he answer his cell phone or show up in the three hours they sat and waited. Finally, Merrick started the engine.

"Change of plan, Princess."

"I'm coming with you?"

"You're coming with me."

"What about the supplies you need?"

"I know a place I can get them. But this worries me."

They crossed the border between Celestia and Avernos in the early hours of the morning. Merrick parked near the location of Alyssa's abduction. Once he had the car secured, he reached into the back for the equipment he'd purchased. His wife stood patiently by while he helped her strap on a pair of night vision goggles and instructed her on their operation. Then he led the way through the woods toward the chapel.

On the edge of the woods, he caught Alyssa's arm and drew her to a stop. "I doubt there's anyone around at this hour. But we don't want to take any chances. So, no talking once we leave the woods. We're going in low and careful. I take point. You follow. Agreed?" At her nod, he continued. "There's an underground passageway near the chapel that leads to an interior courtyard. Are you familiar with it?"

"Yes. The private rooms of the palace surround it. They're keeping my mother in one of the courtyard bedrooms."

"Do you know which one?"

She frowned. "I might be able to figure it out once we're there, assuming they haven't moved her. They kept us separated most of the time. I only had the opportunity to see her once. Considering how upset we both were..." She trailed off and bit her lip.

He wrapped his arm around her and pulled her into a swift embrace. "Don't worry. We'll find her." Of course, then they'd have to get away again, backtrack to the car and drive like maniacs for the border. All in a day's work. "Okay, let's go. Once we get to the palace courtyard I'll need you to show me which room is hers."

The first part went more smoothly than he could have hoped. The chapel appeared deserted and they found the door to the passageway without any problem. It was locked, of course, but he didn't detect any sort of alarm system, cameras or motion detectors, which surprised him. The lock proved a minor obstacle. He had it picked and open in less than a minute. The next phase of the operation promised to be trickier.

They emerged on the palace side and he signaled Alyssa to wait while he checked the exit. He still couldn't find any sign of an alarm system and that bothered him more than he cared to admit. Every instinct he possessed warned that their incursion had been too easy. That it was a trap. More than anything, he wanted to turn around and get Alyssa the hell out of here. But he knew, without a single doubt, that the only way she'd leave without her mother was the same way he'd removed her last time—by physical force.

The landscaping of the courtyard offered plenty of

cover. Trees and shrubs abounded. He made a swift reconnaissance of the area, familiarizing himself with the layout. There were two doors that accessed the building and here he finally found an alarm system. He examined it carefully and it only added to his growing suspicion.

Hell. He couldn't see Tolken using something this basic. Not when a pair of wire clippers and a remote device could disarm it. They'd both been trained better than that. He returned to the passageway.

"What's wrong?" she whispered the minute he crouched beside her.

"It's a trap."

"Where? How?"

"The alarm system is too dated. I can punch through it in no time."

"But that's good."

He sighed. "They know we're coming and they're waiting for us. We should leave."

"Not without my mother." And then she played the one card he couldn't trump. "You promised. You gave me your word."

"I did. And I'll keep it. But I want you out of harm's way."

Her mouth tightened. "You mean, you want me to return to the car."

"And leave if I'm not back within thirty minutes."

She shook her head. "Good try, but I'm staying."

"Alyssa—"

"We're wasting time, Merrick. Let's get in there,

grab my mom and get the hell out before we're discovered."

He could feel her anxiety, sense how close to the edge she'd slipped. If they had any hope of succeeding, they needed to act. Now. Catching her hand in his, he lifted it and kissed her ring. It sparkled in the subdued light, a rainbow flash of joy that mirrored his memories of their wedding night. It helped center him, filling him with determination.

"Okay, Princess. Listen up. Once we're in the courtyard, I'm going to give you a moment to get your bearings. There are two doors. One will be to your left, the other directly in front of you. See if you can remember which is closest to the room where they were keeping your mother. Ready?"

At her nod, they exited the passageway and slipped into the deep shadow of an ornamental cherry tree that overhung a koi pond. She scanned the area and then pointed toward the door to their left. As promised, he disabled the alarm in minutes. He went through the door first, ready for anything.

The corridor was empty. Not good. It only heightened his sense of dread. This wasn't going to end well. He knew it with a gut-deep certainty. The worst part was putting Alyssa at risk, which was why he'd deliberately left his weapon behind. At the first sign of trouble, he intended to surrender. In the meantime, he'd let it play out and hope he could negotiate a reasonable resolution if the situation went sour.

She tugged at his arm and pointed to a room farther

down the corridor. He nodded in acknowledgement. Keeping her behind him, he approached the door she'd indicated. Ever so carefully he turned the knob. It held firm. Precious seconds were eaten up as he picked the lock. The deadbolt snicked home and he eased the door open. The room lay in total darkness and yet with his night vision goggles he could see a woman standing rigid in the middle of the room. The only thing she lacked was a sign hung around her neck that read, "cheese."

Before he could stop her, Alyssa brushed past him and darted toward the woman. "Mom!"

He swore. Instantly, the lights flashed on, blinding him. He tore off his goggles, not that it helped. His vision was gone and all he could do was brace himself for the inevitable. They took him down. Hard. They'd left nothing to chance this time. There were a full dozen men who moved with a fluid coordination that warned that their attack had been expertly planned and executed. He didn't fight them. There was no point. They finally dragged him to his feet, not too bruised, his hands cuffed behind him.

Tolken stood beside the two women, both of whom were weeping as they embraced. "This was the second most foolish thing you've ever done, Your Highness," he commented.

"And the first?" As if he didn't know.

"Abducting Princess Alyssa, of course."

Merrick would miss their friendship, could hear the finality of its passing in Tolk's voice. "I'd have to disagree with you there." He attempted a smile, then winced as it tugged at his newly split lip. "That may have been the smartest thing I've ever done."

"You will change your mind after Prince Brandt is through with you."

Merrick's smile faded. "Or he'll change his when I'm done with him."

Tolken escorted Merrick and the two women through the palace. They ended up in a large, richly appointed office. Von Folke sat behind his desk, nursing a drink. He stood as they filed into the room, studying each of them in turn. His attention settled on Alyssa.

"Are you all right, my dear? Montgomery didn't harm you?"

His undisguised warmth surprised her, as did the tenderness underscoring his words. What in the world was going on? "I'm fine, thank you," she replied cautiously.

His gaze shifted to Merrick and all warmth and tenderness vanished. Raw fury gleamed in the inky darkness of his eyes, fury he barely held in check. "You stole my wife, you son of a bitch."

Alyssa shuddered. She'd heard a similar tone used only once before. Ironically, it had come from Merrick when Tolken and his men had burst into their bedroom that first morning at the cottage and one of the guards had dared to put his hands on her.

"I stole your bride," Merrick corrected. "There's a difference."

Brandt lunged before his men could stop him. He grabbed Merrick by the throat and slammed his back against the wall. "She isn't just my bride, you bastard. She's my wife. You dare deny it?"

"Your wife? Hell, yes, I deny it." To Alyssa's relief, Merrick didn't fight back. She suspected if he had, Prince Brandt would have taken him apart, piece by precious piece. "What are you talking about?"

"You snuck into my home in the middle of the night and you took her from me. She was with you when my men found her. In your bed." A primal rage exuded from von Folke. "You may have taken advantage of her since our wedding night but that doesn't change the fact that she's my wife. You put your hands on my woman. And I will see that you burn in hell for that."

Merrick's eyes narrowed. "Yes, I abducted her, but not in the middle of the night." He spoke slow and clear, a hint of cold arrogance bleeding into his words. "And FYI... She's not your wife."

Brandt's hand fisted and for a split second Alyssa was certain he intended to use it to pound Merrick's face. Gathering himself, he released Merrick and took a step back, the breath heaving in and out of his lungs. His fight for control was impressive to watch. Bit by bit he regained command of himself, banking the fierce anger that held him in its grip in order to consider the situation logically.

"I've never before known you to flat-out lie, Merrick," he said after several endless minutes had passed. "In consideration of our former association and out of respect for the faithfulness with which you have served our country, I'll give you a single opportunity to justify your actions. After that, I promise you, life will become very painful."

In response, Merrick pulled himself up into a military stance, wincing as he did so. "First, you didn't marry Alyssa Sutherland. I can't be any clearer than that. As for justifying my actions, you know damn well why I took her from you." His voice held undisguised condemnation. "The people of Verdonia deserve a fair election, not one orchestrated by you. I was honor bound to stop you, and I did. End of story."

"I have no intention of debating politics with you. That can wait for a more opportune time. At this point, all that matters is the harm you've brought to my wife and the lies you're telling about her." Brandt stalked across the room and took a stance at Alyssa's side. "I married this woman two weeks and one day ago. Bishop Varney performed the ceremony. Afterward, she retired to her room where she remained…attended to the entire time."

"You mean, under guard?"

The taunt sent dark color sweeping across Brandt's cheekbones. "I was with her that night. I should know who I married." He laced Alyssa's hand in his. "She even wears my ring."

She lifted the hand he held for everyone to see. Her amethyst and diamond studded wedding band glittered in the subdued light. "You're mistaken, Prince Brandt."

He gripped her fingers, staring in disbelief. "What

have you done with the wedding ring I gave you?" he demanded.

"You never gave me one."

"Explain!"

"Merrick's right. I never made it to the ceremony. He abducted— I mean, I escaped with him before the wedding took place."

"That's not possible." Brandt said the words automatically, but they lacked his former heat. "You were there. At the ceremony. We said our vows."

She shook her head. "I wasn't. I never married you."

"The earrings. The tracking device." He struggled as though finding his footing on shifting sand. "That's how we located you after Montgomery's abduction later that night."

"You gave me those earrings before we married," she reminded him. "Think back. Did you see them on at any other point? During the ceremony? Afterward? When we were together on our wedding night?"

He shook his head, his mouth compressing. "How do I know you aren't lying?"

"I have no way of proving what I say, if that's what you mean. But I assure you, I'm not lying. I've only ever married one man and it wasn't you."

"Who?" His infuriated gaze shifted. "Montgomery? You married him?"

Merrick took the opportunity to shrug off the guards restraining him. "Yes, she married me. Now take your damn hands off my wife!"

Brandt stilled, his expression icing over. "Everyone out." He signaled to the guards. "Escort Mrs. Barstow to her room. Princess Alyssa will remain behind."

"No!" Angela cried. "I want to be with my daughter."

Brandt dropped a hand to her shoulder and gave it a gentle squeeze. "It's only for a short time." To Alyssa's surprise, the prince's manner had softened perceptively. "Please don't worry. This will all end very soon and then you may return home."

"Do you promise?"

He inclined his head. "I promise." He glanced at Tolken. "You and Prince Merrick stay, as well."

They waited while Alyssa's mother and the guards exited the room. The door clicked loudly in the sudden silence. "Hold him," Brandt ordered Tolken, indicating Merrick.

As soon as Merrick was secured, he turned to Alyssa. "Allow me to apologize in advance, Princess. But I need to verify your claim."

Her alarmed gaze slammed into Merrick's. "How?"

Brandt gestured toward her jeans. "Unzip them."

Merrick's howl of fury raised the hair on the back of her neck. He fought Tolken, fought with a wild recklessness that terrified her. It took all Tolken's strength to restrain him. If it hadn't been for the cuffs, he wouldn't have succeeded.

"Stop!" Alyssa cried. "Merrick, don't. It's not worth it."

His eyes were crazed, the gold burning so bright it hurt to look at them. "I swear to God, von Folke, if you touch her, I'll kill you."

"He's not going to touch me. I won't let him." She ripped at the snap of her jeans and yanked down the zipper. She glared at Prince Brandt. "There, I've done it. Now, what do you want?"

He stood in front of her, blocking her from the view of the other two men. "Show me your left hip. The woman I married had a tattoo there."

She did as he requested, tugging the denim along her side down an uncomfortable few inches. An embarrassed flush stained her cheeks. "Satisfied?"

"The other hip, if you will." As soon as she'd complied, he stepped back, thinking hard. "There are such things as temporary tattoos, are there not?"

"Yes," Alyssa acknowledged, refastening her jeans.

"Then there's no way to be certain yours wasn't temporary, unless..." He faced her with stony resolve. "Again I must apologize, Alyssa. If there were any other way, I'd take it."

"What are you going to do?" she asked warily.

A slight smile softened the harshness of his features. "Make your husband—assuming he is your husband—extremely angry."

Her chin shot up. "And me, as well, I suspect."

He inclined his head. "And you, as well."

He didn't give her time to retreat. Cupping her face between his hands, he bent down and, with Merrick's curses ringing in their ears, he kissed her. He took his timc, tracing her lips with his, first gently and then with a hint of passion. She stood, enduring it, praying all the while that Tolken was a hell of a lot stronger than Merrick.

After an endless moment, Brandt straightened and took a step back. Then he turned and faced Merrick. "It would appear your wife is telling the truth. She's not the woman I married." His attention shifted to Tolken. "Your men have some explaining to do."

"Yes, Your Highness. I'll get the facts as soon as we're done here."

"Give me a timeline, Montgomery," Brandt ordered. "When, where, how."

"Very well." Merrick shrugged free of Tolken's grasp. "May twentieth, thirteen-thirty. I infiltrated the woods behind the chapel garden. Your bride and one of her guards moved from the courtyard into the garden. I disabled him and—" A hard, fierce smile tugging at the scar on the side of his mouth. His anger had subsided, though not by much. She could still hear the remnants of it, undermining the tattered scraps of his self-control. "And liberated your bride-to-be."

"I cooperated fully," Alyssa insisted.

Brandt held up his hand. "Good try. But considering your mother was my…guest, I doubt you'd have willingly left without her."

"Merrick insisted you wouldn't harm her."

"Did he?" The question held a trace of amusement. "And you believed him?"

"Yes."

"Admirable." He gestured to Merrick. "Continue. You forgot to mention the men you had with you."

"I operated on my own."

"A lie, but an understandable one, given the circumstances." He addressed Tolken, not bothering to conceal his intense displeasure. "Clearly, one of your men neglected to report this. You'll find out who and deal with it."

"I used a modified tranquilizer dart," Merrick offered. "The subject is only rendered unconscious for a short time. He could have believed he'd fainted or blacked out for some reason, and since your bride was still present and safe when he came to, he was too embarrassed to report it. Regardless, I drove Alyssa to the safe house where your men found us the next morning."

"At which point you—how did you refer to it before? Ah, yes. You liberated my helicopter and flew to Celestia."

Merrick inclined his head. "We appreciated the loan."

Alyssa stifled a groan. "For God's sake, do you have to go out of your way to provoke him?"

"When did the two of you marry?" Brandt asked.

"Two days ago."

"I assume you can prove the legality of it?"

"I can."

"In that case, I only have one final question."

Merrick bared his teeth in a mock grin. "Always happy to help."

"Just out of curiosity…" Brandt strolled closer, the expression in his eyes causing Alyssa to shudder. "Whom did I marry?"

Nine

Merrick shrugged. "Some woman I picked up. I don't remember her name."

"Try."

He pretended to consider. "Sorry, doesn't come to me."

"Perhaps time in a jail cell will assist your memory."

Merrick planted his feet as though in preparation for a blow. "Don't count on it."

Brandt stopped in front of him. "I married this woman you 'picked up' believing her to be Alyssa. I took her to my bed and made love to her." He lifted an eyebrow. "You react to that. Interesting. So, you do know her. And for some reason you don't care for the fact that we were intimate. I'd suspect she were a former lover of yours, except for one small detail."

"What's that?" Merrick asked through gritted teeth.

"My mysterious bride was a virgin."

Merrick's fury burst through his self-control. "How dare you put your hands on her. You had no right!"

"I had every right. She's my wife." He leaned forward, speaking in a low, intense voice. "Do you think I took her by force? If so, think again. Now tell me who she is and why you're protecting her."

Merrick gathered himself. "It's my job. I got her into this situation. It's my responsibility to ensure that no harm comes to her."

"Then you shouldn't have put her in harm's way." Brandt stepped back and signaled Tolken. "Take Prince Merrick and his wife to the Amethyst Suite. And Tolken?" His black eyes held a warning. "Make sure it's secured. No more surprises."

Merrick paused by the door, determined to have the last word. "She left you, Brandt." He tossed the comment over his shoulder. "Your wife could have stayed. But she didn't. You might want to think about that."

Apparently, he wasn't to have the last word, after all. "And you might want to wish your own bride a fond farewell," Brandt shot back. "Because I intend to make certain that this is the last night you spend with her for a very long time to come."

Alyssa and Merrick were escorted to their room. As

soon as the door locked behind them, she walked into her husband's arms. "This is all my fault."

"No," he corrected. "It's von Folke's."

"You warned me it was a trap. I should have listened to you."

"Okay, that's true."

She shook her head in disbelief. "Amazing. Here we are, captured, locked in a room, the threat of jail hanging over your head. How can you make light of it?"

"What would you rather I do?"

"Hold me." He tightened his arms around her, willing to do whatever necessary to ease her mind. "You were right about one thing."

"I'm right about most things," he informed her with impressive modesty. "Which one did you have in mind?"

"Did you see how Prince Brandt treated my mother? He was so...gentle with her. So careful. She usually has that affect on people, but even so I suspect he'd never have hurt her. You told me he wouldn't, but I didn't believe you."

"You couldn't take the risk. I understand that."

"I'm so sorry, Merrick." Her arms encircled his neck. "I can't bear the thought that you'll be condemned to prison because of me. What are we going to do?"

"Give von Folke time to come to terms with what's happened." He released his breath in a long sigh. "Which will give me time to come to terms with it, as well."

"That won't be easy." She hesitated, lowering her voice to a soft murmur. "What about Miri?"

"We keep silent about her. Do you hear me, Alyssa? Not a single word to von Folke."

She frowned. "You're not going to tell him who he married?"

Was she kidding? "Not a chance. I don't want him anywhere near my sister any more than I want him near my wife."

Alyssa hesitated, and he could tell she was picking her way through their conversation. "She stayed with him, Merrick. If Prince Brandt is telling the truth, she chose to sleep with him. Did you tell her to do that?"

He jerked back as though she'd struck him. "Hell, no! How could you even suggest such a thing?"

"I didn't think you had," she hastened to placate. "But the point is, it happened. She wouldn't have slept with him just to give us more of a head start, would she?"

"No."

Her hands dropped to his shoulders, massaging the clenched muscles. "Is that a 'No, I hope not because I can't handle the guilt if she did' or 'No, it's not in her nature to ever do such a thing'? I hate to ask the question, but does Miri have as strong a sense of duty as you? Would she have slept with Prince Brandt for king and country?"

He swore, long and virulently. "Yes, she has a strong sense of duty. No, I hope to God she wouldn't do anything as foolish as to sleep with von Folke in order to give us extra time to get away, or even worse, out of obligation."

He didn't dare consider the possibility that there

might be another reason, not when he was holding on to his temper by a thread. Still, he couldn't help remembering the conversation he and Alyssa had the night he'd abducted her—the one where they'd discussed the possibility that there'd been a personal aspect to Miri's insistence on participating in the abduction.

"So, what now?" Alyssa asked.

"Now we do as von Folke suggested. We make the most of the time we have left together."

"Don't say that," she protested in alarm. "You're not going to prison, not if I have anything to say about it. I'll deny I was abducted. They can't prove I didn't go with you willingly."

"This isn't the United States." He tried to break it to her gently. "Despite the fact that you're Princess Alyssa, duchess of Celestia, von Folke governs this part of Verdonia. His word is law. He can throw me in prison, if that's what he chooses and there's little anyone can do about it. My best guess is he'll leave me to rot in jail for a while before banishing me."

"But just from Avernos, right? Surely, he can't banish you from the entire country?"

"He can—and will—if he takes the throne."

"No! I won't allow that to happen."

He regarded her with regret. "You won't be able to stop it." He brushed a kiss across her brow. "Since we can't predict what tomorrow will bring, there's no point in worrying about it now. We still have tonight. Let's not waste our few remaining hours."

Tears filled her eyes. "What if I want more than just one night?"

"Our relationship was never meant to be permanent. That was our agreement, remember?" He tilted his head to one side, hoping against hope. "Or has that changed?"

"And…and if it has?" Her chin shot up and a hint of defiance gleamed in her eyes. "What if I said I wanted more than a temporary relationship?"

He had to hear the words. "How much more?"

She took a deep breath and he could feel her square her shoulders. "What if I said I wanted our marriage to be a real one? What would you say then?"

He hardened himself against her pleading gaze. "I'd say that wasn't enough. I want more from my wife, from the woman I commit to spend the rest of my life with."

A tremor rippled through her. "Then…what if I said I loved you? What if I told you that I love you more than I thought it possible to love another person?"

He closed his eyes, wanting to shout in triumph. "Are you asking? Or are you saying the words?"

"I love you, Merrick." No hesitation this time. No doubt. No ambiguity. Just a hint of wonder and a infinite quantity of joy.

"That's all I need to hear." He cupped her face. "I love you, too, Princess. You are my beginning, my middle and my end. More than anything, I want to spend the rest of my life with you."

Dragging his head down to hers, she took his mouth

in an urgent, hungry kiss, one that devastated the senses. Her hands caught at his T-shirt, shoving it up and out of her way until she hit hot, bare skin.

Her desperation poured over him in waves, her need ripe and edgy. Demanding a response. Teetering out of control. She so clearly wanted to lose herself in him. He followed her lead, taking his mouth off hers only long enough to yank her thin cotton shirt over her head and toss it aside.

She was beautifully naked underneath, her breasts milky white and topped with sweet raspberry buds that begged to be tasted. He took a quick biting sample and she went rigid in his arms. A thin, keening wail caught in her throat and she vibrated with a frenzied yearning that nearly proved his undoing. He slid his hands along endlessly bared skin to the snap of her jeans, ripping it open.

"I've never wanted a man the way I want you." She swept a hand down his chest until her hand hovered at the heavy bulge beneath his belt buckle. "I can't seem to help myself. I can't seem to get enough. I want more."

"No problem." It took every ounce of self-possession not to grind himself against her hand. He settled for leaning more fully into her, mating them as completely as possible without immediate access to a bed, far fewer clothes and the time and energy to indulge in every hot and sweaty fantasy the two of them could invent. "For you, I have a limitless supply."

"No." Her head moved restlessly back and forth.

"This isn't just about sex. That wouldn't be enough for me."

"Really? I thought it was pretty good, myself."

She fixed her gaze on him, her eyes huge and dilated. "Sex…that's for anyone, anywhere. That's easy. I've never been willing to accept easy. I've always wanted more."

He stilled, understanding what she was trying to say. "But you've been too afraid to grab more, haven't you, Princess?"

She trembled with the effort to speak, to trust him enough to open her heart. "I've spent a lifetime running. My mother taught me that lesson well." Her throat worked for an endless moment, and when the words came they were heavy with pain. "I'm afraid to stop."

"Then pause. Just for one night." He soothed her with a kiss, eased her heartache the only way he knew how. "Savor the moment. You can always run tomorrow."

"You don't understand, because you've always had it. A home. Roots. Security." She leaned into him and closed her eyes, almost chanting the words. "I don't belong. I've never belonged."

"Is it that you don't belong, or have you turned away from the one thing you want most of all because you were too afraid to take a risk?" He pushed ever so gently. "Tell me which it is."

Tears squeezed from beneath her tightly closed lids. "I'm afraid," she whispered. "I want to belong. But I can't risk it. So, I tell myself I can't have it. That I don't even want it."

The answer was so simple. Didn't she see? "It's already yours, my love. You do belong. You belong with me. Now and forever."

He speared his fingers into her hair and lifted her face to his. Her beautiful, tragic face. He kissed away the pain etched alongside her mouth, across her eyebrows, nuzzling the muscle-tense juncture of neck and shoulder, before briefly sampling the raspberries and cream. He trailed his hands up her exposed arms to her shoulders, watching her shiver. Watching her nipples peak with desire while her gold-tipped lashes fluttered open once again. Her skin felt like silk, the sheen from her desire tinting it with the barest hint of sultry rose.

His touch sparked an immediate response. With a sigh of relief she opened to him, gave herself without question or hesitation. And he took what she so unstintingly offered. He lowered his head and captured her mouth once again. Her lips parted beneath his in helpless invitation and she softened against him. It was such a gentle taking, the way he slipped between her lips, the sweep and swirl of his tongue a blatant imitation of a more physical joining. It told her how it could be, if she would just let down her guard and open to him. She responded, tentatively at first, and then with growing ardor.

Instantly, the gentleness shifted and became more passionate. Fierce. Raw. Their desire spinning out of control. Without breaking contact with her mouth, he cupped her bottom and lifted. Her legs parted of their own accord, wrapping around him, allowing him to settle in the warm juncture of her jean-clad thighs. His clothes were a delicious abrasion, the friction of his slow undulations driving her toward the brink. She rocked in tempo with him for an endless minute of pure delicious lust before freezing.

"Please." She tightened her hold, preventing him from moving, while she dragged air into her lungs. "I'm going to lose it."

He brushed his fingertips across her beaded nipples, edging her closer still. "I hope to heaven this suite has a bedroom."

She swallowed, fighting for control, teetering so close to oblivion that he knew the least little movement would send her over. "Find it. Fast. Or it'll be too late."

"It's already too late. We'll do it here and now."

His mouth crushed hers, practically swallowing her whole, as he tipped her onto the floor. Hands got in the way, his as he tackled her jeans, hers as she tackled his. Clothes ripped loose, discarded with blistering haste. The urgency built, pounding at them, firing their blood, reducing them to the most basic, primal essence. Through the roar in his ears he heard her whimper, the breathless plea, the blatant demand. Or maybe they came from him.

The scent of her filled his lungs, the sweet, hot musky odor that was so uniquely hers. It roused him to a fever pitch, proving to him yet again that in this regard, nature forever dominated intellect. He found her ready for him, burning wet, and he filled her, driving into her, sending her up and over. She crashed down, brutally hard, only to scream upward once again as he rode the pain and pleasure.

It had never been like this. Never. "More. More. More!" The words were ripped from him. A desperate mantra that beat out the pace. The music sang through them both, soaring to a final endless note before dying to silence.

The breath shuddered from her lungs and she stared at him, dazed. "That was…that was—" She trembled. "I haven't a clue what that was. But you better be able to play it again."

"Oh, yeah." Maybe. If he lived that long.

Eventually they found the bed and fell into it, exhausted. She clung to him and he read the silent message. She was terrified that any minute now Tolken and his men would come to the door and drag him away. He could only reassure her with his touch. He held her, stroked her, soothed her. The light fragmented off his wedding band, catching her eye and her arms tightened around him in response.

"You're my husband." She said the words, fiercely, laying claim.

"For as long as you choose."

Her fingers traced his features, a delicate exploration before feathering into his hair. "He'll come for you soon."

His shoulders lifted. "We have a little longer."

"I don't think I can handle it when they take you." The admission came hard. "I want you in my life. More than that, I need you."

"I can give you what you need. No question." He said it with absolute assurance.

She smiled, her mouth trembling from laughter to tears. "You don't know what I need or want. You might think you do. But you don't."

The tenor had grown serious and he rolled onto his side to face her. "Then tell me," he urged. "Tell me so I'll know."

She met his gaze and he read the temptation hovering there along with the reluctance. "If you were smart," she whispered, "you'd let me go. I'm not the type to stick around."

"I can't. I won't." He felt the brief yielding of her body and pressed home his advantage. "You say you love me, that you want to be with me. You have a home in Celestia. You have people who love you and need you there. So, stay." To his frustration, he instantly realized he'd miscalculated, a rare misstep.

She stiffened within his arms, wariness creeping into her gaze. "Is this how you negotiate? Use whatever advantage will get you what you want?"

"Yes." He couldn't help smiling. "Though if it makes you feel any better, I only use my sexual advantage on you."

Exhaling roughly, she flopped onto her back. "Of course. After all, it's worked like a charm up until now, hasn't it?" She scrubbed the heels of her hands across her face as though waking from a deep sleep. "What am I thinking? I'm not the type who stays. I can't believe I'm even considering the possibility."

He couldn't resist a final caress, one that left her shivering in reaction. "What did she do to you, Alyssa?"

She didn't pretend confusion, he gave her credit for that much. "It's not my mother's fault. Not totally. I could have chosen a different path instead of following in her footsteps."

"Explain it to me."

"You haven't noticed her hands, have you?" She shook her head before he could answer. "No, you wouldn't have. There hasn't really been an opportunity for you to."

Merrick frowned, picturing Angela during that brief time they'd been in the room together. He'd observed her, of course, and had automatically filed away a quick, detailed image in his mind. An occupational hazard. She'd been slight of build and fair like Alyssa. Paler. Fragile. Eyes the same slice-of-heaven blue. But her features were sharper. Drawn. She'd stood perfectly still, arms at her sides, as though reluctant to draw attention to herself. But he couldn't recall anything specific about her hands.

"No, I didn't notice," he admitted. "What about them?"

"They were broken as a child. Deliberately. Finger by finger."

"Oh God."

"The details aren't important. Let's just say that whatever type of abuse you can imagine happening to her probably did."

Anger filled him, an impotent rage over the helplessness of children trapped in the keeping of deviant, amoral adults. "Was she removed from her parents' custody?"

"Yes. Foster homes followed. A series of them. I don't think she was abused there. At least, she's never hinted at it. She just wasn't helped. When she turned sixteen, she took off."

He closed his eyes. "And so the running began."

"Exactly. She's spent most of her life looking for love and never finding it, always hoping she'd discover salvation around the next corner." Alyssa's mouth twisted. "Or with the next man. Most of her husbands have been older. Substitute father figures, if I had to guess."

It fit. "Like Prince Frederick."

"He was a father figure?" He'd surprised her. "Older than Mom?"

"Twenty, twenty-five years older."

Her brow wrinkled. "I guess my brother must be older, too."

"Forty-five, at least."

"I didn't realize." She released a gusty breath. "So, the pattern was set, even then."

"Apparently." He took a moment to digest everything she'd told him before asking his next question. "Okay, I understand your mother and what motivates her. But how do you fit into all this?"

"I love her," Alyssa stated simply. "I've been the one constant in her life. We've been on the run from the minute I was born, with brief layovers along the way. A couple of cockeyed optimists searching for the pot of gold at the end of the rainbow. At least, that's how she always described it to me."

"So, it's all about honor and duty with you, too. Not to mention protecting those you love." Judging by her stunned expression that had never occurred to her before. "And now? Where do you go from here?"

"I'm so tired, Merrick." Her voice dropped, filled with a yearning that tore at his heart. "I'd like to stop, maybe stay somewhere awhile. Let that rainbow find me for a change."

He brushed a tumble of curls from her eyes. "Maybe stay longer than a while?" he asked tenderly. "How does forever-after sound?"

"That might have been a possibility, if it weren't for one small problem." She smiled, a wobbly effort too painful for words. "The one person I'd have been willing to stay for won't be here, not if Prince Brandt throws you in jail. Now, how's that for irony?"

"Then maybe I can give you something to remember me by."

He left her arms long enough to find his trousers and remove a small velvet pouch from the pocket. He dumped out the contents and returned to the bed, gathering her close once again. Taking her hand in his, he slipped a ring on her finger.

"This is for you," he told her.

The subdued light flashed off Fairytale, the ring she'd admired at the Marston's shop. A ring that symbolized soul mates united in an unbreakable bond of eternal love. With a small exclamation of disbelief, she turned in his arms and clung to him. "How? When? Why?"

A slow smile lit his face. "Why? Because it was meant for you and only you. The how and when were a little trickier. But I found a way." His smile faded. "I'd planned to choose the perfect time to give this to you, but I'm not sure there's going to be one."

She gathered his face in her hands and kissed him. "Then we'll make this the perfect time. Here and now."

And as one by one their final minutes together ticked away, she made those moments more perfect than any that had come before.

Prince Brandt sent for Alyssa early the next morning. She was escorted once again to his office. She didn't know quite what to expect, though she could guess what he wanted.

"Please. Sit." He held her chair with an inborn graciousness. "We need to talk."

"About what?"

"First, I wish to apologize to you. I pulled you into a situation not of your making or of your concern. It was wrong of me."

"You tried to force me to marry you," she replied bluntly. "And you used my mother in order to ensure my agreement. That wasn't just wrong. It was outrageous."

"There were reasons. Valid reasons." He said it without remorse.

Anger swept through her. “Because you want to be king? You consider that a valid reason?”

He started to reply, then hesitated. “I can’t go into it at this point. Perhaps someday in the future.” He regarded her in silence for a moment and then spoke with surprising frankness. “You were a pawn, Alyssa, a pawn I chose to use without taking into account how it would affect your life.”

“You mean without caring.”

He inclined his head. “Without caring.” This time he did show a hint of regret. “If there had been any other way, I would have taken it. But there wasn’t. There still isn’t.”

“You can’t really intend to throw Merrick in prison,” she said, hoping to take advantage of his momentary change in disposition. “You abducted me, remember? If anything, his could be considered a rescue mission.”

Brandt shrugged that off. “My principality, my rules. His prison sentence stands.”

“So, what now?” She struggled to keep her distress from showing. “Is this the point where you threaten me if I don’t tell you who you married?”

“I was thinking more in the nature of a bribe.” He cocked a sooty eyebrow. “Would that work any better? You and your mother on the next plane to New York, Merrick at your side? Any interest?”

“I’ll pass, thanks.”

He sighed. “Don’t tell me Montgomery has brainwashed you with his notion of honor and duty.”

She tilted her head to one side. “You know, a few

hours ago you might have scored with that one. But my husband pointed out an interesting fact to me. I do believe in honor and duty, in protecting the ones I love. Otherwise I wouldn't be sitting here right now, intent on saving my mother and my husband." She smiled coldly. "So, no. He didn't brainwash me. I was pretty much there already."

"Honor and duty? Really?" He looked mildly intrigued. "Are you serious?"

"Dead serious."

"Let me guess." Laughter gathered in his eyes. "You plan on saving Verdonia from the evil prince."

"Hey, if the royal shoe fits."

"And you plan to swear on your honor that Montgomery didn't abduct you."

"Absolutely."

"You cooperated with him."

"All the way."

"In order to avoid marrying me."

"Can you blame me?"

"So when the opportunity presented itself, you ran off with Montgomery."

"I did."

"And let Miri take your place."

"Yes. No. No!" She stumbled to a halt, staring at him in barely controlled panic. She debated backtracking, saying something—anything—to cover up her mistake. But she could see it was far too late. He'd bluffed; she'd fallen for it. She closed her eyes, guilt overwhelming her, and spoke through numb lips. "How did you know?"

"I was pretty much there already," he replied, tossing her own words back at her. "But I appreciate the confirmation. Now, one final question. Where is she?"

"I don't know." She opened her eyes, blinking against tears. "That's the truth."

"Yes. I can see it is. You don't lie very well, Ms. Sutherland."

"You say that like it's a bad thing."

"In my position, it can be. You'll see what I mean in a minute." He picked up the phone and punched a button. "Bring them."

She regarded him with undisguised bitterness. "You'll never know how delighted I am that we never married."

"You may find this hard to believe, but so am I, despite the agenda that made our alliance so critical."

He leaned across his desk toward her. She found his features too austere for her taste, though she couldn't deny they were compelling. And when he smiled with gentle warmth, as he did now, he was downright stunning.

"Don't take it too badly. Despite your husband's ridiculously protective nature, there are few women he'd feel the need to defend with quite such passion and ferocity. His mother. His wife." Something shifted within his gaze, an emotion that he swiftly banked. "His sister. It only required calm logic to reach the appropriate conclusion." He gave a harsh, self-deprecating laugh. "Though I'm forced to admit it took me most of the night to manage calm, let alone logic."

"And why is that, Prince Brandt?"

"Because of Miri," he surprised her by admitting. "And then, once the obvious occurred to me, I needed someone to confirm my guess about her."

Alyssa flinched. What he meant was someone foolish enough to confirm his guess. Before she could snarl a response, Tolken entered the room, followed by Merrick and her mother, as well as a handful of guards.

Prince Brandt stood. "You'll all be pleased to know that Alyssa and I have reached an accord." He gave Alyssa a courtly bow. "Thank-you, Princess, for your assistance identifying Miri as my wife. The three of you will be driven immediately to the airport where I've arranged for first-class seats from Verdonia to JFK."

Merrick, whirled to face her, took one look at the guilt she was certain was written all over her face and charged toward her. He was stymied by the timely intervention of the guards. "What the hell did you do?" he demanded, frantically struggling against his captors. "You told him, didn't you? Why, Alyssa? Why would you do such a thing?"

Ten

Alyssa shook her head, frantic to explain, eaten up with guilt. "It's not what you think."

But before she could explain further, Prince Brandt interrupted. "Part of me envies your future, Montgomery. To live in the United Sates, playing house-husband while your beautiful, intelligent, cooperative wife takes over as Assistant Vice President of Human Relations at Bank International. Quite the life of leisure. Far better than a jail sentence, don't you agree?"

"Take off these handcuffs and I'll show you how well I agree with you."

Brandt shook his head. "Perhaps we'll save that for another time and place." He picked up a packet and handed it to Tolken. "Here are the tickets. The ladies will be riding in the limousine I have waiting. I'm afraid

I don't quite trust you to behave well enough for such an elegant vehicle, Montgomery. Tolken and a few of his men will escort you in a van better suited to the transportation of felons. Not quite as comfortable, but I'm sure you understand the necessity. Just as I'm sure you understand the necessity of the handcuffs remaining on until you're safely aboard the plane."

"I'm not leaving Verdonia."

"I thought you might say that." Brandt smiled. "So, I've arranged for a jail cell for your wife and mother-in-law should you refuse. Your choice, Montgomery."

"You can't do that," Alyssa protested. Her gaze flickered from Brandt to Merrick, and back again. "You can't, can you? Everyone keeps telling me I'm a princess. That ought to count for something."

Brandt shrugged. "Once again…my principality, my rules. I might not be able to lock you up forever, but I can hold you long enough."

Merrick shot her one brief look. "My wife in jail. Tempting."

"But you'll pass, won't you?" said Brandt.

To Alyssa's distress, Merrick had to think about it before nodding. "If it means she'll be out of Verdonia permanently, then yes. I'll pass." Before anyone could prevent him, he took one swift step in her direction. "It's a good thing you run well, Princess. Because when I get free, you better be able to run faster and farther than I can." His gaze, pure molten gold, pinned her in place. "Trust me on this one, you don't want me to catch you."

"Merrick—"

Without sparing her so much as another glance, he crossed to the door and addressed Tolken. "What are we waiting for? Let's get the hell out of here."

"She betrayed you, old friend."

"Shut up, Tolk." The van rumbled onto the highway and gathered speed.

"Don't feel bad. Women are notorious for being weak."

"Some women, perhaps," Merrick conceded. "Not Alyssa."

"So you're saying she's strong enough to resist Prince Brandt's questioning?" Tolken nodded. "That would indicate she chose to betray you. Outrageous. Definitely not the sort of woman to rule Celestia. Verdonia is better off rid of her."

Merrick ground his teeth. "That's not what I meant."

"Tell me. What did you mean?" When a response wasn't forthcoming, he suggested, "Perhaps her betrayal is your fault."

"What the hell are you talking about now?"

"You abducted her for the greater good. Do I have that right? I'm sure you set an excellent example. No doubt she betrayed Miri for a similar reason. Of course in this case it was for her greater good and that of her mother." Tolken lifted a shoulder. "Well…and yours."

Merrick deliberately changed the subject. "I won't get on that plane. You realize that, don't you?"

"I realize it'll take force. It's a good thing I have plenty of that available."

"Even if you succeed, I'll return."

"With your wife?" Tolken tilted his head to one side. "Or without?"

There was no question. "Without."

"In that case, I've been authorized by Prince Brandt to offer you a deal."

"What deal?" Merrick asked warily.

"Simple. Resign your position as commander of the Royal Security Force and return to Verdon. Stay there. Quietly. Live a long and peaceful life out of the public eye. If you do that, Prince Brandt is willing to pretend this incident never took place."

Merrick gave a short laugh. "What you mean is, if I don't tell on him, he won't tell on me. It wouldn't be to his advantage for any of this to be made public, would it? Not before the election." He stared moodily out the window of the van. "What about Alyssa?"

"What about her? She'll return to New York. Not that there's anything Prince Brandt could do if she elected to stay in Verdonia, despite his threats. Especially since the airport is on Celestian soil." He curled his lip. "Just as well she goes, if you ask me. She wasn't suited to play the part of a princess."

"You know nothing about her." The retort burst from Merrick. It felt good to explode, better yet to siphon off some of the anger sloshing around inside him.

Tolken grunted. "I know one thing. She's capable of betraying her husband. No doubt she hid that trait from you. I'm sure you'd never have married her, otherwise. A very devious woman, your wife."

"Just shut the hell up, Tolk, she's not like that. She believes in honor and duty as much as I do. She protects the people she loves. She risked everything to save her mother. Sacrificed everything."

It took a second for him to hear his own words. The minute he did, he groaned. Oh, man. He was a first-class idiot. His head dropped toward his chest. Dammit, dammit, dammit. He did need to resign his position. No one this stupid should be allowed to live, let alone be in charge of a national security force.

"You could be right," Tolken was saying. "I'm not familiar with that aspect of her character. There is one thing I know for certain."

Merrick lifted his head, finally, finally starting to put the pieces together. "And what's that?"

"Your wife is a rotten poker player, whereas Prince Brandt is a master."

Merrick stared blankly. It took a full minute before the implication sank in. And then he said, "Get me out of these handcuffs and give me your cell phone, Tolk. Hurry. I have a plane to stop."

Tolken smiled. "About damn time."

They arrived at the airport and Prince Brandt's guards escorted Alyssa and her mother through security. She delayed as long as she could, constantly checking over her shoulder for Merrick. But he never showed. Once through the checkpoint, they were ushered to a private lounge where she paced off the next two hours, minute by endless minute, step by dragging step.

And still he didn't come.

"I don't understand it," she burst out. "They weren't that far behind us. They should be here by now."

"Maybe they're holding him in the van until it's time to board," her mother said, trying to soothe her. "They probably don't want you having the opportunity to scream at each other ahead of time."

Alyssa spun to face her guards. "You must have cell phones. Can't you call Tolken and find out where they are?"

"My apologies, Your Highness. I'm not permitted to do that," was all one would say.

Another hour passed and a knock sounded at the door. Alyssa flew across the room, waiting breathlessly for Merrick to join them. But instead of her husband, an airport official entered. "You may board now," he informed them.

Deaf to her protests, the guard escorted Alyssa and her mother from the lounge to the boarding gate and then down the gangway leading to the plane. "Wait. Please." She had to try one more time. "I need to speak to Merrick."

"You can do that when he boards, Your Highness."

"You don't understand." She fought to keep from weeping. "He's not coming. I know he's not. He thinks I betrayed him. And he needs to protect his sister. He won't leave Verdonia."

"I assure you, Your Highness, he won't have a choice."

They were shown to their first-class seats in the front of the plane where Angela handed her daughter a third tissue to help mop up her tears. "Listen, baby, as long as you're already crying, there's something I need to tell you." She glanced around, then lowered her voice, whispering, "It's about your father."

"I already know," Alyssa replied, fighting to regain control of herself. "Merrick told me that he was older than you."

"No. That's not it. I mean, there's that. But there's something else that I should have told you long ago. I did marry Freddy because he was older and because he was safe. We only knew each other a week before we did a Las Vegas." She twisted her ruined hands together. "But that's not what I have to explain to you."

No doubt there was a point to her mother's confession, but Alyssa wasn't sure what it might be. Still, it was a relief to focus on her mother, to put her needs first. Anything to take her mind off Merrick. She dried the last of her tears and gave Angela her full attention. "What is it, Mom? What do you have to tell me?"

Her mother bowed her head. "It's about what happened when Freddy and I came here. By then it was too late to change anything. We were already married and I couldn't just leave him. I mean, how would that look after just a week?"

"So, you didn't run?"

"I couldn't. Mainly because I didn't have a plan in

place at that point. Besides…" Her voice dropped to a mere whisper. "That's…that's when I met him."

A coldness crept into the pit of Alyssa's stomach. "Met who?"

"Freddy's son, Erik." Angela's eyes slowly lifted and fixed on her daughter. "Your father."

Alyssa could only stare for a long minute in stunned disbelief. "You're saying…" She drew in a deep breath. "Are you telling me that my brother is actually my father?"

"Yes, to the father part. No, to the brother." Angela's brow crinkled. "Although since he was technically my stepson at the time, maybe he would be both your brother and your father. I get a headache just thinking about it."

"Mom—"

Her face crumpled. "I'm sorry. I'm not doing this very well."

"Is this somehow connected to why you're here in Verdonia?"

"Uh-huh." Her lashes flickered as she glanced at Alyssa, and then away again. She cleared her throat. "After I left Jim, I decided to fly out to Verdonia. I'd heard that Freddy died a few years back and I thought maybe…maybe Erik and I…" She bowed her head, trailing off miserably. "I wanted to see him again."

"And did you?"

"Yeah. Yeah, I saw him, all right."

"Good grief, Mom. What did he say? What did he do when you showed up?"

"Oh, he abdicated."

Alyssa struggled to breathe. "You went to visit Prince Erik, duke of Celestia and he up and abdicated? Just like that?"

"Sort of. He said something about finding these important documents and needing to fix things, or some such. He said if he abdicated, you could rule Celestia and that when he returned he and I could marry. Only..." Her eyes overflowed. "Only Erik disappeared and Prince Brandt arrived and invited me to stay with him. With Erik gone, I didn't know what to do. So, I went with Prince Brandt. As soon as he learned that Erik had abdicated and that you would rule Celestia in his place, that's when everything went to hell in a handbasket. He came up with that crazy scheme to marry you."

It was Alyssa's turn to supply the tissues. "You can still find Prince Erik. You can be with him now."

"No, it's too late."

"Only if you let it be too late."

Angela shook her head. "I've made a mess of my life. I allowed my past to ruin my future. I let it dictate my choices." She faced her daughter, the river of mascara and tears slowing. "That doesn't have to happen to you. You're so much stronger than I am, just like your father. You can take a chance. Have the future you always dreamed of having."

"No, I—"

"Listen to me, Ally." She used a tone Alyssa had never heard before, that of a determined mother. "I want you to leave. Now."

"What are you talking about?"

"I want you to get off this plane and live your dreams." She swiped the dampness from her cheeks. "Don't think about it. Do it. Get up and walk away."

"I can't leave you behind," Alyssa protested. "You need me."

"Not anymore. I've held you back for too long. We've gotten our roles all mixed up. I'm supposed to be the parent. You're supposed to be the child. And yet I've always let you take care of me."

"I wanted to, Mom. It was my choice." She gripped her mother's poor, broken hands, lifted them to her mouth and kissed them. "I love you."

"Ever since I was a child I wanted someone to take care of me. To love me unconditionally. You always did that." Angela broke down for a brief moment again before gathering herself back up. "But it wasn't fair of me to let you. It was wrong and I won't allow it to go on any longer."

"There's no point in getting off the plane. Merrick thinks I betrayed him."

"Then you'll have to set him straight." She released Alyssa's hands. "Take off your wedding rings."

"I don't understand."

"Take them off. There'll be an inscription inside of them."

"How do you know?" Alyssa asked, even as she found herself tugging off the rings.

"It's a Verdonian tradition, a rather sweet one, actually. A private message between husband and wife.

Read what yours says. If it's something pitiful, like, 'You're my hoochy momma' or 'It'll be fun while it lasts' then you know it wasn't meant to be and we'll hit New York City and buy shoes or something." She leaned forward. "But if it's special, really special, then you have to promise me you'll get off the plane. Do we have a deal?"

"Okay, yes. It's a deal."

Alyssa held Fairytale to the light, turning the ring until she could make out the flowing script inside and started to cry.

"Oh God. It says hoochy momma, doesn't it?"

Alyssa shook her head. "No, no it doesn't. I've got to get off, Mom. I have to go now." She half rose in her seat before realization dawned. "The guards. They're not going to let me off the plane."

"Of course they will."

"No, they'll stop me."

"Think, Alyssa, think. If there's one thing I'm good at, it's getting out of a tight spot. And this one isn't even all that tight." Her mother smiled slyly. "You just have to tell them who you are."

"Tell them—" Of course. Alyssa didn't hesitate. She gave her mother a fierce hug. "Come with me. Do it, Mom. You can have the dream, too. We can find out what happened to Prince Erik. And maybe you can have your happily-ever-after ending, as well."

She didn't wait for her mother's decision. It was hers to make. Alyssa had her own life to live, her own future to fight for. She swept to the doorway. The guards were still posted there. They immediately moved to block the exit.

She drew herself up to her full height. "I am Princess Alyssa, duchess of Celestia," she announced in her most ringing, royally-ticked-off tone of voice. "And you will move out of my way."

She'd rattled them, she could tell. They glanced helplessly at each other, uncertain how to respond. Before they could decide, a man in uniform appeared from the front of the plane, either the captain or co-captain, she wasn't sure which.

"Did you say you're Princess Alyssa?"

"I am."

"We've been denied clearance until you're removed from the plane." Annoyed disbelief touched the man's face. "We've been accused of abducting Celestia's princess. So, if you wouldn't mind disembarking..."

"I'd be happy to."

The guards weren't given an option at that point and they reluctantly moved aside. A few minutes later, Alyssa stepped back onto Verdonian soil. To her absolute delight, her mother joined her. She reentered the airport only to be greeted by a wave of people. Clearly, someone had revealed her identity. The minute they saw her, they began to cheer. And when she paused in front of them, every last man, woman and child swept into deep bows and curtsies.

It took her two tries to get the words out. "Thank you," she finally said. "You have no idea how much this means to me."

"Will you be staying, Princess?" one of the women asked shyly.

Alyssa smiled. "Where else would I go? It's my home." And that was the simple truth, she realized.

"And your husband?" a husky voice sounded in her ear. "What about him?"

She spun around. Merrick stood behind her. For a long moment they didn't move, each greedily drinking in the other. There were so many questions she wanted to ask, so much she wanted to say. Apologies to make. Explanations to give. Wounds to heal. But none of it mattered. Not right then. Not when she looked into those beloved golden eyes and saw the fierce glow of undisguised love.

She took one step toward him. Then another. And then she raced into his waiting arms. He practically inhaled her, kissing her mouth, her eyes, her jaw before finding her mouth again. They were hard, fierce kisses. Urgent kisses. Greedy and needy. Telling her without words how desperately he wanted her. And then the tenor changed.

He kissed her gently, a river of passion flowing deeply beneath. A balm. A benediction. A husband gifting his wife. "I didn't tell him," she said, breathless and dazed. "I swear to you, I didn't."

"I figured that out. It took a while, but I got there."

"I couldn't leave Verdonia. Couldn't leave you."

"I figured that out, too." He cupped her face with his magician's hands. "You still haven't answered my question. You have a husband, Princess. What are you going to do about him?"

Her chin wobbled. "My home is within your heart. At least, according to this Fairytale I read not long ago. Unless your ring has a better suggestion."

"Just one."

"Which is?"

A hint of color darkened his cheekbones. "It's trite."

She grinned through her tears. "I can't wait to hear this. Come on, warrior man. What does it say?"

He snatched his wife into his arms, lifting her high against his chest. More cheers broke out around them. "It says, Two souls destined to live as one."

She wrapped her arms around his neck and buried her face against his shoulder until she'd recovered sufficiently to speak. "Let's go home, Merrick."

"Is this your home, Princess? Have you finally found your roots?"

"A home. Roots. Heck, I've even found a father." She laughed at his stunned expression. "I'll explain that part later."

To her delight, Merrick's brother was waiting for them outside the airport. One look was all it took to see the resemblance, both in autocratic manner and old-world graciousness. She looked forward to getting to know her brother-in-law a little better, to form an opinion about the man who would be king. There was hint of a warrior about him, a trait that must run in the family, though the rough edges were a bit more polished than with Merrick.

To her surprise, it didn't take long for Lander to put her at ease, and he had her mother charmed within minutes. He also drove them back to Glynith, and though it rained almost the entire way, Alyssa neither noticed nor cared. There were too many other matters of far greater importance to address.

"How did you figure out I hadn't betrayed you?" she asked Merrick at one point.

"Tolken helped with that." He flicked her nose with the tip of his finger. "Surprises you, doesn't it? Once I calmed down enough to think straight I realized you would never have given up Miri, not even for my freedom. Certainly not for your own."

"Not even for my mother's," she confirmed. "I'd have given him almost anything else, but not that. It was too high a price to pay."

"There's the palace," Angela broke in. Wistfulness underscored her comment. A whisper of bittersweet memories.

Merrick peered out the window, squinting as the sun broke through the rain clouds. He wrapped his arm around his wife. "We can't take up residence there until after church and state have made your position official. But that shouldn't be too long a wait."

"And you? What will you do?"

"I've decided to keep my current job. After my dealings with von Folke, I think Verdonia needs a tough watchdog." He inclined his head toward the palace. "I'll just relocate my base of operations."

Alyssa stared at her new home. This was it. Permanent. No more running. A hint of apprehension rippled through her. Staying involved so much responsibility. How would she manage to handle it all? If it hadn't been for Merrick's presence, she would have been tempted to order Lander to turn the car around and return them to the airport.

And then she saw it. Watched as it formed right before her eyes. From its roots, deep in Celestian soil, a rainbow arched across the sky, a brilliant sweep of color, so dazzling it hurt the eyes. And from where she sat it seemed to burst apart right on top of the palace. Merrick saw it, too. He turned to her, a crooked grin tugging at the corner of his mouth, clearly understanding the significance.

Alyssa caught her mother's hand and directed her attention out the window. "Look, Mom. You were right. Our rainbow was out there. After all these years we finally found it."

And then she met her husband's steady gaze, one that glittered like the sun. She'd discovered what was at the end of her rainbow and it was infinitely more precious than mere gold. She curled deeper into Merrick's embrace. "Take me home," she whispered.

"On one condition."

"Which is?"

"That you promise to live happily ever after."

She pretended to consider. "There's only one way

that'll work." Her expression softened. "And that's with you at my side."

He lowered his head and kissed her. "Welcome home, my love. Welcome home."

* * * * *

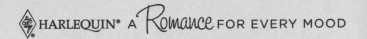

Five hunky Texas single fathers—five stories from Cathy Gillen Thacker's LONE STAR DADS *miniseries. Here's an excerpt from the latest, THE MOMMY PROPOSAL from Harlequin American Romance.*

"I hear you work miracles," Nate Hutchinson drawled. Brooke Mitchell had just stepped into his lavishly appointed office in downtown Fort Worth, Texas.

"Sometimes, I do." Brooke smiled and took the sexy financier's hand in hers, shook it briefly.

"Good." Nate looked her straight in the eye. "Because I'm in need of a home makeover—fast. The son of an old friend is coming to live with me."

She was still tingling from the feel of his warm palm. "Temporarily or permanently?"

"If all goes according to plan, I'll adopt Landry by summer's end."

Brooke had heard the founder of Nate Hutchinson Financial Services was eligible, wealthy and generous to a fault. She hadn't known he was in the market for a family, but she supposed she shouldn't be surprised. But Brooke had figured a man as successful and handsome as Nate would want one the old-fashioned way. *Not that this was any of her business…*

"So what's the child like?" she asked crisply, trying not to think how the marine-blue of Nate's dress shirt deepened the hue of his eyes.

"I don't know." Nate took a seat behind his massive antique mahogany desk. He relaxed against the smooth leather of the chair. "I've never met him."

"Yet you've invited this kid to live with you permanently?"

"It's complicated. But I'm sure it's going to be fine."

Obviously Nate Hutchinson knew as little about teenage

boys as he did about decorating. But that wasn't her problem. Finding a way to do the assignment without getting the least bit emotionally involved was.

Find out how a young boy brings Nate and Brooke together in THE MOMMY PROPOSAL, coming August 2010 from Harlequin American Romance.

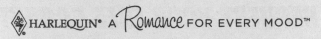